The Ripples of Rebellion

Book 15 in the Border Knight Series

By

Griff Hosker

The Ripples of Rebellion

Published by Sword Books Ltd 2024

SWORD
BOOKS

Copyright ©Griff Hosker First Edition 2024

The author has asserted their moral right under the Copyright, Designs and Patents Act, 1988, to be identified as the author of this work.
All Rights reserved. No part of this publication may be reproduced, copied, stored in a retrieval system, or transmitted, in any form or by any means, without the prior written consent of the copyright holder, nor be otherwise circulated in any form of binding or cover other than that in which it is published and without a similar condition being imposed on the subsequent purchaser.
A CIP catalogue record for this title is available from the British Library.

Contents

The Ripples of Rebellion	1
Prologue	4
Chapter 1	9
Chapter 2	21
Chapter 3	28
Chapter 4	41
Chapter 5	52
Chapter 6	63
Chapter 7	74
Chapter 8	84
Chapter 9	99
Chapter 10	111
Chapter 11	119
Chapter 12	126
Chapter 13	134
Chapter 14	143
Chapter 15	151
Chapter 16	159
Chapter 17	170
Chapter 18	185
Chapter 19	196
Chapter 20	204
Epilogue	214
Glossary	215
Historical Note	217
Other books by Griff Hosker	220

The Ripples of Rebellion
Historical figures

King Henry III of England son of King John
Richard of Cornwall - 1st Earl of Cornwall second son of King John and also the King of the Romans
Prince Edward - heir to the throne and known as **The Lord Edward**
Prince Edmund - putative King of Sicily and brother to The Lord Edward
Eleanor of Provence - wife of King Henry
Eleanor of Castile - wife of Prince Edward (also descended form Henry 2nd)
Henry of Almain - the son of Richard of Cornwall
Gilbert de Clare - Earl of Gloucester
William de Valance - The Earl of Pembroke. King Henry's half-brother through his mother, Isabella of Angoulême
John de Warenne - Earl of Surrey
Guy de Lusignan - King Henry's half-brother through his mother, Isabella of Angoulême
Simon de Montfort - The Earl of Leicester (deceased)
Simon de Montfort the younger - the son of the Earl of Leicester
Guy de Montfort - the son of the Earl of Leicester
Aymer de Lusignan - King Henry's half-brother through his mother, Isabella of Angoulême
King Louis IX of France - also known as St. Louis
Philip, Dauphin of France
Charles of Anjou - King of Sicily and Naples, brother of King Louis
King Alexander III of Scotland (The Glorious born in 1241) - King Henry's son-in-law
Llewelyn ap Gruffudd - Prince of Wales
Lord Rhys Fychan - The Welsh lord given the land of Gwynedd by King Henry
Gilbert de Clare - 6th Earl of Gloucester and the son of Richard de Clare
Roger Bigod - 4th Earl of Norfolk
Hugh Bigod - the brother of the Earl of Norfolk
Roger Mortimer -1st Baron Mortimer of Wigmore
Dugald mac Ruari - King of the Isles
John de Vescy - Lord of Alnwick
Dervorguilla of Galloway - Widow of John Balliol and related to the Scottish Royal Family
Peter II - Count of Savoy and Earl of Richmond

The Ripples of Rebellion

The Land of the Warlord

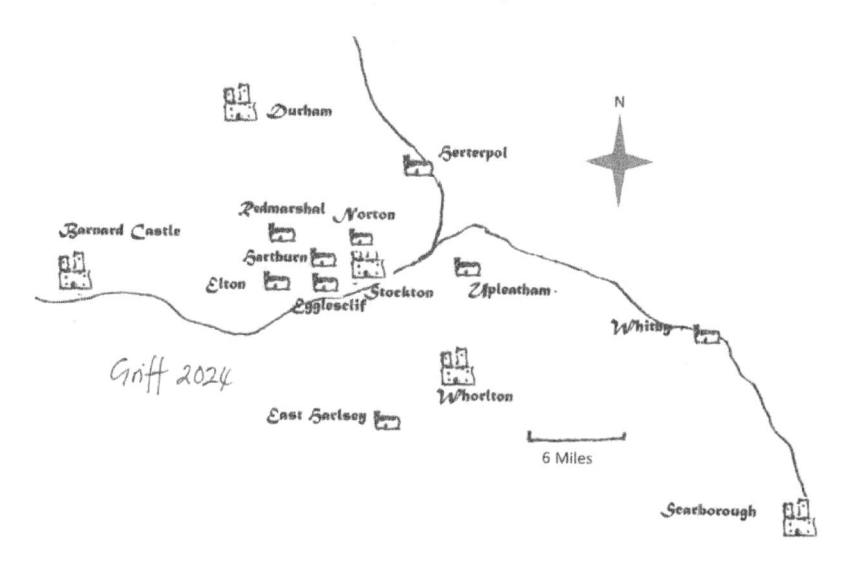

- Durham
- Herterpol
- Redmarshal
- Norton
- Barnard Castle
- Hartburn
- Elton
- Eggleselif
- Stockton
- Upleatham
- Whitby
- Griff 2024
- East Harlsey
- Whorlton
- Scarborough

6 Miles

N

The Valley 1270

The Ripples of Rebellion

Prologue

Sir Henry Samuel

Stockton

The rebellion against King Henry had ended with the Battle of Evesham. That had been just five years ago. Simon de Montfort was now dead. He had been butchered with one of his three sons and Hugh Despenser at the Battle of Evesham. Roger Mortimer had been responsible for the savage end of the French rebel but all of those who had defeated the rebels were tainted by the horrific butchery. The attempt by the Lusignan family to take the crown from King Henry had failed. It did not mean that the land was at peace, far from it. The lands seized from the rebels were a source of contention. New laws forbidding foreigners from owning lands in England were also disputed by the dispossessed but, for us the descendants of the Warlord and those living in our valley, we were, temporarily, at peace. I was now the Earl of Cleveland and lived at Stockton in the home that had risen like a phoenix after King John had attempted to wipe it from the map. My sons were almost ready to be knighted and contentment lay along the valley.

It had taken years to finally make the land secure and to bring order and peace back to England. That peace was still an uneasy one. The Lord Edward had come of age before, during and after Evesham. My knights had helped his cousin clear a nest of rebels from the forests close to Chesterfield. Henry of Almain, the nephew of King Henry, and I got on well. The Lord Edward and I, however, did not like each other and I doubted we would ever be friends, but when his father died and he became King of England I believed that he would be a better ruler and a stronger king than his father. Now, however, he had chosen to take the cross. I did not think that was a good idea. My ancestors had seen, at first hand, the futility of trying to wrest back the Holy Land from the Turks and Egyptians. It was doomed to failure before it began, but The Lord Edward was adamant. King Louis of France was leading the crusade and King Henry had managed to avoid having to go to the Holy Land as The Lord Edward wanted the honour of fighting for Christ and the Pope. We were summoned to meet with the heir to the throne and the other barons. I dreaded the outcome of that meeting. The presence of all of us was demanded. I did not like it but we had little choice. I had wanted to complete the training and knighting of my sons, Alfred

The Ripples of Rebellion

and Samuel, but that would have to wait. I had much to do in Stockton and I resented this summons.

The parliament was to be held in Northampton. It was at the worst time of the year to travel, March. With days that were still too short and the worst of weather it would be unpleasant at best. That was one consolation as we would have a slightly shorter journey than had we been ordered to attend Westminster. Every baron had been invited and both King Henry and his son, The Lord Edward, needed their support to guarantee the funds needed for the expedition. It would be a difficult parliament. The money for the crusade had to be raised and while the church would provide some of the funding much more would need to be raised in taxes. It would not please the Montfortians who had lost lands and money already. We would be travelling through an England that was still reeling from the rebellion. The journey would be hard, expensive and possibly dangerous. We were lucky that the valley was not impoverished, and we could afford the expense. Each knight took his squire but just one horse. Matthew had recently appointed Robert, the son of Joseph of Aylesbury, as his squire. Many nobles chose the sons of nobles as their squires. We had done so too but, as with the Warlord, we also recognised skills and rewarded them. Robert had his father's weapon skills and the build of a warrior already. He would be perfect for Matthew and the two got on well. What was most worrying was leaving the land with just some men at arms and the rest of our archers to watch over it. My brother William would not be coming but he was not a knight. He would be the one who would have to command and I worried about that. He was a scholar. When I discovered that the former northern rebels, led by de Vescy, were also travelling south for the parliament it made me less anxious. The king and his son might have problems at the parliament, but our homes would be safe.

One of the other knights not travelling would be missed by me. My friend, Richard of Hartburn, would not be making the long journey with us. He had been ill for some time and he was still grieving over the death of his eldest son, Alfred. If danger came then he would not be able to do anything to prevent it. His other sons were young and could do nothing to help. His absence would be a loss for he was a good friend and I had always used him as a sort of crutch as well as someone in whom I could confide. My sister would care for him and my two nephews. Things were changing.

We had half a dozen archers and four men at arms as an escort and to watch over the sumpters. We did not travel in mail hauberks, but we took them with us along with our helmets and shields. The rebellion was still a raw wound in the land, and we had to be ready to respond to danger.

My two cousins, Dick and Matthew, flanked me along with my brother Alfred as we headed south. Sir Thomas was with my sons, Alfred and Samuel. I think Thomas felt an affinity to them for he lived in Stockton with his mother and me. He saw my sons every day and they looked up to Sir Thomas. Dick and Matthew had both been my squires and those ties remained.

"So, Earl, do we go on crusade?"

"You know, Dick, that you do not need to call me by my title. We are family."

"I know but it is a good habit to get into. Your elevation is but recent and this will give you an edge over some of the barons. When we return to Stockton, I will revert to Henry Samuel but, on the road, we have agreed to use your title."

I looked at Matthew, "All of you?"

"Aye, Earl, even your sons."

I sighed and shook my head. I had never been one for titles. My grandfather, the great Sir Thomas, had been the same. "To answer your question, I shall not be going on a crusade. This family had their days of glory at Arsuf and in the Baltic. We had success in the Baltic but the Holy Land just sees hopes and dreams dry up and men lose their lives for nothing in an inhospitable land. I am not afraid of failure but I want a possibility, no matter how slim, of success."

"And will we be commanded to join?"

That was my fear. In the past men chose to go on a crusade. King Henry had promised to go and assiduously avoided it. The Lord Edward was keen to go and would want as many knights to travel with him as possible. It would show the other kings of his power and his commitment to the cause. "Perhaps, but the command cannot be binding." I looked at my brother who was the next most senior knight, "This will be your first parliament. It will be as unlike combat as night is to day and yet the outcome can be just as deadly. To achieve the result that they want the king and his son will barter, bribe and deal. The manner in which they do so will be less than honourable."

He nodded, "And how do we vote?"

Alfred was now a baron and he would, unlike the rest of the knights, have a vote.

"As you wish. I will not sway you, brother. I know you and trust you. You will vote as you think right as will I."

Matthew asked, "Then you will not vote for the crusade as the pope wishes?"

The Ripples of Rebellion

"The pope will neither fight nor shed blood. I will vote for the crusade only if the arguments are convincing."

Dick said, "And you do not think that they will be."

I smiled, "No, I do not."

The long journey south allowed us to talk through all the possible outcomes of the parliament and the effect it would have on the valley. The heir to the crown had been clever. He had chosen Northampton because the church of the Holy Sepulchre had been built in the town as a copy of the one in Jerusalem by a knight who had returned from the First Crusade. Even before the parliament had begun we were all invited to a ceremony in the church. The heir to England's crown was stacking all that he could to influence the vote that would tax the people and fund the crusade. We were all addressed by Cardinal Ottobuono. At the end of it The Lord Edward, his brother Edmund and his cousin Henry of Almain took the cross. It was the start of a stampede. Many knights raced to the altar to take the cross. Royalists such as Roger Clifford, Roger Leybourne and William de Valence were not a surprise. The first ones were orchestrated as though this was a pageant but some of the later ones surprised me as they were Montfortians or had been opposed to the king at some point: John de Vescy and Gilbert de Clare were two such notables. There was a euphoric mood as we were all feasted and feted in Northampton Castle. I did, however, notice The Lord Edward casting baleful looks in my direction.

The next day the parliament was almost a foregone conclusion. The arguments were made and when we voted it was clear that the king's son had won. I did not vote for the tax. I felt that the people were heavily taxed enough as it was. It did not make a difference to the outcome but I knew that it had not endeared me to The Lord Edward. He had watched every baron as they voted.

We rose early to head back to the valley but The Lord Edward and Henry of Almain waylaid us in the Great Hall when we ate before the journey. The Lord Edward looked angry, "So Earl Henry Samuel, not only do you try to thwart us at every turn but you also sneak off like a thief in the night."

I was not intimidated by the forceful prince, "My lord, having an early breakfast is hardly sneaking away and as for thwarting…if you mean not voting for your crusade…"

"I do!"

"The rights of barons were won from your grandfather and each baron must vote according to their conscience. I believe that my family has done enough crusading already and I fear that this Crusade will not have a successful outcome."

He glared at me but I held firm. He then switched his attention to my knights. "And none of you thought to take the cross?"

Before any could answer I said, "My brother and cousins are all recently married, and their place is in the north with their families."

He snorted. It was an unattractive gesture. He said, "Are there no bachelor knights then?"

Matthew was both too honest and too honourable and he said, "I am a bachelor, my lord."

"So, what is your excuse for skulking in the north?"

I saw Matthew colour but before I could speak Matthew said, "If you want one knight from the valley then I shall come, my lord, but like the earl, I fear it shall end in failure."

The Lord Edward beamed. He had won. I confess that all I wanted to do was to strike out at the royal bully, challenge him to combat, in fact, anything rather than just accept my cousin's rash decision.

Lord Henry of Almain made it easier for me, "Sir Matthew of Redmarshal, I would be honoured if you would join my retinue. I need good knights and the men of the valley are renowned as doughty warriors and honourable knights." The smile left his cousin's face and made me feel better. Our name had been redeemed. More importantly, I trusted Henry of Almain. I had served with him and knew that he was a good man. The Lord Edward was a vindictive man and I would not have put it past him to use Matthew and put him in harm's way deliberately as a way of punishing me.

Matthew said, "It would be an honour, my lord."

"Good, then I will send word when we are to muster." He reached over and clasped Matthew's arm in a warrior's handshake.

The Lord Edward had won and despite our intentions was taking one of the family of the Warlord to war.

The Ripples of Rebellion

Chapter 1

Sir Matthew

Horses and ships

The earl had always advised me that a man does not make decisions when he is angry. I had been angry that the next King of England was insulting my family and, more importantly, Sir Henry Samuel. My offer was hasty and ill-advised but just as he had warned me of being reckless, he had also instilled in me the belief that having given your word you could never take it back. I would go on the crusade. I was happy that I was serving as noble a man as Henry of Almain. His father Richard of Cornwall, the King of the Romans, would be the Regent and I knew him to be a good man. My cousin spoke highly of him.

No one said a word as we left the castle and took the road north. There was no banter as there normally was and that matched the mood. We had all been insulted and it hurt; the words *'skulk'* and *'sneak'* had been ill-chosen by the next King of England. When we had mounted our horses I had heard whispered conversations between the squires, the men at arms and archers. My brother, Dick, rode close to me and I felt his gaze upon me but silence reigned until we stopped to water our horses fifteen miles north of the castle. A villager hurried out with a jug of ale and we held out our coistrels. The earl gave her coins, "Thank you, Gammer, you are kind to travellers such as we."

Until that moment I thought we had all been struck dumb. "Sir Henry Samuel…"

Henry Samuel held up his hand, "Not yet, Matthew, I still have to work out what to do about this."

As we mounted, however, Dick said, "You were provoked, Matthew."

"We could have left you in Stockton, cousin, and then this problem would not have arisen. You are not a baron and had no vote. We obeyed the summons to the letter and this is the price we now pay."

The earl was a true leader, "Alfred, this is not of Matthew's doing. This is my fault. Even though I thought that The Lord Edward had accepted my explanation of our flight from Lewes, he clearly has not and seeks to punish me." He sighed, "Matthew, we shall have to make the best of this. You will be with Lord Henry and he is a good man and a reasonable one. Even so, you will have to avoid volunteering for dangerous tasks. This crusade is taking place because the King of France is an old man, close to the end of his life and he wishes for some glory. He failed once and this time he is encouraged by the Pope. King Henry has managed to avoid the promise he made to go to war and our future king does not wish France to garner the glory. He goes to emulate the feats of the French."

"You know these matters better than I do. When will we leave? How long do I have?"

"Longer than you think but not as long as you need. You and Robert will need to ensure that you have all that you require before you leave the valley. Crusaders pay more the closer that they get to the Holy Land. Men take advantage of their religious zeal. The muster will be at Portsmouth and then you will have a journey through France before taking a ship to Sicily and then Cyprus. The journey to the Holy Land could take half a year with adverse winds."

Sir Alfred looked at me, "How do you know all this, brother?"

"You forget that I spent a long time with our grandfather, Sir Thomas. That is how I know the crusade is doomed to failure. He took me through every disaster that befell the army and he included the battle of Arsuf. It brought him fame and glory but he saw the deaths it brought to the knights of the valley and the disaster that ensued." He shook his head, "It may be, Matthew, that your sacrifice might save the rest of us. Had no one gone with the next King of England then he has such a vindictive nature that he might have punished us, much as his grandfather, King John, did." There was silence. Then he turned to his sons, "And one of you, when you are knighted and given your spurs, will be required to take over Redmarshal for Matthew."

I saw the grins on their faces as I gave them the confirmation of their knighthood, "Will not Thomas return there?" I had wondered why I was still lord of Redmarshal when it had been the home of Sir Thomas.

The father of Thomas and Isabelle, Sir Robert, had been a bad man. After he died the stories emerged. "There are too many bad memories there for Thomas. No Thomas, I thought to give you the manor of Norton. It has been without a lord for too long. You two need not decide now but one of you must be lord of Redmarshal until Matthew returns."

My cousin Thomas looked pleased. Norton was close to Stockton. There had been no lord there for a few years and I think that Henry Samuel had been waiting for a good hand to rule there. It was another that had lost its lord at Arsuf.

The air was cleared somewhat and the rest of the journey north had more conversation. My family closed ranks around me and offered all sorts of support. My head, by the time we crossed the river to Stockton, was full of all the attendant problems of travelling abroad. Robert and I would need at least four horses. I would need a warhorse and a hackney while he would need a hackney and a sumpter. The earl had provided land and funds so that Osgar and his son Osric could begin to breed animals for us. We had previously bought our mounts from Abel the horse breeder and whilst they were good animals, they were also expensive. If I was to fight in the crusades then I would need a good warhorse. My mail, helmet, shield, lance and sword were adequate but Robert had only recently been appointed a squire and he lacked many things. I began to realise that Sir Henry Samuel was right about the shortness of time.

When we entered the castle the sun was already setting and we would all stay in the Warlord's home. As we passed through the gatehouse the earl said, "It is I who will tell the ladies of this matter. No loose lips."

My father had been the earl, but he had not used that power as wisely as Sir Henry Samuel. My brother, Dick, bore no resentment that Henry Samuel had the title and not him. We all obeyed Henry Samuel.

We had more ladies living in the castle these days and the earl sought them all out and gathered them, even as we were unpacking. By the time we descended to the Great Hall, Henry Samuel had spoken and they all knew of my task. My mother was tearful when I entered the hall and rushed to embrace me. Henry Samuel's mother, Matilda, was the matriarch of the family and she snapped, "Mary, he is not leaving today. Save your tears for when they are needed." She beamed and held her arms wide, "Welcome back, knights of the valley. God has kept us safe and we are glad that you have returned to us."

The words of Henry Samuel and his mother set the tone. We settled back into a life that would have been almost idyllic but for the spectre of the impending crusade. The problem we had was that there had been no date given. I had been told that I had to leave for Portsmouth as soon as I received the summons. In the end, we had less time than we had thought. A messenger arrived on the 1st of August with the missive to join the crusade at Portsmouth. We had ten days to reach the port of embarkation.

My brother was incandescent with rage, "That is barely enough time for you to say your goodbyes."

The earl merely shook his head, "This will not be the doing of Henry of Almain. As soon as The Lord Edward had the backing of parliament and the funds it was clear that he would quit England. His father is ill and all that remains is for the regent to be confirmed. Richard of

The Ripples of Rebellion

Cornwall will be that regent and he is a good man. Matthew is as prepared as it is possible to be. We will hold a feast this night and tomorrow we shall bid farewell to one who will follow in the footsteps of great men like Sir William of Ouistreham, Sir Samuel of Stockton and Sir Thomas, the hero of Arsuf."

The knight who trained me was right and I was as ready as it was possible to be. Osgar had a warhorse for me, he was appropriately called Warlord. The two hackneys we had and the sumpter were well-schooled and I hoped that the journey would not tax them too much. Joseph, Robert's father, had given him a mail hauberk he had taken at Evesham and the weaponsmith had made him a good helmet. The earl gave him a sword and with the blue livery of Stockton upon our backs, we looked like warriors.

Even though we left as soon as the sun rose the whole family came to the ferry to see us off. As we stood and watched them waving from the quay I wondered if I would return or would my bones be bleached in the lands of the east. I knew that all those crusaders named by my cousin would have felt the same and that gave me comfort. I was the right knight for this for I was without a wife. I left no children. If I was killed then I would be mourned but I would not leave a fatherless family.

Robert was excited about the journey. He had seen barely eighteen summers and had yet to fight in any battle. The prospect of fighting for God seemed to inspire him. As we passed East Harlsey I said, "Robert, as a squire, your job is to hold my spare horse and wait with the baggage. You may not have to draw a sword."

He smiled, "My father told me that your grandsire, Sir Thomas, was a squire at Arsuf and defended the body of his knight."

I nodded, "So, you wish me to die so that you can enjoy the glory and the fame?"

His face fell, "No, my lord, I…"

I laughed, "I am teasing you, Robert. I doubt that we shall be in such a position. Lord Henry of Almain and the king's sons will not be at the forefront of any fighting. At best I may have to defend them but that day is a long way off. We have more than three hundred miles to travel in England and then another six hundred miles through France before we take a ship. Then we will have a thousand miles across the Mediterranean before we even reach the Holy Land. This may well be tedious and dull. Let us make the best of it and enjoy travelling through England when the sun is shining and the people are happily harvesting."

He nodded, "Aye, my lord, and I am sorry. This is all new to me."

The Ripples of Rebellion

"And to me too. I am used to following the earl into battle. I know him; Henry of Almain and his cousins are unknown to me."

I knew that I was insignificant in the wider scheme of things. There would be earls and barons closer to the action than me. I might end up being little more than a messenger sent by Lord Henry to fetch and carry. Two men travelled faster than a mesne and we made good time. All routes led through London. It was as we passed through London that we heard the news that we were no longer leaving from Portsmouth. Instead, due to unfavourable winds, we were directed to head to Dover. It did not bode well. If we sailed from Dover then we would have a longer journey through France than had we landed at Bordeaux. The advantage was a shorter crossing.

We reached Dover eight days after leaving the ferry in Stockton. Osgar and his son had raised and schooled good horses but I made sure that we found a piece of land where they could graze and recover, for the bulk of our journey lay ahead of us. The journey we had made was but a shadow of the one they would have to endure in France. Robert was given the task of watching them. I would not need him while we were in Dover. While I had a chamber in the castle, one I shared with another three knights serving Lord Henry, Robert had to make do with a hovel close to where our animals were tethered. It did not bode well. It was not the glorious life he had expected. I briefly met the three knights and I liked not one of them. They were arrogant, aloof and thought me a country bumpkin. The journey would seem longer than it actually was.

Lord Henry and The Lord Edward had yet to arrive but the castellan of the castle had tasks for us. The fleet that would carry a thousand men across the Channel to France was already gathering, having been diverted from Portsmouth. The largest of the ships was for the heir to the crown along with his wife and family. Princess Eleanor was travelling to war too. The second largest ship was for Prince Edmund and so I was tasked with the job of ensuring that the *'Maid of Rye'*, our ship, would be ready when Lord Henry arrived from Portsmouth. The reason that the lowliest of tasks was given to me was that the other knights were all older than I was and had served Lord Henry since Chesterfield. Added to that they did not like me. I would be treated as little more than a squire.

The captain of the cog looked like a pirate, albeit a rotund one. He had lost an eye but did not wear a patch. Instead, he had a scarred hole where the orb had been. His other eye seemed to make up for the lack of a partner by constantly dancing around. It was most disconcerting to speak to him. However, he was a good sea captain and appreciated that I had taken the time to find out what was needed.

The Ripples of Rebellion

"Normally, my lord, horses would be secured below deck. They do not like it, but had we travelled from Portsmouth then it would have been necessary. We can cross to Calais in half a day and so, with Lord Henry's permission, we will secure horses here." He pointed to the bolts on the side of the main deck, "It means that we will need men to watch them for my crew will be too busy watching the rest of the fleet."

I nodded, appreciating the candour, "And how do we get the animals aboard, Captain Furze?"

He smiled, "There are two ways: if the horse is well schooled then we use a double gangplank and they walk aboard." He shook his head, "While that is the easiest way I doubt that we shall enjoy such luck. Most will need a sling rigging and that takes time. They have to be hoisted aboard. Whichever method is used we shall need all the horses aboard the night before we sail. It may well take all day to manage this feat. Do we know how many horses there will be?"

I shrugged, "I have four. I am guessing that the other knights will also have four and then there will be Lord Henry's. There could be thirty or more."

He sighed, "Then I hope they pay a good price in Calais for horse dung!"

I laughed. I liked the man and the more I talked to him the less obvious became the empty socket. "And our war gear?"

He nodded towards the open hatch. "We have plenty of cargo space, my lord. I also have cabins although, unless we have a storm, we should not need them."

"I hope you are being well paid for this, Captain?"

He grinned, "Aye, my lord. We negotiated a good price and this voyage will be easier than travelling across the Bay of Biscay to Bordeaux."

The castle filled up on the fifteenth of August when the royal family arrived. The Duke of Brittany and his wife were also travelling. I was just pleased that Lord Henry was not taking his wife. I hovered with the other household knights as we waited for Lord Henry to have the time to seek us out. When he did, he had a raft of questions, "So, which is our ship and what are the loading arrangements?"

The other three household knights, Sir Walter le Grange, Sir Marmaduke Fitzwilliam and Sir Leofric de Lacy all looked at each other blankly. They had spent the time in Dover drinking and playing dice. I did not jump in immediately but when a frown appeared on Lord Henry's face, I had no choice and I volunteered the information. "It is the *'Maid of Rye'*, my lord. Captain Furze seems to know his business. We are to load the horses the day before we sail. Thus far no one has

The Ripples of Rebellion

given us the date. The war gear can be stored below decks. The horses can be hoisted aboard by sling or, if they are well schooled, walk aboard."

He smiled, "You are the newest of my knights, Sir Matthew of Redmarshal, but it is clear that you know your business. Well done."

I saw the scowls from the others. I had made no friends there.

He continued, "I believe there are still some knights to arrive. I cannot see us leaving for three or four days. I leave the loading of the horses to you, Sir Matthew. I have six horses. My squire, Karl, will assist you. He is a good man with horses. My horse is Bruno and his is called Rock. They are both coursers and well schooled." He turned to the other three knights, "And your squires will also obey the orders of Sir Matthew." They nodded. "Sir Matthew, you may leave us. I have some more mundane tasks for these three. Find Karl and take him to the ship."

"Yes, my lord."

I realised that Lord Henry was more like the knights I was used to and I began to look forward to serving him.

Karl was an older squire and he looked to be in his mid-twenties. That was old to still be a squire. I went with him and Robert to the ship and showed them the places where the horses would be tethered. Karl had served Lord Henry for some time and knew his horses well. I explained to them both, as we headed for the quay, what was involved. Karl nodded, "If we hood the horses, my lord, we should be able to get them all aboard using the gangplank. I have seen horses hurt by slings and even if they are not hurt they are always distressed."

"Good, for that will speed things up."

I showed them the places we would tether them and they both seemed happy. As we headed back to the castle I noticed that Robert and Karl got on well. That was good for the squires of the other household knights had shunned Robert in the same way I had been. They seemed to have much in common with their masters. At least Robert would have company for the two-thousand-mile journey ahead of us.

Lord Henry spent most of the time we were in Dover in the company of Prince Edmund and his brother. I noticed that the Montfortians were kept away from the royal party. That did not fill me with confidence about the success of our venture. At least the Earl of Gloucester was not with us. He had withdrawn from the crusade alleging that Llywelyn ap Gruffudd would take advantage of his absence. Henry Samuel had never trusted de Clare who had changed sides during the civil war. Such inconsistency was not a good thing for a leader. I found myself a

The Ripples of Rebellion

watcher. The other three household knights, keen to make up for their chastisement at the hands of our lord fawned around him. I waited patiently until I was summoned. This was not what I had expected but as I had been taught by Sir Henry Samuel, patience would always be rewarded.

Two days before we were due to sail, I was in my usual place. Henry of Almain was speaking to The Lord Edward. He waved and the other three household knights leapt forward as though released by a spring. Lord Henry waved an impatient hand, "Not you three, the one with his wits about him, Sir Matthew."

When I joined the two cousins The Lord Edward waved away all within earshot.

He did not smile at me but at least he was not glaring, "My cousin tells me that you are a resourceful knight."

"He is kind to say so, my lord."

"I hope that you are for you are the one who will be guarding him when we go to the Holy Land."

I was shocked and my answer showed that, "Me, my lord, a bodyguard?"

He did allow himself a rare smile, "The knights of the valley may well tax my patience but the one thing that has to be said for them is that they are the best of warriors. From what I have been told you are a typical northern knight. My cousin has already seen how resourceful you are and you will need those skills. The other household knights are dressing and are here for political reasons. We do not know their worth. You, I do. You shall guard my cousin when we are in the Holy Land and on the long road through France."

"I hope that I can serve Lord Henry well."

His face had lost its smile, "And if you do it might go some way towards alleviating the distaste I have for the treatment I received at Northampton." He waved a hand and I was dismissed.

As I went back to the wall, I reflected that Henry Samuel was right. The Lord Edward bore us a grudge.

We were ordered to load the horses a day after my meeting with the two nobles. The other three knights found places to be but they obeyed the command of Henry of Almain and sent their squires to us. As they led the horses from the castle I reflected that our four, having been grazed, cosseted and cared for by Robert were in much better condition than the others. Robert and Karl had managed to acquire four hoods and the two of them used those to take the horses aboard. As was expected the ones belonging to Henry of Almain were boarded first but then it was the turn of my four and they managed it easily.

The Ripples of Rebellion

A good warhorse cost more money than the finest mail hauberk and a good squire ensured that it was well cared for. The problems began with Sir Marmaduke's horse, Caesar. The knight's squire was a lazy youth and was not firm enough with the horse. It baulked and slipped. Karl and Robert were quick thinking and they grabbed the reins and managed to manhandle it aboard but the damage was done. There was a long cut along the horse's foreleg where it had scraped it on the gangplank. Karl tended to the wound but the horse would never be the same. That night, when he came aboard and discovered the injury, Sir Marmaduke beat his squire. It took the intervention of Henry of Almain to stop it.

Sir Marmaduke glared at me as though it was my fault. In his eyes I had been the one in charge of the loading of the horses. My position was not improved when Lord Henry ordered the knight to leave the ship with his squire and horses. He said that he would rather travel with one less knight than have one who treated his squire so badly. Henry of Almain pointed to me and said, "Here is a true knight, who understands the needs of his horses and his duty to me. Sir Matthew of Redmarshal should be your model, gentlemen, and not one who does not deserve his spurs such as Sir Marmaduke."

As the knight left the ship I saw the glares from the other two knights, Sir Marmaduke's friends. I was the one that they blamed. It was Robert and Karl who managed to take the horse ashore. They did so without it being hurt on a second occasion We had little time to reflect on the incident as we left the moment the gangplank was raised. We sailed for France but it was an ominous start.

As we headed across the water Karl confided in me. "I knew that Sir Marmaduke was a bad 'un, my lord. He fought on the rebel side in the civil war. He lost his lands and this was his way of ingratiating himself with Lord Henry and getting back his lands. He swore that he regretted his actions but you can tell, can't you, my lord, when someone is not telling the truth. He swore loyalty but a leopard does not change its spots. It is good riddance."

"And the other two?"

He nodded, "Fought for de Montfort, my lord, but they weren't at Evesham. They were garrisoned at Kenilworth. I am not sure that they lost as much but I don't trust them either."

I hated politics and I could see that the crusade was not the simple one I had expected. The rebels were being kept close to the leaders. Now I knew why I was to be the bodyguard. I was the one that was trusted. I was also young and expendable.

The Ripples of Rebellion

The voyage was a short one but that did not mean an easy one. It was fortunate that the nights were shorter at this time of year but, even so, some of the horses became restless. Karl showed his skills when he sang to them and they calmed.

"Karl, why are you not a knight?" Robert was young and naïve and asked questions that wiser heads such as mine did not.

Karl did not seem to mind answering. He shrugged, "I have been offered my spurs but I like Lord Henry and I enjoy the life I lead. If I was a knight, Robert, then I would not enjoy the same freedom I do now."

"Freedom?"

"Aye, your master, Sir Matthew here, has to obey orders while I just serve a kind master. I have orders but none of them cause me to do anything I do not wish to do. I look after his horses and that is a joy. When we ride to battle then my only task is to ensure that his horses are ready. All is good. If I have to fight then I know that I can but we have been fortunate and not needed to since Chesterfield."

I nodded, "I remember that campaign."

"It was where Sir Henry noticed you and the other knights of the north, my lord. He admired the earl and how he led."

I now understood my inclusion. His cousin had seen it as a punishment but Lord Henry had made a deliberate choice. I had liked him before but now my admiration grew.

Disembarking the horses was easier than the loading had been for the squires were all mindful of the accident that had befallen one of the horses. We landed in daylight and that helped too. It took many hours to organise the column of men who would ride south to the port close to Marseille. I knew that we were lucky as, serving Lord Henry as we did, we would be at the fore of the column. The Lord Edward would be the first to arrive in any of the places where we would sleep and we would have the first choice of grazing, beds, food and shelter. For those at the rear, it might be a journey of hovels.

The ladies who accompanied us necessitated the use of wagons but as we had some men on foot the wagons did not delay us. When we, eventually, headed south I was able to see that The Lord Edward, for all his martial manner, had a soft side. He was clearly enamoured of his wife, Eleanor of Castile. I could see why. She was the gentlest of ladies and was kind to all. She had learned our names quickly and made a point of addressing us. She even knew the names of the squires and seemed quite fond of Robert. He had a young fresh-faced look and whenever we stopped she would seek him out to look out for the horses. Both he and Karl were in great demand. The loading and unloading of our horses had given them a good reputation. Princess Eleanor was thoughtful and did not like horses to be abused. Her animals were well looked after.

We stayed in abbeys, monasteries and castles as we wound our way south. We made surprising speed and reached our destination by the end of September. We had covered six hundred miles in just over a month. A prodigious feat.

It might have been pleasant but for my two companions. When we stopped it was inevitable that we would have to share a room. If Robert also had to share the chamber then it was bearable but left alone with the two men I found my hands clenching into fists, and I had to tell myself that if I did that which I wanted then I would be punished by The Lord Edward and Henry of Almain would lose his bodyguard. I held my tongue.

I knew from our conversations with Lord Henry that we were supposed to meet up with King Louis and his brother, Charles of Anjou, the King of Sicily. However, delays in England and the long journey meant we were very late in arriving. When our outriders returned, shortly before we reached Aigues Mortes, it was with the disappointing news that King Louis, his brother and his son had sailed already. Even worse was the news that they had not sailed for Jerusalem as had been planned but Tunis. The Holy Land was still a distant dream. None of our leaders were happy although Henry of Almain took it philosophically. The two sons of the king thought that it was all a personal insult from the King of France and Charles of Anjou, the King of Sicily and Naples. It was an ominous start.

The Ripples of Rebellion

The 8th Crusade 1270

Chapter 2

Sir Matthew
Disease and Death

I was privileged to be a fly on the wall as The Lord Edward, his brother Prince Edmund, the Count of Brittany and Lord Henry debated what they would do. Along with the other bodyguards of the king's sons, we stood guard close to the door.

"Brother, we should sail for Jerusalem."

The heir to the throne smiled at his younger brother and shook his head, "We have one thousand men, Edmund. Do you think we can retake the Holy Land with such a number? We have just over two hundred knights. King Louis has almost four hundred and his army is ten thousand strong. No, we must follow him to Tunis."

Lord Henry shook his head, "But why Tunis?"

"I think, cuz, that is the work of Charles of Anjou." He nodded to both his brother and his cousin. "You should know that Sicily was offered to your father, Henry, but he refused the offer and then you, Edmund, were offered the crown. Wisely was the poisoned chalice spurned. Charles is made of different metal. He wishes for an empire and having Flanders and Provence he persuaded the pope to back his claim for the island. I have spoken with the lord of Aigues Mortes and he told me that it was Charles who persuaded his brother to sail to Tunis. He wishes the Emir of Tunis to pay the tribute that is owed to Sicily and Naples." He shook his head, "King Louis is an old and honourable man. He has done this for his brother."

I watched the men take in the information given by The Lord Edward.

It was Henry of Almain who broke the silence that followed, "And how do we get to Tunis? Where are the ships?"

His cousin gave a sad smile, "I am already trying to gather them. My wife has some influence in this part of the world and we may be able to gather a fleet."

Edmund shook his head, "And as the French left even before we landed in France it is likely that we will be too late to take part in this crusade."

"King Louis will still wish to take Jerusalem, brother. This is merely a diversion."

The Ripples of Rebellion

It took until the start of November to gather the ships and then we sailed south. I had never sailed in the Mediterranean Sea. It was nothing like the seas of the north. The waters were bluer and the waves were not as terrifying as those closer to England. I found it a pleasant experience. When we reached Tunis, we saw that the French fleet was being embarked. They were leaving. We had arrived too late.

Lord Henry shook his head, "This is all the fault of that parliament. Had they promised the money quicker then we would have been part of this crusade from the start. We will leave the horses aboard. Matthew, you can come with me and we will follow my cousin ashore. It seems pointless to put the animals through the process of landing if we are to sail again."

We boarded the small boat and were rowed ashore. This was Africa and it was both hot and dusty. My mail, even though it was covered by a surcoat, was hot to the touch by the time we climbed up the ladder to the quay. Already the yellow gryphon was fading as the sun bleached it. The pale blue background was almost white too. The Lord Edward and his brother were already heading for the palace, surrounded by bodyguards. Lord Henry just had me, Karl and Robert. The language we heard, as we strode to the palace, was French. French knights were going the opposite way to board their ships.

I could speak some French and recognised the insults from some of the French knights. They were calling us tardy cowards. Even as my hand went to my sword Lord Henry said, "Peace, Matthew. We know we are not cowards and have made all haste to get here. Once King Louis is apprised of the situation then all will be settled."

It was when we reached the palace that the full scale of the disaster was revealed. Dysentery had raced through the Crusader camp. It had already claimed the life of the French King, one of his sons and many other nobles. Philip would now be King of France and he was taking his army home. The crusade was over before it had even begun. This time I was not privy to the conversation between the monarchs. Lord Henry was invited and we stood without where gossip and rumours were rife. I still got on better with Karl and Robert than the knights and I stood to talk to them. For once Karl lacked confidence.

"That is the end then, my lord. It is clear we cannot go on to the Holy Land. We must return to England. King Henry and his sons are doomed never to fulfil their crusader oath."

I shrugged, "The Lord Edward seems to me to be a strong-minded man. He may persuade King Philip to fulfil his father's promise. King Louis failed once to take the Holy Land. This may be the time for his son to do what his father could not do."

The Ripples of Rebellion

When the leaders emerged it was with the decision that we would sail to Sicily and there make the necessary decisions. It made sense for it took us a little closer to the Holy Land and away from the disease-ridden camp. I was right in one respect. As we boarded the ships Lord Henry told me that the next king of England hoped to convince the French that the crusade could still succeed.

The French fleet left first. The Lord Edward decided that we would head for Palermo. King Charles had invited him to stay at the palace there. Our poor horses had not been landed and some were becoming distressed. Unlike the other knights, I stayed on deck to help the squires to keep them calm. Once more it was Karl and his songs that helped. What did not help was the storm which brewed up as though from nowhere. It was just hours after we left Tunis harbour. The normally benign and blue sea became black and flecked with white. The waves which usually barely rippled the sea, rose as high as the ones I knew wrecked ships off Biscay. The sky was as black as night and the captains were forced to reef their sails to avoid collisions. We were following the ship of The Lord Edward and it was barely visible. As we plunged into troughs, we could see little of the cog which, like us, had reefed sails. The winds drove us north into the darkness of a violent sea. The horses were most agitated and Lord Henry ordered every man on deck to help us calm them. That was easier said than done as the slippery deck made it hard to keep a footing. Robert and I stood between our four horses and I found that holding the ropes that tethered them to the rings on the side helped me to keep my footing. Karl and Lord Henry were equally successful at keeping their feet but Sir Leofric's squire, Henri, did not and was swept overboard. I prayed that he had a quick death. The thought of being battered against the hull of the ship did not bear thinking about.

The day turned to night and I think that dawn might have broken but the skies were so dark that it was hard to tell. I just knew that I was exhausted. My hair and skin were rimed with salt and my hands were red raw from holding onto wet ropes. I heard the cry from the lookout who shouted, "Land to the southwest, Captain." I almost wept with relief.

That had to be Sicily. Any hopes of a safe landing were dashed when the captain ordered sea anchors to be thrown out and all the sails reefed. Karl asked, "What does this mean, my lord?"

Henry of Almain said, "It means that while the land is within touching distance, we will not risk a landing in the dark and we dare not sail further. We will have to ride out the storm here."

Sir Walter shouted, "Will this storm never end? We are cursed."

The Ripples of Rebellion

"Sir Walter, you are a knight. Behave like one."

"My lord, we risk being swept overboard as was the fate of poor Henri. I beg you to make the captain land us."

"Sir Walter, I am no seaman and the captain is. We are in his hands and in God's. Trust to God and all will be well."

Lord Henry was a religious man. On our journey through France, he had visited every church that we passed and prayed. The last church had been in Aigues Mortes and I knew that he would visit one the moment we landed. It was his way.

Although Sir Walter and Sir Leofric carped and complained as much as ever I was aware that the shore to the south of us was giving us some shelter. The motion of the ship was less exaggerated. It was far from pleasant but I detected hope. When the sun appeared that hope was realised. The port of Palermo lay just a few miles to the south of us and when the captain ordered the sea anchors raised and then the sails lowered so that we could sail into the harbour, I knew that our ordeal was over. This time, when we landed, we disembarked the horses. It was easier than the boarding and it seemed to me that the horses were happy to be leaving the torture chamber of the cog.

"Bring your war gear too. The captain tells me that the ship will need repairs. We may be ashore for some time."

One advantage of being with Lord Henry was that we were asked to follow The Lord Edward to King Charles' palace in Palermo. Although it was crowded we had rooms. The disappointment for me was that I had to share with Sir Leofric and Sir Walter. However, their attitude and lack of mettle on the voyage meant that they were embarrassed and ashamed. They were sullen and silent, rather than arrogant and insulting; that suited me. We spent the first day just recovering. Lord Henry asked me to go with him to the cathedral dedicated to the Assumption of the Virgin Mary. There was a chapel in the palace, the Cappella Palatina, but Lord Henry did not wish to use what was, in effect, the chapel of the King of Sicily. Instead, we went to mass at the cathedral. Lord Henry was still on his knees even as people began to leave and I left the church, along with Robert. Karl knew his master well and he stayed with him.

Outside the cathedral Robert and I were able to look at the buildings. They were totally different from anything I had ever seen. There were parts that looked Arabic and others that would not have been out of place in London or Paris. William, my uncle, would know the reason for the disparate styles of architecture but they just intrigued me. When Lord Henry and Karl emerged, we headed back to the palace. He was always silent when we had been to church and I knew better than to intrude. Robert and Karl, however, chattered behind us.

"The land smells more like Africa, Karl, and yet we are close to Italy."

Karl said, "It was ruled by the Arabs at the same time as the Crusaders were trying to take Jerusalem the first time. I think when this island was recovered it gave hope that the Holy Land would soon follow."

"Sir Matthew, will we still go on crusade?"

"I confess, Robert, that I know not. What is clear is that the storm means we cannot leave any time soon. The storm will have hurt the French too. I think that we will be seeing a little more of Sicily."

It was two days later that we heard of the disaster that had befallen the French fleet. They were either unlucky or cursed for while we had found the safe haven of Palermo they had been dashed upon the rocks at Trapani some fifty miles to the west of us. King Philip arrived with the survivors. There were not enough of them to go on a crusade. I was at the feast to celebrate their survival although, after the death of his father and brother and now so many knights, it was a sombre celebration. The Lord Edward still wished to go on the crusade. It was sad to watch his vain attempts to persuade the other leaders to join him. King Philip, although he had yet to be crowned, was adamant that he would go home. "I have my father's bones with me and I would bury him."

King Charles said, "And I have a brother to bury. I will travel with my nephew. Besides, Prince Edward, we do not have enough men left to succeed."

"Had you not gone to Tunis then we would have twelve thousand men and King Louis would be alive."

Even I knew that was the wrong thing to say. What had been done was done. The ten thousand men led by King Louis, our one thousand men and the thousand Sicilians might have been able to succeed but we could not change the past.

King Charles shook his head, "Prince Edward, I know that you wish to fulfil your crusader vow but if you do so then it must be alone. I give you and your men permission to stay here in Sicily until you can arrange for your ships to take you home. My nephew and I will take the land route to France." He patted the hand of his nephew. "Your father's heart and intestines will be buried here, in Palermo. We will leave when that is done."

The heat in Tunis had meant that the ceremony known as mos Teutonicus had been performed. The heart and intestines of King Louis

The Ripples of Rebellion

had been removed and then the flesh rendered to allow the bones to be carried back. The burial of the heart was a necessary ceremony.

Lord Henry said, quietly, "Cousin, let us talk alone. We three can make the decision." I saw Prince Edmund nod.

The Lord Edward sighed, "We are confounded at every turn. You are right. Let us speak on the morrow."

While preparations were made, the next day, for the interment, I was put to guard the door to the small chamber used by the three men. I was able to hear all that they said and I took it as a compliment that I was trusted. I knew that it was Lord Henry's doing. I noticed that The Lord Edward had three bodyguards who stood with us. Two were knights but one was an archer. I had heard of the man. He was called Gerald Warbow. I wondered how an archer could have become a bodyguard. That said, he was the toughest man I had ever seen. He looked like he could handle himself.

It was his master, the heir to the English crown, I heard speak first, "I would still go on the crusade. I can support the Prince of Antioch and the Count of Tripoli. We still have more than two hundred knights. Perhaps more might come from England and Normandy."

"But it is now winter, cousin. The storm we endured might well be the precursor of worse."

"We have eight ships and thirty galleys, Henry. When they are repaired I will consult with their captains. I promise that I will only travel when they think that it is safe."

Prince Edmund said, "And you have our support, brother. We will show the French what English courage can do."

I heard his voice change as he dashed the hopes of Henry of Almain, "I want you, Henry, to travel to Gascony." He looked to me, "Sir Matthew, check that none are listening without."

I opened the door. Karl and Robert were seated a little way down the corridor, "None can hear, my lord." I closed the door.

"I do not trust the French or Charles of Sicily. I hear that he has employed the sons of de Montfort and they serve in his mesne. I want you to take command of my lands in Gascony. If nothing else, you can encourage more men to travel to the Holy Land. You will be the Lieutenant of Gascony."

"I am not afraid to come with you to the Holy Land, cousin. My words of warning were not spoken out of fear."

"I know and your courage is not doubted. I need someone I can trust. That has to be you or my brother, Edmund. Your father was on a crusade here and your blood has committed to Christ. My family needs us to do what my father failed to do. I will give you written authority."

The Ripples of Rebellion

He pointed over to me, "Take just Sir Matthew. Your other knights can swell the numbers going to the Holy Land. I will speak with the two kings. If you travel with them then you will be not only safe but also privy to any conversations that they have. I do not trust either of them and believe that they may cause mischief in our Gascon lands. Sir Matthew has shown himself, like the rest of his family, to be resourceful. You will need that."

"Very well, cousin. I will obey your command for I am an Englishman and like my father, we serve England."

Sir Walter and Sir Leofric did not want to go on the crusade but they had little choice in the matter. The Lord Edward was in no mood to be baulked. I would not have to endure their insults for much longer. Once the burying of the heart and intestines was over the matter of our accompanying the bones back to France was broached. It was then I saw the clever, some might say the cunning side of The Lord Edward. He made it sound as though he was honouring King Louis by sending the son of the King of the Romans, and he even apologised for the few knights he could send back. He told them that he also intended to honour the memory of King Louis by carrying on to the Holy Land. Lord Henry and I were given permission to travel with the royal party.

The night before we left we dined, not with the French and Sicilian kings, but in a small dining room and Princess Eleanor, clearly pregnant, was present. She was a very religious woman and her background in Castile meant that she supported the idea of a crusade. Spain had been under Arabic yoke and it had taken many years for the Aragonese, Navarrese and Castilians to rid themselves of the invaders. When I saw the love between husband and wife I was touched. The wife of The Lord Edward would give birth in the land where Christ was born. We all knew how significant that would be. This time I dined with the family. Princess Eleanor insisted. I said little and was mindful of how I ate, drank and spoke. When the meal came to an end Lord Henry embraced his cousins and Princess Eleanor. I realised then that they were as close as our family and that, perhaps, we were not so different.

Chapter 3

Sir Matthew
Murder at the Mass

    We had rested the horses enough so that they coped with the short journey to Messina. From there it was a ferry across the straits. It all took time, however, as we were moving at the speed of a wagon carrying the bones of the king and loading and unloading the ships took longer as due reverence had to be shown. Each village and town paid their respects to the king who had been so saintly. The four of us were made less than welcome by the others. I am still unsure if this was deliberate or just a sign of the grief they felt. King Louis had been old and widely revered as a devout man. He had famously said, before he left France, '*Déjà vieux, j'entreprends le voyage d'outremer. Je sacrifie pour Dieu richesse, honneurs, plaisirs... J'ai voulu vous donner ce dernier exemple et j'espère que vous le suivrez si les circonstances le commandent.*' He knew he might die but hoped his death would inspire others. I believed that his son, the new king, was grieving but King Charles was cut from a different cloth. As we travelled north through his kingdom, it was as we passed towns and villages that he adopted a look of melancholy and sadness. For the rest of the journey he and his knights happily bantered. We English were at the rear with the baggage and travelled in the dust of the others. Household knights flanked the funeral wagon.

    Lord Henry spoke of the task we faced in Gascony, "I know it is not a crusade, Matthew, but we shall be serving England. It is strange, is it not, that the last knight I chose for my household should be the one I kept with me? Now I see the folly of choosing knights who sought only glory. I fear that my cousin is right. King Philip is not his father and may seek to take the contested parts of the Vexin and Gascony from us. I am also more than a little unhappy that there are some knights who followed the Earl of Leicester in King Charles' retinue." We had all spotted them and we kept apart from them. Wearing the livery of Naples and Sicily they were protected. We were not.

    Each time we stopped the first thing we did was enter a church. If there was a mass then Henry of Almain attended, otherwise he prayed for far longer than we did and often he remained within while the three of us retired outside. Lord Henry did not seem to mind kneeling. He was a religious man. He always gave his sword and dagger to whoever waited outside. Sometimes it was Karl but when he stayed within then that was my task. It was a fine sword.

We rested for a week in Naples. It was Christmas and we had travelled up the coast of Italy through a cold and wet land. We needed a rest. There King Charles seemed to revel in the glory associated with his revered brother. King Louis had, as Lord Henry told me, been a truly charitable man. He had founded the Third Order of St Francis and they served food every day to one hundred poor in Paris. Often the king would serve the beggars. He was, in every sense of the word, a Christian King. Lord Henry admired him. After feasting in Naples we continued our journey north. When we reached Rome there was no pope to greet us. Since the death of Pope Clemens, the cardinals could not agree on a new one. There seemed to be more about politics in Rome than religion. We spent a couple of weeks in Rome and that was mainly so that the two kings could speak to their representatives in Rome. It was more politics.

We explored the ancient city. Lord Henry spent hours each day in St Peter's. When he did emerge, he was happy to wander around the ruins that had been Imperial Rome. Robert and I could not believe the number of stone buildings. Back in England, the majority of houses were still largely made of wood. We had longer in Rome than in Naples. King Philip and King Charles used their time there to try to influence the cardinals in their choice of pope. A pope's influence could be useful to a king.

It was March before we continued our journey north. I was tired of the journey already, but the frequent stops meant that the horses had time to recover. We all got on well and Karl and Robert had become like brothers. Karl taught Robert all that he had learned in his years of serving Lord Henry and I could see a difference in my squire. Karl also gave him sword skills. We were lucky that he was such a kind man. Robert could now speak a little French as well as Italian. The son of the man at arms could have passed for the son of a noble.

The twenty miles from Castellan, north of Rome, to Viterbo were some of the hardest we had endured. This was a mountainous country and the large lake of Lago di Vico necessitated a long march around the enormous body of water. We reached the town in the late afternoon and such was the exhaustion of the animals and the two kings that it was decided to wait there for a few days to allow us all to recover. King Charles had a large house in the town looked after by a caretaker and his granddaughter but it did not matter as King Charles travelled with his own cooks and food. He was a man with a healthy appetite for fine food.

As soon as we arrived the four of us went to the Chiesa di San Silvestro where Lord Henry insisted that we pray. It was as we came out, in the half gloom of twilight, that I saw a column of knights wearing the livery of Naples and Sicily. They were heading to meet their king. King Charles must have ordered men to meet us there. We had left one of his fiefdoms, Naples, and the next was Provence. Between those parts of his domain, we had to pass through Florence, Pisa and the other city-states. Such was the rivalry that it was understandable that the king would need more protection. Even though we carried the body of a revered king it did not guarantee our safety. The body was placed in a nearby church and we stayed in the house which had formerly been owned by an enemy of Charles of Anjou but was now the property of the King of Naples. The man had to have been a rich one for it was well apportioned and whilst my room was one normally used by servants, it held both Robert and I. King Charles' servants travelled with us and they took over the house. They were adept at producing good food quickly and we ate well. We learned that the previous owner, a Neapolitan, had been executed by King Charles.

We had a lazy day after our late arrival and enjoyed the comfort of the palatial house. After another good night of sleep, we rose and breakfasted well before we left the house to go to the church for it had been some days since Lord Henry had attended a mass. As was our usual practice Robert and I took mass and then left. Karl stayed in the church with Lord Henry. We took their swords with us. It was as we came out that I saw some knights wearing the livery of Charles of Anjou. There were four or five knights and half a dozen squires. I might have ignored them had they not studied us closely. Two marched up to us and one said, "Where is Henry of Almain?"

It was at that moment that I recognised them. It was Guy and Simon de Montfort. They were the two remaining heirs of Simon de Montfort.

I was Henry of Almain's bodyguard and these were enemies. They had fled England and King Henry would have them executed if they returned. "And what business is it of yours?"

"We serve King Charles and are charged with his protection." It was Simon, Simon de Montfort's son, who spoke.

"And we have travelled with your king since Palermo so I think we can safely say that he is under no threat from Lord Henry."

I was already reaching for my sword when Guy shouted to his companions, "Seize them." He and his brother raced into the church.

The Ripples of Rebellion

Had all the knights obeyed the command then Robert and I would have died there and then but only their squires, the rest of the squires and another knight drew their weapons. I had the chance to shout, "Treachery!" before they were upon us.

I drew my dagger as well as my sword and managed to block the attempt by two of the squires to grab me. I raked the dagger across the back of the left hand of one of them. It was then that the knight stabbed his sword at me. I deflected it with my dagger but it still gouged a hole in my chausse and cut deeply into my leg. Robert was strong and no coward and, protecting my back, he hacked at one of the squires with his sword. He sliced across the squire's arm. From inside the church, I heard shouts and a cry of, "Mercy!"

Then I heard a Norman voice shout, "You had no mercy for my father and brothers!" There was a scream.

I punched at the face of the knight with my sword and was rewarded when my hilt broke his nose. I stabbed at his side with my dagger and my blade slipped through the mail, his gambeson and his flesh. The other squires jumped at me, and I slashed with my weapons to keep them from me. Robert guarded my back. Before I could do anything else the other knights, who had been watching, took a hand. They raced to pinion me and the knight I had wounded brought his sword down to hit my head. I wore just a coif. I would have died there and then had another of the knights not blocked the blow with his own sword.

I heard as I slipped into blackness, "Enough. We hold them. Enough blood has been shed."

I was not out for long. I heard, "On your feet!" and I felt hands lifting me. I saw that Robert was one of those helping me. The knights were looking in horror, not at the man I had stabbed, but at Simon de Montfort and his brother. In Simon's hands, he held the severed head of Henry of Almain and his manhood.

"Now is my father avenged."

The knight I had wounded shouted, "Kill these two, as well!"

Before any further action could be taken, I heard hooves and more riders appeared. They were also dressed in the livery of Charles of Anjou. "All of you, hold. This is unseemly. What has gone on here?"

I managed to say, "Murder most foul," before the knight I had wounded punched me in the face with the pommel of his dagger. Once more darkness consumed me.

When I came to I was back in the house used by the two kings. I saw that Robert was there but of Guy and Simon de Montfort, there was no sign. A doctor was tending to my leg. I saw the knight who had ridden up but of the rest, they had gone.

The Ripples of Rebellion

Robert said, "I am pleased you have awoken, my lord. You have been unconscious for an hour."

"Where are the murderers?"

King Philip shook his head, "Fled, along with the man you wounded. I fear you gave him a mortal wound. There may be repercussions."

King Charles said, "I have discharged the two of them from my service and the cardinal has excommunicated them."

"But they murdered the nephew of the King of England."

King Charles said, "And he can punish them. We have to get the body of my brother back to France." For the first time, there was a hint of sympathy from the Frenchman. "This means, of course, that you can no longer travel with us. There will be bad feelings and, besides, you will need to take the body of Lord Henry back to England. The men who deal with such things are preparing the bones for you."

"How will we get the body back to England?"

He shrugged and all sympathy disappeared, "That is not my concern. This is not Neapolitan land. You may use this house once we are gone but there will just be the old caretaker and his granddaughter. You will have to find food for yourselves. When you leave the house, it will be sold for I no longer need it. My agents will deal with that." I stared at the man who did not seem concerned that the nephew of the King of England had been murdered in a church, decapitated and emasculated.

The doctor said, "In any case, your leg has been stitched. You will not be able to leave here for a week."

"Where is the body of Karl, the squire?" I did not know what had happened to Karl but I could not see him sitting idly by while his master was murdered. I assumed that he too had died.

King Charles just shrugged but the knight who had ridden up said, "I know where it is to be found."

I made to rise but the doctor said, "You cannot move."

Robert said, "I will go, for Karl was my friend." The knight led Robert from the house.

I was carried by the doctor and his assistant to the small mean room at the rear of the house that Robert and I had slept in the previous night. I was clearly of no importance any longer. This was a horror I had never expected. Nothing that Sir Henry Samuel had taught me prepared me for this. I had a great responsibility. If I did not discharge my duty properly then my family would have to endure the enmity of The Lord Edward. Left alone I prayed for help from the Almighty. The doctor had given me a draught and I slept. My dreams were not pleasant ones and when I woke, I was sweating; I was also alone in the room and the house was filled with the cacophony of King Charles' party preparing food. They were eating and drinking as though nothing had happened.

The murder did delay the funeral party. They did not leave until the next day. I do not think it was out of any consideration for Henry of Almain but King Charles had planned out the stops and they were designed for his comfort. Nor was there any farewell to me. Instead, the first I knew of their departure was the silence in the house when I woke, and then the appearance of Robert.

"How is the leg, my lord?"

I hadn't even thought of it until that moment but as soon as it was mentioned I felt an ache. "A slight pain but it is nothing."

"The doctor was a kind man, my lord. He left a bottle with a draught to ease the pain. Would you like some now?"

Shaking my head I said, "I will endure it for I may need the draught when I sleep." I tried to rise but as I did, I felt dizzy.

"The doctor said that the blows to the head will have an effect. You need to rest as much as possible."

"How can I when I have so much to do? There is Karl to bury and the body of Lord Henry to prepare for travel."

"Karl was buried last night and Lord Henry's bones will be ready to take back in three days. They are with those who deal with the dead." He made the sign of the cross. Such men were not popular, but they were necessary.

"I should have been at Karl's funeral. He deserved to be mourned."

"You were asleep and we had to bury him. In this land bodies soon begin to stink. He was mourned. I was there and the priest."

"That was all? A man should have more than that at his leaving of this earth."

"Thomasina came to pay her respects."

"Thomasina?" The name seemed vaguely familiar but my recollections of the previous days were hazy.

"You remember? She is the granddaughter of old Luigi, the caretaker. She and Karl got on well the first night we arrived. The day before he was murdered."

"That was kind of her."

He looked around the room. "This is the meanest room in the house. Thomasina is cleaning the master bedroom for you. The doctor said you would have to stay in bed for a week. The least we can do is to make you comfortable."

A better bed seemed irrelevant. "The horses?"

"I have taken care of them."

The Ripples of Rebellion

"And it will not be a week before we leave. As soon as I can stand, we leave."

"And go where my lord?"

"Back to England."

"By land?"

The thought of a two-thousand-mile journey with the body of Lord Henry seemed horrific.

Robert said, "The man you wounded, died. He bled inside. My lord, he was a Montfortian. He had lands close to the valley, at Upleatham. There were murmurings from some of the others in the king's party. It is good that we are here and they are gone. We would have needed to sleep with a dagger beneath our pillows."

My squire was right. There were just two of us now and we had an onerous task. We had to get Lord Henry's body and possessions back to England. "Lord Henry's chests, are they still in his room?"

"Nothing was moved, so aye."

"He was given a chest of coins. We will use that and take a ship. Pisa has a fleet of ships and we can hire one to take us."

"That will cost a fortune, my lord."

"And Lord Henry deserves it. I am the last of his knights and I will bear the responsibility."

Just then the door opened and the young woman appeared. I confess that I had not noticed her before but now I saw that she was a lovely young thing. She smiled and said, in English, "I have made up your bed." She beamed when I nodded as she finished the sentence. "My English is poor." She added.

I spoke slowly, "Better than my Italian."

Robert said to her, "You have changed." She looked confused for he had spoken quickly. He waved a hand at the dress. "Your clothes."

She gave a broad smile, appreciating that it had been noticed. "While you stay, I am to care for you. I must look…" I saw her struggle for the word, "presentable." I nodded and she smiled. "Roberto," when she used my squire's name it sounded exotic. She pointed upstairs.

"Right, my lord. I shall try not to drop you."

"I can walk!"

Thomasina put her hand on my chest and wagged her other hand at my face, "Doctorrie Galbini, he says no! Roberto." I noticed that when she had time to think her English was perfect but when she rushed, it was not.

Robert picked me up. I was a big man but he was strong and he made it look easy, "Best not to argue with her, my lord, she is strong-minded this one."

The Ripples of Rebellion

She opened the door and led the way. I spoke quietly to Robert as we were led from the servants' quarters to the more opulent rooms on the first floor. "How is it that she can speak English so well?"

"Her mother was English. She was the daughter of a mercenary who served the old ruler of Naples, King Manfred. The old man is her grandfather on her father's side." He added quietly, "He is not healthy either, my lord, although in his case it is old age, rather than a wound to the leg." Robert smiled as we entered the huge room, "The king himself used this room."

The bedchamber was enormous. There were tapestries on the wall and curtains hung around the bed. A fire burned in the hearth. It was bigger than the Earl's bedroom in Stockton. Thomasina plumped up the feather pillows and Robert laid me down gently. Even so, I felt a pain course through me as the injured leg touched the bed.

"Sorry, my lord."

"Not your fault. Now go and bring Lord Henry's things in here."

"But your breakfast."

"Can wait."

He left and Thomasina smiled, "I will fetch your food."

I felt dizzy once more and I closed my eyes. I didn't sleep but the darkness felt comfortable. I heard the door open and, opening my eyes, saw Thomasina backing in with a tray of food. There was a table next to the bed and she placed the tray upon it. She waved a hand over the tray, "Not English food but ...good....yes?"

I saw that there was fresh fruit, bread, ham and cheese. I smiled, "Good."

"This is beer." She handed me the beaker. "My mother taught me how to make it."

I drank some and made the appropriate noises. "Good."

She took a knife and sliced me some bread. She spread butter on it and held it to my mouth.

"I can eat myself."

She looked hurt, "I thought to nurse you. Everyone says you are the brave knight who fought many others. Robert said so too."

I noticed that the more she spoke English the better it became. "I am sorry. It is the wound."

She nodded, "And that is why I will feed you."

Robert was right. There was no arguing with her. She fed me. While she was doing so Robert came in with the belongings of Lord Henry. "There are Karl's too. Should I bring them in here as well?"

"We will need to sort them and as I cannot move then this is the best place. We cannot take everything back with us."

"I will fetch it all then."

He finished his task by the time I had eaten. Thomasina frowned at the mess that was accumulating in the room. "This was tidy."

Robert cowered before her gaze, "And it will be again, Mistress, I promise."

"Good. I will go now and buy food for our evening meal." She paused, "King Charles left one gold piece."

Her meaning was clear. When that was spent there would be no more. "I have money."

She looked relieved, "Good. And, Roberto, Sir Matthew does not leave the bed."

"Yes, Mistress."

She had just left when I said, "We have to break that rule, Robert, I need to make water."

He nodded to the urn in the corner. It was not a tall one but elegantly made for the purpose. "I will carry you."

I shook my head. "Until you fashion me a stick I will use you as a crutch but I will not be carried like a baby. I promise not to put weight on the leg."

Even though he took all the weight the journey of a few paces to the urn was painful and, once again, I was dizzy. When I had finished and was returned to the bed, I closed my eyes.

"I tell you what, my lord, I will sort through Karl's chests and you have a nap. By the time you are awake, we can do the same for Lord Henry's."

Robert had been raw clay when he was appointed to be my squire but now he had grown. I knew that much of that growth was down to Karl. It was right that Robert should be the one to sort through his belongings. I did not sleep long but when I woke I saw that Robert had made two piles. He nodded to me and pointed to one of them, "This is good quality, my lord, and I thought to take it for me." He paused and waited for my approval.

"Of course."

"The boots fit and his hauberk is a better one than mine as is his sword. I thought of selling the rest in the market and my old hauberk and sword. We have not yet counted the money from Lord Henry. If there is not enough…"

He was being practical. We spent the next hours sifting through the belongings of Lord Henry. I say, we, but it was largely Robert who picked things up to show me. This was not the same as Karl's belongings. The travelling clothes we could sell but his rings, seals, weapons, better clothes and mail, would have to return to England with him. I dreaded telling his father of his death although I assumed that by the time we reached England then he would know the news. The chest with the coins was more than enough to get us back to England. I had Robert count it all out and he fetched parchment so that I could keep a tally. It would need to be accounted for. I was no thief.

"The money you get for Karl's belongings, use it to have a mason make a stone. Karl was a warrior who deserves to be remembered."

I could see that pleased Robert, "A kind thought, my lord, and one I should have had."

"You have done more than was expected of you."

When Thomasina appeared with the food Robert was dismissed but in a kindly fashion, "Roberto, you can eat in the kitchen with my grandfather. Make sure he eats. He drinks more than he eats and that is not good."

"Yes, Mistress."

Once more she fed me and this time I did not argue. She seemed to enjoy it. "Your grandfather is not well?"

Her eyes looked sad, "He is dying, my lord. We both know it. When you are gone then the agents of the king will sell this house. I hope that my grandfather is in a better place by then."

I stopped mid-chew, "And you? What will become of you?"

She smiled cheerfully, "Oh, do not worry about me, my lord. I can work as a servant, if not here in Viterbo, then in Rome. My English is useful."

Until that moment I had been desperate to leave Viterbo and begin the journey back. The longer we stayed would benefit the couple.

Thomasina was a wonderful nurse. She was gentle and thoughtful. She told me of the funeral of Karl, "Roberto, he sang a lament, it made me cry for it was a beautiful song and well sung. They were close?"

"They were close and I am sorry that I was not there for I liked Karl too."

"What those men did…" she shuddered, "murder, in a church. They will burn in hell."

"Did you hear where they went?"

"You cannot have revenge, my lord, they would kill you."

She was right but I had no intention in seeking them out. I shook my head, "No, I will not seek revenge but I do not want them to cause us trouble on the way home."

She looked relieved. "The gossip at the market is that they have fled Italy." I nodded and continued eating as she fed me, "And how will you get home, my lord? Over the mountains and through France?"

The Ripples of Rebellion

I shook my head, "A ship. I plan on hiring a ship to travel to England."

"Ah, then that would be from Pisa. It lies one hundred and fifty miles to the north of us. The weather may be better by the time you leave." I had finished eating and she wiped my mouth with a cloth. She smelled fresh and fragrant. Her soft fingers brushed my cheek and a lock of hair fell to her shoulder. She stood and tidied herself, "I will be sad when you go. It has been good to speak the language of my mother. She died five years since and I thought I had forgotten the words. Your arrival has opened the dam in my head and it is as though my mother is still alive."

"Then come back to England with us. My uncle is an important lord. We can find somewhere for you."

Her eyes told me that she liked the idea but the shake of her head and her words did not match her look, "My grandfather cannot leave and…I am his only kin. It is my duty to care for him." She smiled again, "But thank you, my lord, that is a kind offer."

She left.

Over the next few days, I grew stronger and I was able to begin to walk. My Italian improved a little but it became unnecessary as Thomasina's English became more fluent. It was only halting when she was upset and rushed to get out the words. We kept the news that I had begun to walk from Thomasina. Henry of Almain's bones were brought to the house three days later. King Charles had paid for the service, and all had been done well. The bones were in a chest. The chest weighed less than the chest with Lord Henry's mail. Was that all a man was when he died? Robert had the chest, along with the other things we would take back, placed in the antechamber to the room I used. It was where he slept. We then began to plan our journey. We involved Thomasina and she was more than useful. We learned that Pisa was ruled by Ugolino della Gherardesca. His family had gained the upper hand on the powerful city-state and, his sister having married into the Visconti family, had money and powerful connections.

When I had first been wounded I could not wait to leave but now the thought of leaving Thomasina and her grandfather without a roof over their heads made me wonder. Was there a rush to get home? The more I thought about it the less necessary seemed the long journey.

When the agents of the king came they had expected me to be gone. My Italian was not good enough to be the one who spoke to them and so it was Thomasina who took on that responsibility. I discovered that they had someone who wished to buy the house and wanted us gone as soon as possible. I played the wounded soldier and said the leg needed

The Ripples of Rebellion

longer to heal. I was a knight and they did not argue with me. Ten days after the murder I was able to walk about the house. The stitches would need to come out in four days' time and Thomasina had recommended a doctor who would take them out. I sent her with a message to the agents to let them know we would need another four days.

When she returned, I asked her what her plans were. She looked distressed but put on a stoic expression, but her voice faltered "We will manage. My grandfather is sick but he is an old soldier."

Over the last days, he had rarely left his bed and Thomasina had been torn between tending to him and our needs. Robert showed his kindness by offering to cook for us. She reluctantly agreed. The night before my stitches were due to be removed we had enjoyed a good feast for, if we left the next day, Thomasina and her grandfather would be evicted. We finished off the wine. The king had a good cellar and we enjoyed it. Luigi was asleep and I asked Thomasina to join us. At first, she was shy and quiet but as the wine flowed and Robert cheered us with a song she brightened and, by the end, was laughing like a giddy girl. I was pleased and sad at the same time. We had brought a little joy into her life and yet, at the same time, we were abandoning her.

We were woken in the middle of the night by a wail. I struggled out of bed and found the stick that Robert had bought in the market. By the time I reached the ground floor, Robert was with Thomasina, comforting her. I saw that her grandfather had given up the fight and had died.

Thomasina gave me a sad smile, "His mind still worked, right until the end. He knew of our proposed eviction and said that we would find somewhere. He even joked about helping you to take the bones back to England."

I looked at Robert and our eyes spoke the words our voices did not. The old man had decided to die. Robert's father had told him of old soldiers who had done that and I had seen it too. "Perhaps, Thomasina, it was not a joke. My offer of protection on the way to England and a home there were not empty words. When your grandfather is buried come with us."

She looked down at the old man. All the pain had gone and there was the hint of a smile on his face. She knelt and kissed him, "I was his only grandchild and I know he loved me. He could be gruff and silent but I know that he would want me to have a life. I will travel to England with you and be your servant. Thank you, Sir Matthew."

When the agents arrived, the next day, even they were not hard-hearted enough to evict her that day. We buried her grandfather and his grave was next to Karl's. The stone was not yet in place but it gave me the chance to say goodbye to the faithful and ill-fated squire. I had my stitches removed in the late afternoon and we spent the rest of the time packing. Luigi would have to be mourned at some other time. We left Viterbo as dawn broke for we had a long ride ahead of us.

Chapter 4

Sir Matthew

The Road Home

22nd of March 1271

Thomasina could ride and that was a good thing, for Robert and I had our hands full with a horse laden with mail and the bones of Lord Henry, as well as our sumpter and a pair of warhorses. They were too valuable to leave and while we had sold two of the horses, we did not sell those two. Thomasina had little to take. The mementoes from her mother and grandfather were carried in a small bag and her clothes in a slightly larger one. Her horse had no difficulty in coping with her weight and her belongings.

Robert rode Rock, Karl's horse. He knew that when we reached England it would be returned to Richard of Cornwall but until then the courser could cope with the mailed man. Thomasina was cold as we rode north. To Robert and me it seemed quite mild but although born to an English mother, she had been raised here in Italy and was more used to the Italian climate. It was lucky that Robert had kept Karl's cloak. We had learned that oiled cloaks such as the ones we wore were as valuable as gold. Although too large for her it kept both her and Mary, the hackney she rode, warmer. I rode next to Thomasina while Robert dealt with the other horses. At first, it was to ensure that she would not fall from the back of the horse but then it became comfortable. She had spoken more with Robert in the king's house. Now she was able to chatter with me. I think that much of it was nervousness and excitement. She had lived her life in Viterbo. Firstly, with her mother and grandfather and latterly with just her grandfather. As far as I could tell she had no friends and had little contact with people outside of the house.

I did not mind what, at times, was merely a torrent of words filling a silence. After much such chatter, she paused and asked, "So what is Stockton like, Sir Matthew?"

"Nothing like this land." We were heading towards Tuscany which was mountainous. "There is a river and although we are just a few miles from the sea, it can take two days to sail from the mouth of the estuary to my home. To reach the castle from the south you need to take a ferry for there is no bridge. The weather we are enjoying now would be a normal day in summer. The land is colder. That means, of course, it is not as hot in summer." I for one did not wish to burn beneath the sun as we had in Africa and Sicily. "We do not grow olives and we make beer not wine."

She was, briefly, silent and then she asked, "And what would I do in Stockton?"

I deflected the question, "You may choose to live with your mother's people. Where did she come from?"

"I do not know if any of her family live. Even if they were alive then I would not be welcome. My father was a mercenary who served the Earl of Pembroke. His good looks made my mother fall for him. They ran away together. My mother never regretted marrying him even though he was killed in battle when I was just four years of age. I can barely remember him." I nodded. "If you think there is no place for me in England, my lord, then I will leave you in Pisa. I am sure I could find employment there."

I knew that she would but it would be of the wrong kind. She was more than pretty, she was stunning. It was hidden beneath dull clothes and hair tied back in a bun but I knew that she would soon be taken and used by unscrupulous men.

"I did not mean that. I was just aware that England, my England, can be cold and is not what you are used to. As for employment… you could be a lady's maid. We have many ladies in the valley; my mother, sister-in-law, aunts, and the wives of my cousins. You could be a tutor for children."

"A tutor?"

"Aye, you could teach Italian. You could cook. I have tasted your food and it is delicious. Let us worry about what you will do when we reach Pisa, cross the sea, find Richard of Cornwall and then ride back to Stockton. Our arrival at my home is many months off."

Strangely, my answer seemed to please her. We then chatted about her life in Viterbo. The man who had previously owned it had been something of a criminal. He had also plotted against Charles of Anjou. That explained both his untimely death and the taking of his property and riches by the avaricious Frenchman.

We rode just twenty miles that first day. It was not only a consideration for Thomasina but also for me. The wound was painful whilst riding. We reached, after passing the enormous Lago di Bolsena, San Lorenzo alle Grotte. It was an important village and had an inn. We stopped, when we arrived, at the church of San Lorenzo Martire. The priest had heard of the murders for the excommunication edict had been

The Ripples of Rebellion

sent to all the churches. He was happy to have the bones of Lord Henry in his church. Word spread in the village and when we ate, in the inn, we were sought out. I have found that people are ghoulish and relish the grisly. They asked for confirmation of the manner of the death. Thomasina was invaluable. Robert and I could stumble through a few sentences of Italian, but Thomasina became the storyteller, and she showed a natural talent for doing so. That became the pattern all the way to Pisa. We would find a church where the bones would be safely protected and then we would find an inn. The story became better as Thomasina grew into the telling. The reactions of the audience, for that is what they were, encouraged her to make minute changes. It also made a change in Thomasina. She was doing something brand new but she found that she could do it well. It gave her confidence. For my part I found myself captivated by her voice and her smile. Her laughter made me, quite naturally, laugh.

We were all almost sad when we reached Pisa, for the journey would now be completely different. We had not moved as quickly on the road as other travellers out of respect both for Thomasina and the bones we carried. The result was that when we reached the walled city, we were met by a delegation from the Doge who had heard of our progress. We were invited to stay at his palace. We could not have refused even if we had wanted to. Ugolino della Gherardesca was a political animal and ruled that part of Italy. Thomasina had hinted as much on our journey but when I met him I could see that power, money and influence were the lifeblood of the Pisan ruler. He wanted us to stay with him so that he could say that he had watched over Henry of Almain's bones. I did not like him but I happily accepted both his hospitality and his help. Once again Thomasina's Italian proved to be invaluable. Once he discovered that we needed a ship he put one of his own vessels at our disposal. The Pisan fleet at that time was only rivalled by the Genoese. He refused to accept payment although I knew there would be an ulterior motive. There was, as I discovered later.

We stayed with the Doge for four days and that was mainly so that the ship could be prepared for a voyage which would take it beyond the Pillars of Hercules. Normally ships from Pisa did not venture into the deep dark sea that stretched to the end of the world. Our vessel needed fresh ropes, spare sails and, of course, supplies. It was as we boarded the ship that Thomasina discovered the ulterior motive. She overheard a conversation between the captain of the ship, Giacomo, and the steward of the Doge, Paulo. We were carrying a cargo and the doge hoped to make money by buying sheep skins from England. We had been given a

The Ripples of Rebellion

sealed letter from the Doge addressed to Henry of Almain's father, the Regent of England.

    The ship was like the ones we had sailed from Agues Mortes. They had been Genoese but the design was similar. This time we were given three cabins in the bow castle. Robert and I had much more room than when we had sailed to Tunis. After we had put our bags in the cabin we went back on deck and watched the lines as they were thrown aboard and neatly coiled by the crew. I led Thomasina up the ladder to the bow castle. We were out of the way of the crew and had a fine view ahead. Captain Giacomo tacked his way out of the harbour to the sea and once clear we turned to larboard and began our voyage. We watched dolphins darting out of the water ahead of us and the cries of the sea birds as they swarmed behind the returning fishing boats. Thomasina giggled at the antics of the birds. Robert was in good humour and, as was his wont, sang a song. While Thomasina had never heard it, for me it was a memory of home.

    It was getting on to dark when the sails were reefed a little and we descended to the main deck. The fact that the ship's owner had commissioned the voyage for us meant that we were treated like royalty. The crew knuckled their foreheads and gave way as we headed down the deck. We made our way to the aft cabin, the captain's. We ate with the captain and his officers and Thomasina was given the respect of a great lady. They stood as she entered the cabin. Once more her confidence soared.

    As we ate we chatted about the weather and the food and then I asked a little more about our voyage, "So, Captain, what is our course?"

    I risked a little Italian but it soon became clear that I could not carry out a complicated conversation about such matters as our course and the dangers. Food and the weather were safer grounds. Thomasina translated.

    The captain sighed and waved his spoon to the north, "The Genoese are to the north and while the passage along the Provence and Castilian

The Ripples of Rebellion

coast is safer, the Genoese would take us. It means that we are forced to sail south and pass the Arabs of Tunis and Algiers." He shrugged, "You may have noticed that we carry almost as many warriors as sailors and that is because we fear an attack. The Emir pays tribute to Charles of Anjou but he makes back that tribute by taking ships such as ours. Once we pass Corsica we will sail directly for the passage between Africa and Andalucia and pray that they miss us." He gave a sad smile, "Life as a galley slave on a Barbary pirate does not appeal."

Even as she translated, I saw the fear on Thomasina's face as she had not expected this. I now understood why The Lord Edward had chosen the land route over France. It was safer.

The first mate added, "We will sail quickly during the day and travel as far as we can. We will be like a young boy racing to play with his friends. At night we reef the sails and travel at the speed of an old man with a stick." The picture made Thomasina smile. She was resilient.

The ship and the sea were engulfed in darkness as we made our way to our cabins. I saw what the first mate had meant. Our motion was sedate. We were still moving but not as fast as we had been. There were two men at the steering board as well as a lookout, another was at the top of the mast in a precariously placed wooden basket and, as we neared our cabin, I saw two men at the bow. They waved as we entered the bow castle. We would edge along slowly for safety reasons. The captain estimated it would take a month or perhaps two for us to make England. We would have to get used to this.

The three cell-like cabins were next to each other. Fire was a risk on ships and we had been given one candle which was contained within a glass vessel. That first night at sea, I held it so that Thomasina could see her bed. Unlike the ships we had sailed in before, our cabins had small beds. There was a wooden rail to prevent its occupant from falling out. Thomasina entered hers and looked nervous. I handed her the candle. "You keep this. Robert and I are old campaigners and can undress in the dark."

She looked relieved, "You are kind, my lord. I thought all nobles were arrogant men who looked down their noses at the likes of me but you are different. Are all English knights like you?"

Robert answered, "Mistress Thomasina, there are arrogant knights in England too but you will find, in Stockton, that the knights are all cut from the same cloth as Sir Matthew."

"Thank you, Robert."

"Sorry, my lord. Goodnight." He entered his cabin.

Thomasina still looked nervous. "Close your door and I will wait without until you are in bed."

"There is no need."

"I will wait."

She closed the door and I heard the sounds of her undressing. Eventually, she said, "I am in bed now, my lord. All is well. Thank you. As my mother used to say, *'Goodnight and God bless.'*"

"Goodnight and God bless you, too, now blow out the candle."

I saw the light go from beneath the door and went to my cabin. I undressed but it was some time before I managed to find sleep. It was not the dangers of pirates or the voyage that kept me awake but Thomasina. She was in my head.

The sails were billowing as soon as dawn broke and that woke us for it was not just the snap of the sail but the motion of the ship that made us rise. The air off the sea and the early hour necessitated cloaks and Robert and I were dressed and on deck before Thomasina. "I will go and see to the horses, my lord."

"And I will wait for Thomasina."

With just one squire for our horses, Robert would be kept busy. He would have to muck out twice a day, feed and water them and lead them for a short walk. They were not on the main deck but the captain had allocated the foredeck hold to them. The deck above had been removed so that they were not confined as some of the horses had been on the voyage from Aigues Mortes. It made a difference. I was watching from above when Thomasina arose. Framed against the low sun she looked stunning with the cowl of her cloak around her ears.

"It is cold, is it not?"

I smiled, "When we pass the pillars it will seem like winter to you."

She looked down and saw what Robert was doing, "I could help him, my lord. It does not seem right that he has to do all the work."

"It is the lot of a squire. I was a squire once and I had to clean out the stables and serve at the table. It is preparation for knighthood. One day Robert will be a knight and hopefully, this experience will make him a better one."

"Does it work?"

"Sometimes, but as we said on the road there are some knights who are naturally bad."

We waited until Robert had finished his work, washed his hands in seawater and joined us on the main deck before we went for food. The food was laid out in the captain's cabin. The officers had already eaten but there was plenty of food left. He had told us that we would not put in again until we reached Lisbon. Portugal was safe and was at a halfway point on our voyage. We would take on more water and supplies there. The captain had a cargo to unload. The road route to

The Ripples of Rebellion

Portugal was fraught with dangers and the Doge had seen this voyage as a chance to test the water.

The days took a pattern. After we had eaten we would walk around the deck. The seas were blue and we could see, first to the west and later to the north, the islands of Sardinia and Corsica as we passed them. We saw fishing ships aplenty and many Pisan ships. These were safe waters but I could see why there was a need for reefed sails at night. A collision would be fatal. We ate in the captain's cabin but the officers only joined us for the evening meal when, with reefed sails, a small watch would stare into the dark. Despite my words, Thomasina insisted on helping Robert with the horses. She did not muck out but she fed the horses and groomed them. It seemed to be mutually satisfying. I found myself admiring her more and more. I thought of some of my cousins at home. Lovely ladies though they were, they would never have thought to help a squire. Thomasina was special.

We were a week into the voyage when we noticed a change. It was not just the weather which became more threatening but the crew became more watchful. We could feel the heat of Africa on the larboard bow. It lay to the southwest of us. Antonio was the first mate and when I saw two crossbowmen ascend to the mainmast, I asked him why. Others had whetstones and were sharpening the boarding pikes that were attached to the mainmast. My Italian had improved and I could understand a little more. The crew were sympathetic and spoke slowly to help us.

"We are now in the waters of the pirates, my lord. The Barbary coast lies to the south of us. They live in their lairs and when they see a sail such as ours then they hunt in packs, like dogs. Now is the time for you and your squire to arm yourselves and to keep the young lady close. When they attack it will be both sudden and deadly. They use oars and need not the wind. They wait in packs and when they come they attack from many directions. We have high sides and they are low to the water but, even so, they have many men aboard and can overwhelm us if we allow them to close with us."

I found Robert and told him to fetch our swords and coifs. Thomasina was watching some dolphins as they swam close to us, "Are they not wonderful creatures, my lord? They seem to fly out of the water."

"They are that, Thomasina. Listen, the first mate has told me that we are now in the waters where the pirates wait. When we see them, you must go to the cabin."

"Will you?"

The Ripples of Rebellion

"No, but I am a warrior and I can fight. Without being rude, you would get in the way. I have never fought on a ship before but I imagine the confined space makes for a confusing fight." We had given her a dagger before we had left Viterbo. "You still have your dagger?"

She nodded, "If they come for me they will find I can fight."

"Good, but hopefully, it will not come to that. I cannot see them taking the captain and his ship easily."

The captain had impressed me with his planning. He was no fool. He had a wife, children and grandchildren in Pisa. He was a rich man and had a half-share in the ship. This one voyage and the profits from trade with England could mean he might be able to leave the sea. He would do all that he could to keep alive and that meant we had more chance of survival too.

It was at daybreak two days later, as we turned to sail west towards the Great Sea which lay beyond the Pillars of Hercules, that we heard the words we had dreaded, "Sails to the south."

We dressed hurriedly and raced from the cabins with swords hanging from our belts and coifs on our heads and shoulders. I banged on Thomasina's door, "Stay within until we return." I did not wait for an answer but wondered if there would be a return. Even as we emerged, we saw the decks being replaced over the horses. They would have to endure the Stygian darkness and the noise of conflict until the battle was over. We would have to spend time calming them…if we survived.

I looked south and felt the wind in my face. I saw the dots in the distance. The Arab ships, all three of them, were low and sleek. Each one was smaller than we were but I could see weapons bristling and glistening in the sun. With the wind behind them, they would not need as many men on the oars and that would mean more men available to fight us. They would surround us. The captain had full sails and we were flying but the Arab ships had the wind, too, and it would be a race.

Robert looked up at the crossbowmen who were already lining the sides of the two castles and the small wooden nest on the mainmast. "They can hurt the Arabs, my lord."

"I would rather have archers and as they are loosing into the wind they will have to wait until the pirates are close. Remember how long it takes to reload." I nodded to the boarding pikes stacked by the mainmast. "Let us take those."

We each selected one of the shafted weapons that would give us a greater reach. Half a dozen English archers would have made a difference. I shook my head. Henry Samuel had taught me that asking for what you did not have was of no help.

The Ripples of Rebellion

We walked to the side closest to the Arab ships. I noticed that all the crew were now armed. The main defence would be the twelve crossbows but there were another ten men armed as we were. This was the reason for their inclusion and now they would earn their pay. They each had a short sword at their waist. Our swords, whilst better weapons, were a little too long to use aboard a ship. We would all use the pikes to keep the attackers at bay.

One of the sailors pointed, "See, one is ahead of the others. He is the leader."

Now that they had closed a little with us they were much clearer. I saw the slightly larger boat with the black flag. It was using more oars and fairly flew through the water. I wondered where she would attack us. She could pick wherever she liked. I guessed that it would be at the rear where the captain and helmsmen stood. If they took that then the ship would be theirs. Robert said, "My lord, there are stones stacked here."

I had not noticed before but there were nets hung along the gunwale and inside were stones. They were the size of a child's head. "I am guessing we use these to try to sink the pirates." Our one advantage was the height of our ship. It would tower over the pirates and any stone dropped from our side could hurt both men and ship.

The captain was using all his experience and guile to give us a chance. He turned us to head north and west. Not only was that away from the Arabs but it also gave us more wind. I saw a gap begin to appear and the three ships had to deploy more oars. It meant the leading Arab began to draw away from its consorts for it had a bigger crew. The respite we gained was short-lived and the leading ship drew closer to us. However, it began to open a gap between the two consorts. The crossbowmen at the stern would have the first chance to hurt the enemy. Those in the bow castle and on the main mast would have to wait until the pirate was alongside. Then, however, they could do serious damage for they would be able to clear the Arab's stern and the helmsman who held on to the rudder on the steerboard side. I knew from talking to the captain, that the pirates liked to use archers but having every oar manned meant that advantage was denied them. The cracks from the crossbows punctuated the air as our first line of defence tried to hurt the Arab ship. At best they would be able to hit half a dozen men and from a tossing ship that was all that we could hope. I guessed there were forty pirates on each ship. All that they needed to do was to get one alongside and grappled and we would be doomed.

One effect of the bolts was that the leading pirate changed his course to run a parallel one. I was no sailor but the warrior in me told me that

The Ripples of Rebellion

they could then turn and either strike at our bows or simply ram us. The captain saw what they were doing and he turned once more to give us back the advantage. I could hear the beat of the drum as the pirate captain ordered an increase in speed. The first mate had told us that the ship was not crewed by slaves but by men who were cruel and savage warriors. They would endure the extra work knowing what rewards lay ahead.

When the pirate turned and headed for the middle of our ship, I was astounded at both the speed and nimbleness of the Arab vessel. The crossbowmen on the mainmast and bow castle did not release straight away. The billowing sail of the Arab leader headed for our vulnerable stern. The Pisan crew needed no orders to be given. Every hand except for the captain and the helmsman rushed to the larboard side, ready to repel all boarders. When the pirate turned, I heard the crack as eight crossbows sent their bolts towards the enemy. Four were lucky. I saw the helmsman and the man next to him fall and the leader of the pirate crew, wearing mail and a helmet, clutch his shoulder as he was struck. Even as more sailors ran to take over the helm, I could hear the crossbows being reloaded. The pirate had not managed to touch our sides. The other two, seeing how close the leading ship had come were racing towards us, eager to take advantage of the situation. The pirate under control, she came back but this time every crossbow on our ship was released and the range was so close that each bolt struck flesh. Not all would be mortal but we had seriously hurt their crew.

When the Arab hull ground next to ours grappling hooks were thrown to secure the two vessels together. None were close to us. The rest of the crew tried to sever the ropes. Robert and I picked up stones and hurled them to the ship below. Robert's rock hit a climbing pirate who plunged silently between the ships. Mine cracked into the deck and thus encouraged, we each threw a second. I heard the noise of the ropes holding us close to the Arab being cut. They twanged as they were severed. The pirates climbed as quickly as they could up our steep sides, and I picked up the boarding pike. It was like a halberd and I had used one before. I swept it at the head of the first pirate who tried to grab hold of the gunwale. He wore a helmet but the edge of the pike was sharpened. The dent became a crack and he fell screaming to be crushed between the two ships. Men were pouring aboard us and every Pisan was wielding a weapon as though their lives depended upon it. A huge half-naked warrior stood above me, his feet on the gunwale and his left hand on a stay. I lunged with the pike and it tore into his middle. Dropping his sword to the deck he clutched at his middle and in his falling, he dragged the pike from my hand. I drew my sword and dagger. The spear that was hurled at me struck me with a glancing blow to the side of the head. My coif and arming cap saved me. Robert's pike ended the life of the spearman. I could see the other two Arab ships. They were just five lengths from us.

It was at that moment that the first mate appeared from the stern cabin. He held in his hands one of the oil lamps which lit the captain's cabin. He ran to the side. I flanked him as a pirate swung an axe at him. My sword was sharp and I severed his hand which fell, still clutching the axe to the deck. My dagger deflected the pike that came at the first mate's side. He hurled the lamp at the Arab ship's deck and shouted, "Sever the lines!"

Crossbows cracked and swords and axes sliced down as the crew obeyed the order. A wall of flame rose from the pirate as the burning oil set fire to a tinder-dry deck. The captain turned our helm and we began to draw away, no longer tethered to the stricken pirate. Ships, especially in the Mediterranean, are bone dry and the fire raced up the mainmast and ignited the sail. The men who were trying to board us fell screaming into the sea as the fire scorched their backs. There were half a dozen men left aboard. Two leapt overboard while the other four were butchered. The last two pirate ships now had an obstacle in their path, their burning consort, and even as they tried to navigate around the doomed vessel we began to pull away. It soon became clear that they had given up. We spied the circling sharks as the survivors were picked up. We had won. I sheathed my weapons and clapped a beaming Robert on his back. He had survived his first real test and was now a true warrior who had been blooded.

I went to Thomasina's cabin and knocked on the door, "It is over."

The door was flung open and a terrified-looking Thomasina threw her arms around me and kissed me hard on the lips. To say I was shocked would be an understatement. She stepped back and looked at me, "I could hear the screams and the battle. I was sure that you would die." She suddenly seemed to realise what she had done. "Oh, my lord, I am sorry but…"

I embraced her and kissed her back. This was not the chaste kiss I gave my mother and cousins on the cheek, this was a kiss of passion. We held each other tightly and our lips were locked. The battle had, it seemed, changed everything.

Chapter 5

Sir Matthew

A New Beginning

I heard Robert's feet as he raced along the deck and flung open the door to our cabins. We just had time to part. He was framed in the light and we were shadowed in the dark. "We won, Thomasina, and slew many pirates. The captain says we can share in the bounty."

I smiled, "That is good." I wanted to be alone with Thomasina for we needed words to explain the kisses.

Robert took Thomasina's hand, "The bodies are gone. Come on deck, away from this darkness."

She gave me an apologetic smile and allowed Robert to take her out. I did not follow immediately. Had I behaved honourably? Thomasina was not a child and she had kissed me but I was a knight. I should have had more self-control. I tried to think what Henry Samuel might have advised and realised that was pointless. Dick had been his squire when he had met and married Eirwen. I did not know how he would have behaved. The crew were swilling the decks with water to clear away the blood as I emerged. The four crewmen who had been wounded were being tended to and the bounty of the attack, jewels from fingers, purses, swords and mail were being gathered. I would not take any, of course, but Robert would. He had earned it.

The captain shouted down, "You and your squire did well."

"As did the crew."

He beamed, "Aye, they did, didn't they? And we suffered no damage. All is well. Carlos, open the deck. His lordship's horses will be terrified. Let them feel the sun and breathe fresh air."

When the deck was removed I saw that the horses were all lathered. Any conversation with Thomasina would have to wait. The three of us climbed down the ladder and spent the next few hours grooming the horses, watering them and calming them. Robert's singing helped. By the time we had finished I, for one, was ravenous and when food was brought out on the deck for the crew to eat we joined them. The conversation was filled with banter and bon homme. We had won and the wounded were not seriously hurt. The crew and Robert told the same tales to each other. Every moment was relived. Men acted out the swashing blows and mimed the falling into the sea of pirates. There was

The Ripples of Rebellion

laughter and joy. They had survived. The two silent ones were Thomasina and me. We both wanted to speak but could not and, instead, we had a conversation with our eyes.

The good mood was terminated when a sudden squall arrived. It came from the south and east. The winds pushed us hard and we had to vacate the deck. Robert and I went to our cabin to change from our mail and put the hauberks in the sheepskin-lined sacks so that they could dry. When we reached home we would need to have them cleaned with sand and polished. That done we went into the captain's cabin and the three of us sat and listened to the rain pounding on the deck. If nothing else, it would wash away the last of the blood. It was awkward between Thomasina and I. Robert was so full of the fight that he did not notice it and he began to speak of the battle. I watched Thomasina's face. She looked torn. Robert took the look to be his fault. "I am sorry, Mistress Thomasina, you are a lady and should not hear such words."

She forced a smile, "My grandfather was a soldier and he told me tales of battles. I was just worried that you or Sir Matthew might have come to harm."

Robert did not notice the inflexion she gave to my name, but I did and as her eyes were locked on mine we spoke with those instead. The rain pounded harder on the deck above, and we sat in silence.

Thomasina broke the silence, "The ship that we destroyed, what would happen to the crew?"

I shrugged, "Some would have been picked up by the other two ships but most would have drowned. I think few men can swim and the clothes they wear are voluminous."

Robert nodded, "And better that than to be eaten by sharks. I saw sharks."

"Enough, Robert. With luck and God's help we have done with pirates." I gestured with my thumb, "It is nature and the weather which will give us our next challenges. This is mild compared with the storms that Biscay can throw at us."

"Where do we land when we reach England, Sir Matthew?"

"A good question, Robert and one I shall ask the captain when we dine this night."

The servants began to lay the table and brought in food as the sun started to set. The rain had relented only slightly and when the officers entered their heads were soaked, but thanks to their oiled capes their clothes beneath were dry. The captain smiled, "An interesting day." My Italian was becoming better and the captain and his officers, when they spoke to us, chose their words wisely and spoke slowly.

"How are the wounded?"

"They will be able to return to work by the time we reach Lisbon. Tomorrow, we pass the pillars." He smiled, "Mistress Thomasina, then you will have to wrap against the weather. Sir Matthew and his squire know what to expect but you do not."

A sudden thought struck me, "When we land in Lisbon, will we stay at all?"

He nodded, "We have a cargo to unload and I will seek one to pick up on our return. We might even pick up something else to trade in England. We shall be there for a day and a night. Why do you ask?"

"There will be a market will there not?" He nodded. "We can buy clothes for Mistress Thomasina there."

"An excellent idea." He smiled at the first mate, "And we will need to buy another oil lamp now that Antonio has discarded one!"

We all laughed, except for Thomasina who knew nothing of the fiery bomb the first mate had improvised. I explained and she smiled.

"And where do we land when we reach England?"

"I assume that you will wish to land in London."

I nodded. That suited me.

That night I did as we had each night and stood with the candle so that Robert could see his way to the bed. "Goodnight, my lord."

"Good night, Robert, you did well today. Your father would be proud of you."

"I cannot wait to tell him. I do not think that he ever fought the Moors."

He closed his cabin door, and I handed the candle to Thomasina. Our fingers touched and I felt a rush of excitement race through my body. All was silent and any words would be heard by Robert. "Goodnight, my lord, and thank you." She stood on tiptoe and kissed me on the lips.

I just wanted to grab her in my arms and embrace her. I did not. "No, Thomasina, thank you."

We stood looking at each other and then she said, "Good night, until the morrow, my lord. I shall have sweeter dreams this night."

"And I, too."

I lay on my bed for what seemed like an age. We needed to speak to each other. I was unused to the ways of love. I suspected from what I knew of Thomasina that she was too. The ship was not the place for talk. We would have to be patient but we still had many days at sea. I knew, from the talk at the captain's table, that the favourable winds had put us ahead of schedule but we could not count on such luck continuing. I would need to find time in Lisbon to be alone with her.

The next day we passed between Africa and Andalucia. To me, the passage looked wide but I knew from the crew that it was fraught with

The Ripples of Rebellion

danger and every seaman was working the ship to ensure a safe passage. As soon as we passed through the straits the motion of the ship changed. When we turned north the waves that struck us from the west were strong enough to make the ship heel hard to steerboard. I saw that not only were the captain and the helmsmen at the steering rudder but also another sailor. This sea needed to be fought. The captain had told us that this would only be his second voyage past the pillars and the first to England. He had bought new maps in Pisa. He had asked my advice but I was no sailor. The maps meant little to me. However, when I had asked him where we would land, he had offered me the chance to tell him my thoughts.

"We need to find a port that we can use to begin trade with England. Where would you suggest?"

"You have a letter from the Doge?" He nodded, "Then that would better be given to a man of importance. I will have to visit with the Regent who rules in The Lord Edward's absence, for Richard of Cornwall is the father of Lord Henry whose bones we carry. Billingsgate is not far up the river and a short distance from London. It is closer to the sea than Queenhithe. I believe that Richard of Cornwall will be at the Tower."

"When I have spoken to other sailors they tell me that the river that runs to London can be tricky. Are there pilots?"

I nodded, "I suppose so."

"Then when we near the coast we shall find one."

As we headed up the coast of Andalucia to Lisbon I began to dream of home. Standing with Thomasina and Robert on the bow castle I began to dream of my life back in Stockton. I had images and ideas in my head but I dared not trust any of them. I had to speak to Thomasina.

Lisbon was a huge harbour and as the captain negotiated the busy entrance, I saw the mighty castle that dominated the harbour. We learned it was called Castelo de São Jorge. It was even larger than Henry the 2nd's castle at Dover. This was a new country. It had only been reconquered from the Muslims in the last one hundred years and that showed. The warships that patrolled the waters were ready to repel any attacker and we saw many armed men on the walls of the castle. It took a couple of hours for us to tack our way through the other ships to reach the quay. While the captain went ashore to negotiate for a cargo the three of us left and went ashore. Robert and I were now used to the different smells that other countries had but Thomasina was not. This land had the smell of Africa. We found the market, here they still called it a souk, but, as it was late in the afternoon, most of the traders were packing up.

The Ripples of Rebellion

Thomasina was more at home in markets than we were, and she said, "We will find nothing of quality left. We know where it is, Sir Matthew, let us return early in the morning."

"A good idea." I heard the bell of the cathedral, the Santa Maria Maior de Lisboa. "Let us go and thank God for our safe arrival and deliverance from the Moors."

With the cowl of her cloak over her head, Thomasina entered the cathedral first. We found a side chapel and knelt at the rail. None of us could read Portuguese but from the statue in the niche above us, I guessed that it was the Virgin Mary. We knelt in prayer. I knew not what the others prayed for but I prayed for a safe return to England and for help to win the heart of Thomasina.

When we returned to the ship we saw that the crew had set up a fire on the quayside, partly to keep away the cold for the night watch but also to cook food and we enjoyed hot food for the first time since Italy. The fish the crew had caught on the voyage after the pillars were augmented with ham that would not last much longer, old onions and spices. The second mate had managed to buy bread and that was a luxury we all enjoyed. We had missed such things as we had sailed west.

The captain arrived as we were eating, sitting on the main deck. He looked pleased, "I have arranged for a cargo to be picked up in a month on our return from England. It means, Sir Matthew, that we will have but a short turnaround in London once I have purchased sheepskins. I will need to find a buyer for my cargo quickly and deliver the letter to Lord Henry's father. Much will depend on you."

"I shall do my best."

"I have also bought more fodder for your horses. It is a shame we cannot let them off the ship but I fear the loading and unloading would distress them."

He was right and I knew that we would have to try to find some way to exercise them on the ship.

"When do we sail?"

"The noontide; we will be taking on provisions from first light."

I knew that we would be able to get better and warmer clothes in England and that they would be cheaper but the weather was already colder and we had barely travelled north.

We went to the market which was busy from first light. The stalls had been set up while it was still dark. I paid the money although Thomasina insisted upon haggling. I always felt uncomfortable doing so. We also bought provisions to supplement the food on the ship. They had a good ham and I bought that as well as some cheese. To pay for it

The Ripples of Rebellion

we sold a couple of the Moorish swords taken in the pirate attack. When we returned to the ship the cargo was half loaded but, more importantly, the forage was aboard as well as some oats. Robert and I had bought some apples and the horses were treated to a well-deserved feast.

As we fed them, I said, "We will have to treat them gently once we land. It is lucky that Billingsgate is close to London. We just have to walk the animals for three miles or so."

We left Lisbon Harbour just after noon. The captain was keen to take advantage of the tide but we barely made the sea before dark, such was the traffic along the river and in the harbour. That night we ate well. Food had been cooked on the quay and kept in pots wrapped in straw. The straw would be reused for the animals. With freshly purchased Portuguese wine we dined like kings and there was a merry atmosphere. Thomasina laughed as though she had not a care in the world and Robert amused the Pisans with his rustic English songs. He had a good voice and he sang well. Thomasina sat next to me and when her hand brushed mine or she leaned in to speak about the songs that were sung I felt my heart rise and my passions were aroused. I did not want the night to end but it did.

That night we retired as normal but when I waited to see that the candle was out Robert came from his cabin and said, quietly, "My lord." He gestured for me to enter his cabin. I feared he had some dire news and I went. "My lord, I am just your squire and if I speak out of turn then chastise or beat me."

I smiled, "You know that is not my way. I am no Sir Marmaduke."

He looked relieved, although it was hard to make out his facial expression in the gloomy cabin. "Mistress Thomasina is enamoured of you, my lord," I said nothing. He hesitated and then continued, "And you, I think, feel the same." Again, I was silent. "Since becoming a squire I have learned to serve and to watch, here on the ship I do not serve. I have watched you since the attack and seen you grow close."

I found my voice, "If what you say is true, then what business is it of yours?"

"I am your squire, my lord. I ask you, as your squire and someone who knows your family, what would they say of the liaison?"

It was a good question. My mother would probably disapprove. My closest other family, Dick, my sister Margaret, Henry Samuel, and Lady Eirwen would be happy, I knew that. It was as I pondered the answer that it came to me. Henry Samuel had married a farmer's daughter from Wales. Eirwen and Thomasina had much in common. The man I respected most in the world would approve if I made Thomasina my bride. I put my hands on Robert's shoulders, "Thank you, Robert, you are truly the right squire for me. Your words have set my mind at rest."

"But, my lord, what did I say?"

"You asked me what my family would think. I believe I know. My troubled thoughts are resolved."

It was easier to sleep with my mind at rest but I could not wait for dawn. I wanted to see Thomasina. Now that Robert knew then we could be open. It felt as though I was going to begin my life again and I could not wait to start. The murder of Henry of Almain had been a low point. Meeting Thomasina and falling in love with her, a high. Now I had to find out if she was willing to be my wife or if she did not relish the prospect. It was much easier knowing that Robert was aware of the situation.

After we had enjoyed breakfast, I gave him a subtle nod and he said, "I will go to see to the horses, my lord."

"Thank you, Robert." I led Thomasina to the bow. The movement of the ship meant I had to hold her arm. She did not resist and my confidence grew. As we looked to the east and the coast of Portugal slipping by I blurted out, "Thomasina, since the fight and that first kiss I have not been able to get you from my mind. I cannot wait to see you each morning and I pine for you at night. I know that this is sudden, like the flash of lightning in a storm, but I believe that you and I are meant to be together. I would, if you will have me, marry you."

I am not sure what I expected but it was not her reaction. She stepped back and said, quietly, "Sir Matthew, I too, feel as you do and my nights are a torment as I dream of your kisses and your arms around me." I beamed but before I could speak she placed a finger on my lips. "I beg you to let me speak for my heart is full. I am from a poor family. We never owned land and my mother spent most of her life in a hovel as she followed my father from battle to battle. You are a lord. You are related to an earl. I will not fit in with the fine ladies." She sighed, "I am happy to be your concubine if you will for I know that there is no other man for me but you."

I took her by the shoulders and held her firmly, "Do not make judgements about my family. We have never judged anyone by their breeding or family. The first Warlord knighted a bandit. Henry Samuel married the daughter of a poor Welsh farmer. I would marry you. I will marry you."

I watched the hint of a smile on her face but the shake of her head made my heart sink, "I will not answer you yet, my lord. We have a long way to travel. Even when we reach London, from what you have said, we still have many leagues to go. When we arrive at Stockton if you still wish to marry me and..." she paused and her eyes locked with mine, "and your family approves then we shall be wed."

It was an answer and I nodded. "Then I have but a little time, a month at most to wait. I am young and I am patient."

The difference was that from then on we could be more open. I could hold her hand. Our embraces and kisses before we went to bed were no longer hidden and secretive. Robert knew all. The days were, despite the increasingly bad weather, pleasurable but I could not wait to get back to England and, more importantly, Stockton.

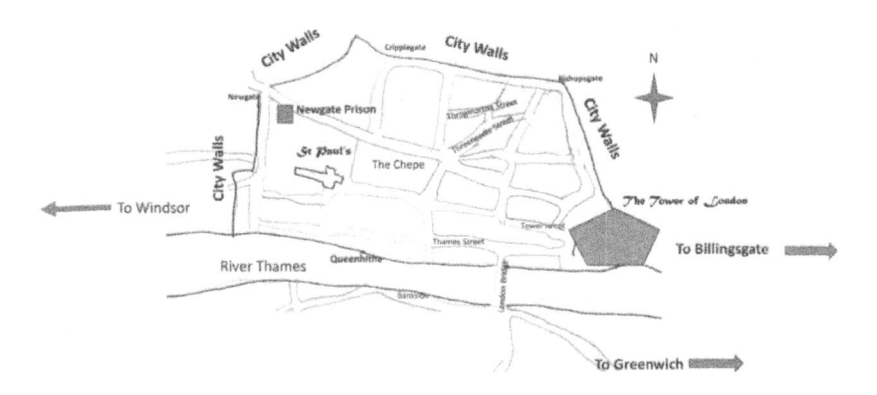

When we reached the Thames, the river was as busy as I had anticipated but the pilot we picked up at Southend ensured that our journey was safe. The pilot wondered why we did not land at Queenhithe, the port closer to Westminster. I explained that we needed to visit the Tower and that the captain did not relish sailing under London Bridge. We found a berth and I went to the port master to ask permission to land. When he discovered my quest he did all that he could to help. Word had reached England of the murder but my arrival was clear confirmation. We unloaded the horses first and Antonio was left in charge of landing the cargo and finding a buyer. Even as we were walking the animals along the quay merchants, hearing of the arrival of a Pisan ship were being attracted to the ship. It would be an auction and that promised greater profits for the captain and his crew. We had grown close and I was happy for them.

We loaded the horses with our belongings but did not ride them. Instead, we walked the three miles along the serpentine Thames. Henry of Almain's bones lay on his horse, Bruno. I had covered it with his standard. As we processed to the Tower a crowd drawn by the banner followed us, so that by the time we reached the Tower they had been alerted to the arrival of visitors. The captain of the guard, seeing the banner said, "Are these the bones of Henry of Almain, recently murdered?"

"They are and I am the last of his knights, Sir Matthew of Stockton. I was charged by King Charles of Naples and Sicily to deliver his son to Richard of Cornwall, King of the Romans and Regent of England."

He nodded, "My master did not wish to believe the news and he hoped for word from his son that would prove the rumour to be a lie. He wanted to believe that this dire deed was a scurrilous attempt to upset England. Your arrival and the confirmation of the manner of the murder will break his heart." He looked at Thomasina, Robert and the captain.

I explained, "These are: my squire, the captain of a ship of Pisa with a message from the Doge for the regent and," I paused, "my betrothed."

He nodded and shouted at the crowd, "The rest of you, begone." He led us through the gate into the ward. Waving over some of his men he asked, "Henry of Almain?"

I pointed to his warhorse and the banner, "His bones, his jewels, his armour and his sword are on his horse."

"With your permission, my lord, we will carry them. You have had the honour hitherto and now it is our turn." The sword and boxes were taken from the backs of the horses and the captain himself carried the chest with the bones and the draped standard.

The cortege wound its way to the royal apartments. Those within had been forewarned and our entrance was facilitated. When we reached the hall in the royal apartments, the shadow of the man who had been Richard of Cornwall awaited us. I took the banner from the bones and said, "My lord, these are the bones of your son who was treacherously murdered by Guy and Simon de Montfort in Viterbo."

He shook his head and it was as though life drained from his face, "I hoped beyond hope that the news was wrong. I am just glad that his mother is not alive to see it. They will be reunited in heaven. Thank you, Sir Matthew, for returning him to me." He turned to the captain. "Have rooms prepared for these guests."

I said, "Captain Giacomo d'Albini, my lord, is a representative of the Doge. He brought us from Italy but his business is commercial."

The Regent nodded, "Captain, I thank you for service and if I can do anything in return I shall but you must understand that this night is not the time for such debate."

Thomasina translated for Richard of Cornwall spoke quickly and the Pisan captain bowed, "Of course, my lord." He had learned a little English from me.

The Ripples of Rebellion

We were taken away and, as the door closed, I saw Henry of Almain's father sink to his knees before the box containing his son's bones.

The room I was given was palatial and even the ones given to the other three were more than comfortable. I sat on the bed and felt a wave of relief wash over me. I no longer had the responsibility of watching the bones of my murdered lord. As soon as I was released by Richard of Cornwall, Regent of England and King of the Romans, I could head north and begin a new life. I knew that Thomasina's fears were groundless and that she would be welcomed by my family. It was our way. Robert knocked on the door and when I gave him permission he entered. He helped me to dress. We waited until a liveried servant fetched us and we were taken to a small dining room. I saw that neither Thomasina nor Captain d'Albini were there. The servant said, "The other guests are in the main hall. His Majesty wished to dine alone with you. He asks that your servant also dines in the main hall."

I nodded and, after I was admitted, Robert was whisked off. I waited until Henry of Almain's father entered. He waved me to a seat. "Tonight, Matthew, there will be no formalities." He waved the letter from Charles of Anjou, that I had given to him. "You were the only one of my son's men with him at the end and from the letter I know that you tried to save him and were wounded for your pains. I need to speak with you about my son's last days. Sit."

We sat and food was fetched. It was fine food and well cooked but Richard of Cornwall pecked at it like a bird and I was too nervous to enjoy it. The efforts of the cook were wasted.

"Karl, what happened to him? There was no word and I know that he was close to my son."

"He was murdered too. I had him buried in the church in Viterbo. There will be a headstone."

He looked at me and tears welled in his rheumy eyes. He put his blue-veined hand on mine, "Like all your family, you are a true knight filled with honour and chivalry. Now tell me all from the moment you left England."

I told the tale. It was punctuated by the encouragement of the earl for me to eat. I concluded with the death and the excommunication. He shook his head, "That they will be punished in the next life is a comfort but I would have some retribution now." He sat back and closed his eyes. I said nothing. When he opened them he said, "And your plans?"

"I will return to Stockton, my lord."

He smiled, "My son's horses are yours for I shall not need them and he has no sons of his own. His sword and his mail I would keep. The gold that remains is yours also. You have more than earned it. I would also reward you. There is a manor close to Stockton without a lord, it is called Egglesclif. Indeed, there has been no lord this last fifty years." He shrugged, "An oversight. One of my clerks discovered it when I first heard that my son had appointed you as a household knight. I asked for a manor that was vacant, close to Stockton. I thought to reward you. I knew that he chose you while the other three were appointed by my nephew, Edward." He smiled, "It was one of the manors that belonged to my father, King John. I know that he was vindictive towards your family and perhaps this will make up a little for his cruelty."

"Thank you, Your Majesty."

He shook his head, "I said, Matthew, that tonight it is Richard and Matthew. It is the least that can be done. When you leave, I daresay, tomorrow, there will be the deeds and a purse of gold to recompense you."

I was distracted by his generous gift and did not think to thank him for the purse of gold. I knew of the manor but it was a tiny hamlet of less than ten houses and, as far as I knew, there was no manor house.

"If I may ask, my lord, if there has been no lord of the manor, who has been collecting taxes and ensuring that the men attend archery practice?"

"The Bishop of Durham took it upon himself to do so."

I had never seen any archers or fyrd when we had gone to war. How had they avoided that? It lay close to the Tees and the river, when it was low, could be crossed there.

The earl leaned forward, "This murder of my son and his brave squire are not isolated incidents, Matthew. Take care when you travel north and tell your uncle that the rebellion is not over. We have not snuffed out that candle. The knights of the north need to be vigilant. The king, my brother, is unwell and with my nephew in the Holy Land I fear that mischief and mayhem will still abound." He shook his head and his eyes welled up again, "And my son, the hope for the future is not here as my rock. He is gone." Silence filled the room and I did not interrupt until he smiled, "I think you understand this too. Tell me about this young Italian lady you have brought back."

We chatted briefly for a short time as I told him her story and then, when we reached the part about her grandfather dying, he sighed, "Old age is a terrible thing, Matthew. I shall retire to bed." I stood as did he. He clasped my arm, "Thank you. If ever you need a favour then it is done."

"Thank you, Your Majesty." I was going home and I had done my duty. I could not wait to fly up the road and get home as soon as I could.

Chapter 6

Henry Samuel

Oath to a dying man

Stockton

When Matthew left and crossed the river to head down the road south I was riddled with guilt. My cousin was bearing the cost of the prince's ire and I wondered if I could have done anything to prevent it. I had been less than diplomatic in my response to the next king of England. I was not a political animal; I was a warrior and I tended to act more assuredly than I spoke. A man cannot change his nature. I doubted that my grandfather would have acted or spoken any differently. He had defied King John.

The castle seemed emptier after my former squire's departure. Even when the family came down to breakfast there was a subdued atmosphere. It was almost as though no one wished to speak Matthew's name. My mother was fussing over Lady Mary, Matthew's mother. She was the frailest of the ladies in the valley while my mother was the rock. The right words would be said by my mother. Dick, Samuel and Alfred, as well as my brother William, were all watching me. I knew why. They were wondering what I would do about Matthew's manor. On the way back from Northampton I had given Norton to Sir Thomas and he and his bride were there now trying to make a home from the long-abandoned hall. With Matthew gone, I had promised Redmarshal to one of my sons. I suddenly found Stockton constricting. Normally, my home was a place of comfort and refuge but the walls, filled with the tapestries of my forebears and their great deeds, seemed to mock me. I had let the newest knight shoulder the burden of upholding the honour of the family.

"I will go hawking. Have the birds readied and we will ride to Hartburn Woods. I was told that the magpies and pigeons are wreaking havoc there. We can visit with Sir Richard at the same time."

The others looked at each other and then nodded. Dick said, "Rafe the Codger will be happy that you fly the birds. I will go and tell him."

Samuel said, "I will organise the squires."

"And I," said Alfred, "will see to the horses."

I could not help but smile. It was as though they all wanted something to do. Perhaps they missed Matthew as much as I did.

The Ripples of Rebellion

William was wise. He was no warrior, but he was the cleverest man I knew. He should have been a priest, but I was glad that he was not. He smiled as he stood to head to his cell-like study where he would continue to write the history of our family. "Brother, Matthew's quest is but another chapter in the rich history of our family. There was nothing that you could have done to prevent it and you know it. God watches over us. Henry of Almain is not like his cousin, the next king. When our forebear William went to the Holy Land the Warlord feared for him, but all was well and he returned with a bride and two children. We sprang from their union and their seed. Who knows with what Matthew will return?"

I nodded, "You are right, but the weight of the Warlord sits heavily upon my shoulders."

"And while I cannot wield a sword for you, I can give you support for that weight. Is there aught I can do?"

"Dick, Samuel and Alfred need manors. Who should get Redmarshal?"

He smiled. He had this way of making everything seem simple with a smile and his calm and soothing voice, "You have already told your sons that they are to be knighted and that one of them will be given Redmarshal or have you forgotten?"

He knew me so well and I shook my head, "You know that I have not. I have procrastinated. I have yet to make that decision."

"Aye, yet if this was the battlefield you would not have done so and trusted your judgement."

"I thought that there was no rush to knight them and now…"

"Are they ready for their spurs?"

"Spurs, aye. A manor? Of that, I am not sure."

"Then let me offer my help. I have an organised mind. I will ride to Redmarshal and speak with the reeve there, Paul. The running of the manor in times of peace does not need a sword. I will assess the problems, if there are any, and make a suggestion to you. That gives you time to knight your sons, appoint squires and then choose." He gave me a cheeky smile, "I will facilitate your procrastination."

I laughed, feeling better already. William was doing what he did best, offering sage advice. I nodded, "Thank you, William."

I went to my chamber and changed into hunting clothes. I was not one of those knights who needed a squire to dress him. Roger of Whorlton and my sons would be better occupied preparing horses and the codgers. Rafe the Codger was both the hawk and hunt master but he had four youths who assisted him. This would be the first time I had hunted with my uncle's peregrine falcon, Erasmus, and I was looking forward to using the bird. The bird had been named by my uncle after the doctor who lived in the manor. He said they both had the same serious faces. The buzzard I had used before, Percy, would still be flown by me but only when the falcon tired.

We used hackneys and the horses were all eager to be ridden. We mounted and with the cadge carried by Rafe, we headed on the road past the well towards the Ox Bridge and the woods to the west of Hartburn. My friend, Sir Richard, had been ill and we would visit with him but only after we had hunted. I knew that mornings were the worst time for him. Doctor Erasmus had seen him regularly but he did not know the cause of the ailment. The knight alongside whom I had fought in the north grew both weaker and thinner each day. I had visited with him when we had returned from Northampton but the departure of Matthew had meant we had not spoken since. I knew that I did not want to see my friend dying from within but I owed it to him to visit.

We passed the farm at the Ox Bridge, waving to Edmund who farmed there, and took the track that led to the woods. The woods lay between Elton and Hartburn. I saw the men working the fields. As we passed them they saw the hawks and one of them, Egbert, shouted, "That is what we need, my lord, your birds. Our slings bring down the odd thief but the others plague our planting. They take two seeds out of every three."

I nodded, "Then by way of compensation you shall have two birds out of every three that we take this day."

"Thank you, my lord."

The grins that came my way were gratifying. The meat would augment their diet of beans and greens. We did not need the extra birds as we had a dovecote and a fishpond, not to mention the fish from the river. We ate well and far better than the yeomen who struggled to produce enough food to feed their families. We stopped at the edge of the woods and the squires tethered our horses. It felt good to be out in the woods. They were only hunted by either me, Sir Richard or my brother Alfred. As such they were havens for wildlife and when we hunted, it was always rewarding. I donned the glove I would use and held out my arm. Rafe took the hood from Erasmus and gave a treat, a piece of sparrow. I held it out and the falcon hopped onto my arm to devour the meat. Dick had a saker, a new falcon called Jude. He took his bird. Our squires would not be flying their lanner falcons until we had flown ours. There was a protocol for hunting.

Rafe knew the woods. When he was not caring for the birds he walked the land. He and the gamekeepers we employed knew every inch of the land around Stockton. We followed him, knowing that he would find game. We headed to the edge of the woods which lay close to the tended fields between the two becks. We spied the flock of pigeons, gorging on the freshly sown seeds. The farmer who had just sown the seed was too far away to chase them. I lifted my arm and Erasmus soared. Jude also took to the air. The two of them circled high and then plunged to earth. The two pigeons did not know what hit them. The rest of the flock disappeared. The two falcons dropped their pigeons close to our feet and waited for the treats we held for them. The boys took the pigeons and put them in the game bag.

I turned to Rafe, "Let the squires fly with us. There are enough birds for us all."

He nodded, "It would be better, my lord, if we spread out. Erasmus is a jealous bird and does not like competition."

I looked at my sons and Roger, my squire, "Are you confident enough to do this?"

Samuel grinned. He was the more confident of my sons, "Aye father. Rafe, give us the treats."

The three squires each took their hawks and one of the boys. They headed off into the woods to hunt. Our birds had the freedom of the field and the skies. I wandered a little away from Dick and sought more prey. I saw a flock of magpies. Farmers hated them as not only did they take seeds but they were also seen to be unlucky. I did not mind them knowing that they had a job to do. Like the crows, they cleared the carrion. The magpies were also eating the seeds.

"Erasmus, show me your worth. My uncle thought you were the finest of hunters. Let us see how many you can take."

I lifted him and he rose into the air. As soon as he did so the magpies took off but it merely gave him the chance to take the largest while it was in the air. He plucked it easily from the sky and, as he landed close to me, killed it. He did not wait for a treat but soared again. The magpies had not gone to roost but were circling, waiting for him to devour his prey. We managed to take three birds before they took to the trees. I wandered back to the others and handed the dead birds to Roger. I let Erasmus hop onto the cadge and took Percy. Percy was eager to be in the air and when I saw that the pigeons had returned and lifted him, he went like an arrow to make his first kill in a heartbeat. He had not hunted for some time and he happily thinned the numbers of pigeons for us. By the time the magpies and pigeons had realised that we were hunting in numbers and had left, it was almost noon.

"Rafe, I will go to visit Sir Richard. Give the farmers their bounty and take the hawks and the others to the castle. The squires and my sons can go with you."

The Ripples of Rebellion

"Yes, my lord."

"Dick, do you wish to visit with me?"

He nodded, "Aye, Dick, for I feel guilty that we have not visited before."

The rest of our party headed back to Stockton and we rode the short way to Hartburn. The trail through the trees ended at a stand of chestnut trees and there lay the small manor of Hartburn. There were fewer houses than Elton but there was a beck which ran through it and that had enabled a fishpond to be made. Those who lived in the village farmed strips of land although there was a rope maker who had chosen to live in the village. Those who fished and the ferryman found the ropes useful and he often sold them to ships that came up the river. I had often wondered why he did not make his ropes in Stockton but Agmark, who was a Norseman by descent, seemed happy enough in the village. Ethelred sold the ropes for Agmark and it seemed a happy arrangement. He waved to me as I passed. He, his sons and the rest of his family were making a hawser that would be used by a cog. The manor had a wall around it and a gate. It would not have stopped a determined attack, but it was a defence, of sorts. The gate was open, and I saw my old friend's steward, Ralph, and the two labourers toiling in the hogbog.

"Sir Henry Samuel, good to see you."

"How goes it, Ralph?"

"This is a job that needs doing once a year, my lord. We do not enjoy it but when it is done then we can forget it until next summer. We have much work in the manor but it is rewarding."

"His lordship is within?"

A frown creased his face, "He has not left his bed since Christmas, my lord. Each time I see him he looks more like a wraith than the fine knight I remember." He stopped, unable to continue.

We dismounted and two of the men working with Ralph took our horses and led them to the trough. Eleanor, my only sister, appeared at the door. She, too, looked thin and old. The death of their eldest, Alfred, killed when he fell from a horse whilst hunting, had sucked the life from both my oldest friend and my sister. She was, like all of our family, strong but the death of a son was something that tore the heart out of any mother and Eleanor was a good one. She smiled, "It is good to see you, Henry Samuel."

"Where are the boys?" Henry and Geoffrey, her other sons, were no longer boys but I thought of them as such.

The Ripples of Rebellion

She shook her head and looked older, somehow, "I know not. Both are wilder now that their brother is with God and they do not listen to me."

I frowned. Like it or not I was the head of the family and I would need to do something about it. Dick looked at me, "Go within, Henry Samuel, I will ask Ralph where they are to be found."

I went inside the house. It smelled of sickness and death. "How is he, Eleanor?"

"He dies by inches. I thought, at first, that it was Alfred's death that brought on the melancholy, but it was not just that. He coughs up blood. Had he been wounded recently then I would have understood the cause but this…"

"What did the doctor say?"

"Doctor Erasmus is mystified. He tried leeches but they did not work. Gammer Grange gave him a potion she made and that helps him to sleep and seems to slow down the deterioration but it does not cure."

I went into the bed chamber and the light from the candles gave Richard a sort of golden glow but as I neared him I saw that he was a pallid grey colour. He stirred as I approached. He tried to rise.

"Richard, lie back for you are ill."

He gave me a weak smile, "I know not what sin I committed to be thus afflicted. I thought my end would be on a battlefield fighting at your side and not wasting away like this. I have no life within me."

I nodded and after sitting, took his hand in mine. Despite the blankets, it felt cold. You do not lie to a shield brother and whilst I knew that others might have said there was hope, Eleanor's words told me that there was none. Richard would die but he needed to know that I would not forget him.

"Is there anything that I can do for you?"

He was serious as he said, "I would ask for a warrior's death but I know that would upset Eleanor. I will endure the pain and smile when I am nursed. I wait for the angel of death to come calling. I have been absolved of all sins and here in this bed I can commit no more. I will see God and my son soon enough."

"Your other sons should be here."

His face darkened and he shook his head, "They are wild, Henry Samuel. You ask if there is anything you can do for me, here it is. Make them into men for in that I have failed. Perhaps I made Alfred too well and did not give them as much attention. If so, I have been punished. I thought I had prepared them well but it is clear that there is some blood in them that makes them behave like animals."

The Ripples of Rebellion

I nodded, "I swear that I shall do all in my power for them to become more like their father."

"Perhaps I should have sent them on crusade with Matthew."

I gave a sardonic laugh, "I think that our cousin will have enough on his shoulders without worrying about two such wild boys. Fear not, I have a plan." I was always one to see something half full and since Eleanor's words, my mind had been working out what to do. Just then the door opened and Eleanor appeared, "Dick is back, Henry Samuel."

"Good. I will let Dick speak to you for he, too, has been concerned."

We passed in the corridor, and I shook my head. He nodded.

I saw the two boys waiting. Both had a sly grin on their faces. Eleanor said, "Dick found them teasing Ralph's dog. He thought they were trying to torture the poor animal." She gave a weak smile, "I will sit with my husband and Dick." I knew that Dick would have chastised them for their cruelty, but their grins told me that they thought they had got away with it.

Henry had seen twelve summers and Geoffrey, thirteen. They were large-framed but there was no muscle. Dick had obviously scolded them and when I frowned and shook my head, their grins changed to insolent glares. They thought to challenge me. I sat opposite them and stared at them. At first, they tried to out-stare me but when they failed they looked down at the table. After a suitably awkward silence, I said, "You know that your father is my best friend." They said nothing and I snapped, "I am Earl Henry Samuel and you will look at me and answer or I shall have you whipped at St John's Well."

Their heads came up and I saw the terror in their eyes. A public punishment would be humiliating. They answered together, "Yes, my lord."

I forced my voice to be gentler and calmer although inside I seethed. A whipping would be the right punishment. "You are a disappointment to me. The blood of the Warlord should run through your veins, but it seems that, in your case, it is water. When Sir Richard found you, he said you were teasing a dog." Their guilty looks were enough of an answer. "Is that seemly behaviour for the sons of a knight?"

They murmured, "No, my lord."

"I owe it to my friend and my sister to do something. I am the lord of this land and dealing with two creatures such as you takes me away from duties upon which the lives of hundreds of people depend. I cannot be coming here every day to ensure that you behave. I want you to gather your belongings and then wait here in the kitchen."

Henry looked horrified, "What will you do with us, my lord?"

The Ripples of Rebellion

"You will find out, but I will take some of the worry from your mother, at the very least."

I returned to the bed chamber. Richard was sleeping. I closed the door. "I have spoken with them, Eleanor. Richard asked me to do something and I shall. I will take them with me to Stockton and make men of them."

I did not know what her reaction would be but when she threw her arms around me and hugged me I knew I had made the right decision. "Thank you, Henry Samuel, you are the best of brothers. I knew you would know what to do." I looked down at Richard. "I will tell my husband when he wakes."

"And I shall return more frequently and when I do then your sons will be with me. Perhaps we can make a change in them at Stockton." I chuckled, "At the very least they will have to endure my mother's glare and her discipline. That usually works."

When we got to the kitchen the two youths had their belongings wrapped in a cloak. It was summer and the winter cloak made a convenient bag.

Eleanor said to Dick and me, "You must be starving. I will feed you before you leave." She called for her servants who were in the pantry making butter. "Food for their lordships."

I turned to the boys. "You have weapons?" They nodded. "Then fetch them." They ran off.

We sat at the table and were given a beaker of ale, some bread, cheese and ham.

The boys returned with a short sword and dagger each.

Dick and I ate the food. The women had just made the butter and the ale was fresh too. It was like a feast. I did not offer any to the boys.

"Thank you, ladies, that was fare fit for a prince."

They giggled, "Thank you, my lord." As the table was cleared, I said to the youths, "Now bid farewell to your mother."

Eleanor held her arms wide and the boys gave her a perfunctory hug. I felt my anger rising. She smiled, "Now, be good for Earl Henry. Mayhap he will make men of you. God knows that I have failed."

That was the moment they could have redeemed themselves in my eyes and said some conciliatory words to my sister but they did not. I snapped, "Dick, take them outside." I embraced Eleanor, "You should have asked for my help earlier, little sister."

She smiled, sadly, "Henry Samuel, it is my failure and I thought to rectify it, but I could not."

The Ripples of Rebellion

Once outside I said, "Follow me." We strode to the water trough. Ralph and his men were there waiting. I turned to the two boys, "And what have you to say to Ralph?" They looked at me blankly.

Dick was as angry as I was and he smacked them both hard on the side of their heads, "You were tormenting his old dog. Apologise!"

Henry said, "I am sorry, Ralph. We meant no harm."

Ralph's face showed me that he was angry too and his words confirmed it, "That old dog is coming to the end of his life and he has guarded you and your family since he was a pup. Do not lie to me and say you meant no harm. I know that you did and I hope that his lordship is ready for your tricky ways. If you were not the sons of such a noble knight then many in the village would have given you a good hiding already."

I mounted and said, "Farewell, Ralph, hopefully you will see a change when next they come." He nodded. I said to the two boys, "Now, keep up with us, I have pressing matters at the castle."

Dick and I trotted in the direction of Stockton. After running for half a mile, Geoffrey said, "For pity's sake slow down, my lord."

I turned in the saddle, "This is part of the preparation to make you into a man. This will be a regular exercise to harden your body and teach you obedience." It was at that moment that Henry chose to run away. We were close to the Ox Bridge, and he took off like a greyhound in the direction of Norton. I could see a stand of trees ahead and he was clearly heading for them.

Dick said, "Leave him to me."

My former squire was a superb horseman and even on a hackney knew how to manoeuvre well. He got ahead of Henry easily and, turning his horse sharply, made Henry swerve. Dick had calculated well and the youth tumbled into Lustrum Beck. It was summer and not deep but he was immersed in the green water and came up coughing and spluttering. Dick waited as Henry pulled himself from the beck and trudged back to join us.

I had no sympathy for him, "Now you will run again and this time you will be wet."

By the time we reached the castle Henry was weeping such was his discomfort. The sentries at St John's gate smiled. The fact that his lordship was treating two youths this way told them all that they needed to know, and they enjoyed the sight of two young nobles being humiliated.

Alfred and Samuel appeared in the inner bailey. They looked from the youths to me and back. "These two will sleep in the warrior hall. Take them there and tell Joseph of Aylesbury that we are to make

71

warriors of them." Henry and Geoffrey looked at each other and I said, "Tell him that they are not to be trusted and should be watched. If they try to run, they are to be punished at Joseph's discretion." Joseph was a hard man and the fact that they were the sons of a noble would not spare them the rod.

"Yes, my lord." Alfred's voice had steel in it as he said, "Follow us."

We dismounted and as we took our horses to Osric, Dick said, "What do you plan?"

"Joseph and the men at arms can work them until I am ready to knight Alfred and Samuel. I have a mind to make these two into squires."

"Is that fair on your sons? Henry and Geoffrey might be kin but I do not like them."

"Let us say, Dick, that this is a test for my sons. I hope that they will succeed but if they do not I will not blame them. I was lucky with you and your brother. Do not worry, I will take a close hand in their training. We will not relent for I owe it to Richard and Eleanor. It is also a test for us. As you say they are kin and they have the blood of the Warlord in their veins. They are not like Sir Robert. Let us see if we can find the jewel that lies within them and make them shine."

"And I will help you also."

I went directly to the Great Hall where the women were sewing. They were all gathered there: my mother, Aunt Mary, Eirwen, Lady Rebekah, Lady Isabelle, Lady Margery and the young women of the family.

"Did the hunt go well?"

It was my mother who asked, and I nodded, "It did. We called in at Hartburn and Sir Richard is not a well man."

My tone made them all stop. Eirwen said, "I visited last month and hoped that the warm weather might help him."

"It has not. He asked me to take charge of Henry and Geoffrey. There is no easy way to say this but they are wild boys. They angered me so much that I wished to have them whipped."

My mother was shocked, "Henry Samuel!"

Eirwen shook her head, "Mother, that shows how bad things are. If Henry Samuel considers whipping the pair then it has reached the point of no return."

"That is exactly it. I will have my men at arms train them but I have other plans. Do not misjudge me, Mother, I intend to make them into knights that grandfather would respect. I will do all in my power for Sir Richard is a dying man and I made a promise to him."

The Ripples of Rebellion

I changed and when I returned to the hall the ladies had vacated it and the tables were being laid for our evening meal. Alfred and Samuel both entered. I poured the three of us some ale. It was a warm day. "Well, what did you think of them?"

Samuel said, "It has been some time since I saw them. In fact, now that I come to think of it not since Alfred their brother died, and that was at the funeral. They seem, to me, to be sulky little brats. I am sorry to say, Father, that I did not like them."

Alfred said, "Nor me."

I nodded, "You know I would knight you?" They nodded, "It will be on All Saints and that is some way off but there is something I would have you do for me. I wish the two youths to be your squires and for you to change them. I want you to redeem the lost boys."

The smiles were wiped from their faces. "Could we not go and fight a dragon, Father, or seek the Holy Grail? Both those seem more achievable than turning what seems like base metal into gold."

I nodded, "I know, and Sir Richard agrees with you. You do not need to do this. I can leave them with Joseph, but I thought that as they are family…"

Samuel nodded, "And we are the blood of the warlord…I will do it."

Alfred sighed, "And I too. I can now understand the weight that comes with being descended from Sir Thomas and Sir Alfraed."

I laughed, "Joseph will have them until the knighting. Say nothing to them."

"Of course."

And so began the task of making two who might become villains into warriors. It was not an easy task I had set my family.

Chapter 7

Henry Samuel

Sir Samuel and Sir Alfred

That first month was the hardest. After a week they both tried to run away. Joseph caught them and I said that unless they swore to stay, I would have them shackled in the stables each night. They swore that they would. The humiliation of being shackled like a criminal, by a man at arms, was too much. William proved to be invaluable again. He was very knowledgeable and to help Joseph, he began to give lessons in the afternoon. He would teach them the history of the family. At first, the two thought that this was a soft option and that mild-mannered William would be easy on them. They soon learned otherwise. The work was not physically hard but it exhausted them. He had them copying texts which, as they read them, told them of their heritage. My mother also weighed in and she gave them a weekly lecture on the responsibilities of children to parents. She also gave them lessons on how to dress and eat. Gradually, we ground them down and removed the rougher edges but, even by the time Samuel and Alfred were due to be knighted, there was still much work to do.

William had spent time with Paul, the Reeve of Redmarshal and he had a clear picture of what was needed. We sat in my solar and he went through what needed to be done. When he finished he said, "If you were to ask me who would make the better Lord of Redmarshal, then I would have to say, Samuel."

"Why do you say that?"

"He is the calmer of the two and the one who sees solutions to problems. Alfred may well get there but now, a month or two before they are knighted, it is Samuel."

I smiled, "I thought so too but it is good to have that confirmed."

Now that I was an earl it would have been easy enough simply to summon them to the Great Hall, dub the two boys and give them their spurs, but that had never been the way of our family. The great Sir Thomas had been knighted on the battlefield of Arsuf but the rest of us had learned to play a rote, compose a song, serve at table and pass the knightly tests of spearing the quoit, hitting a bird in flight with an arrow and, finally, spending a night in vigil in our chapel. Once they knew they were to be knighted, my sons worked hard and succeeded in

The Ripples of Rebellion

passing each and every test. All Saints Eve was a propitious time to be knighted.

The date was set and I went with them to the chapel where lay the bodies of those knights who had died in England. For the ones like Sir Thomas' father, Sir Samuel, there were stone markers to commemorate their deaths. It was a sombre yet peaceful place. Now, lit by a pair of candles, I could feel the fear in my sons as the weight of their forebears seemed to lie on their shoulders. I had felt it too. This chapel seemed to be filled with the ghosts of the past. We knelt at the altar rail and prayed. I stood and faced them. They knelt with drawn swords held, like crosses, before them.

"A knight endures a vigil so that he can be close to God. Here, in Stockton, we are luckier than most for our ancestors are here. Their memories are here in this chapel. Do not fear the dark but embrace it. When you are a knight you may face horror and death. This night will steel you against such days. You are lucky that there are two of you and you will not be alone but do not abuse that. Remember, a vigil should be silent. There is no one to check that you obey this rule but yourselves, and God. He is watching along with the Warlord and Sir Thomas. It is part of the test. I will return at dawn and your vigil will be over. Know that I am proud of you and I know that, once the vigil is over, you will join the illustrious brotherhood of we knights of the border, we defenders of the north who are of the blood of the Warlord." I hoped that my words had stirred them.

I left the chapel, my words echoing from the walls and closed the doors. The castle bailey was quiet. There were a couple of sentries but they were silent. In the distance, towards the woods of Thornaby, I heard the screech of a hunting owl. I pulled my cloak tighter about me and hurried back to the castle. As I walked through the doors of the keep, closing and barring them behind me, it was as though I was alone in the world. Walking through the corridors I thought of my sons and that led me to think about the last knight I had dubbed, Matthew. He would be far away. On the road to the Holy Land who knew what dangers he faced? The royal family had enemies. Many remained in England but I knew that there were others who had fled abroad. As a household knight to the nephew of the King of England, Matthew would be in more danger than most.

Edgar the steward stood patiently by the doors of the hall, "Will that be all for tonight, Sir Henry?"

"It will. All is ready for the ceremony and the feast tomorrow?"

He nodded, "The cook has two men roasting the beef already, my lord. We shall have a most pleasant aroma at breakfast. The rest of the food is prepared and once we have eaten breakfast, we shall transform the hall."

"And rooms for the guests?" I did not know if any would wish to stay but it was as well to be prepared.

"All is in hand, my lord."

"Then I bid you goodnight."

"Goodnight, my lord."

Eirwen waited for me in our bed. She smiled, "So, tomorrow our sons become lords. Have you decided which one will move to Redmarshal? I only ask so that I can ensure that the one chosen will have all that they need."

"I think Samuel is the right choice. Alfred, well, he is closer to William and still enjoys sitting with his mother and grandmother. That will change, I know, but for the while let us keep one chick close to the nest."

I had undressed while I had been speaking and I knelt next to the bed to pray silently. I prayed for Matthew and my sons. Slipping into bed I kissed Eirwen.

"You are the best of lords, my husband, for you are thoughtful. However…"

I looked at her, "However, you are worried about Henry and Geoffrey." She nodded. "I believe that Samuel and Alfred will succeed where Eleanor and Richard have failed. They will give them discipline. What you cannot know, my love, is the bond that builds between a squire and his lord. Dick and Matthew feel as close to me as my sons. I am hoping that the bond will change Henry and Geoffrey."

"And if it does not?"

"Then we have all failed and they will become reluctant men at arms."

"What does William say?" Like the rest of us, Eirwen had the greatest respect for my brother.

"He believes that they can be salvaged. He told me that had we brought them here earlier then the task would have been easier but he says there has been a change already. It is only slight but small steps mean that they are less likely to fall."

I woke before dawn. It was the warrior in me. I dressed quickly for it was cold in the bed chamber. In summer we did not light fires. Now warmed I left a sleeping Eirwen and slipped down the stairs to the doors and unbarred them. I could hear movements in the kitchen and knew that the servants were preparing not only breakfast but also the feast we would enjoy later on. I took my cloak which hung from a peg and with that wrapped around me to protect me from the early morning chill, I

The Ripples of Rebellion

stepped out. I raised my hand to wave at the white face of the sentry who peered from the gatehouse tower. It was good that my sentries were vigilant. I saw, behind him, the setting moon in the west. I walked to the east wall and ascended the steps to the fighting platform. I stared east towards the sea. The fresher air told me that the wind was from that direction. The day would be cooler. I watched for the glow that would tell me it was a new day. Matthew, if he was already in Africa would see, so my grandfather had told me, the sudden flaring of the sun because it rose more quickly further south. Here in the north of England, it was a slow and gentle dawning. A man could appreciate its glory more. This day I would not stand, as I often had, to admire it but would use it to mark time. As soon as I saw the sun rise over the eastern horizon, I descended the steps and went to the chapel. I slipped the door open silently. There was no sound from within. I hoped that they had not failed and succumbed to sleep. When two faces turned at the sound of my boots on the stone I was relieved and I smiled.

"You have passed your test and now you may speak."

They stood and sheathed their swords. Samuel spoke first. "Being silent was the hardest task, Father. Perhaps that was a lesson I needed to learn. I was able to listen to my heart beating. My eyes grew used to the gloom so that it felt like daylight and I studied the chapel. I thought I knew it but spending the night within its walls told me that I did not."

"And you, Alfred?"

He shook his head, "Does it make me seem a failure in your eyes, Father, if I say that I was terrified?"

"No, Alfred. I admire your honesty for that is also a lesson learned. A vigil is different for every knight. You were terrified and yet you did not flee. That will stand you in good stead." I waved a hand around the chapel, "While we are in this most holy of our places I need to ask something and now seems an opportune moment. You know I need a lord for Redmarshal while Matthew is away?" They nodded. "I have made my decision."

Before I could continue Alfred blurted out, "Not me, Father. I am not ready and…"

I smiled, "And you have made my decision easier, I had already chosen Samuel and it is good that you not only accept the decision but embrace it. Come, you will need food for whilst the vigil is over, this day will be a long one."

We left the chapel and the autumn sun bathed the keep in its golden rays. It made my sons beam as brightly as the sun itself and they strode cheerfully towards the welcoming door of our stronghold.

The Ripples of Rebellion

Sir Thomas and Lady Anne arrived by terces for Norton was not far away. My brother and his wife, Eleanor, shortly after. Eleanor was pregnant with their third child. My sister and Sir Richard would not be coming. Although Richard had not deteriorated as fast as his doctor had expected, travel was out of the question. Dick and I now saw him every week, as did my sons. We had not taken Henry and Geoffrey to revisit their home for they were not yet ready. There was still much work to do. We had invited important men from the town and by noon the hall was filling up. This was a time for dressing up and both my mother and Lady Mary stood like sentinels to make sure that all the family passed muster. Poor William was sent back to clean, more thoroughly, the ink from his fingers. Joseph as captain of my guards was present and he had with him, scrubbed combed and dressed as pages, Henry and Geoffrey. I saw from their faces that they were awed by the occasion. We still had to tell them of their new positions. I went over what they would be doing with Samuel and Alfred, as well as my present squire, Roger of Whorlton.

I nodded to them, "They are a credit to you, Captain Joseph."

"Kind of you to say so, my lord, but there is still much work to do."

I nodded and turned to my nephews, "Today you will learn new tasks. You are part of the family and today you will act as pages. Roger here will guide you. You will serve the table. Every eye will be upon you. Lady Matilda and Lady Mary will pick you up on every misdemeanour. You will fetch and carry until all is done. Roger, my squire, will tell you when you may eat. Do you understand? Today, Roger is your master."

I saw what Joseph meant. There was still defiance in their eyes but they both nodded. They were kept in order by fear and that was not a good thing. My sons had a monumental task and I hoped I had not set them an impossible one.

I had invited the Bishop of Durham but was not surprised when he did not attend. While we were closer to the Palatinate than we had been it was still an uneasy relationship. Our priest, Father Albert, would lead the prayers but most of the service would be conducted by me. The spurs I had ordered to be made by our weaponsmith were on two blue cushions. Also, there were their new swords. They had come from Evesham and we had kept them for just such an occasion. They were made from the finest steel and Eirwen had commanded new scabbards to be made for them. Decorated in blue and embossed with gryphons they added to the richness of the gift.

My sons were kept apart until all was ready. Sir Richard and Sir Alfred, as senior knights, fetched the two and I felt pride when they entered. They were both fine young men and moved confidently with assurance. The contrast with their cousins, Henry and Geoffrey, could not have been more marked. The smiles that could not be kept from my sons' faces and the warm reception from the family were a testament to their elevation. Out of the corner of my eye, I could see Henry and Geoffrey. They were looking bored.

It was not a long ceremony but my sons' swearing of an oath on my sword, the sword I had inherited from my grandfather, and laid on a Bible was, a blood oath apart, the most binding of oaths and I knew from their faces that they would not break their knightly oath.

I touched their shoulders and said, "Rise Sir Samuel of Redmarshal and Sir Alfred of Stockton." The giving of the manor was my surprise. I was pleased when I saw the smile and the nod from my mother. The gift of the manor would only last so long as Matthew was a crusader, but as that could necessitate an absence of years Samuel would have the chance to learn to be a lord of the manor. I had done so in the north and it had made me a better knight. There was a spontaneous outburst of cheers and shouts. Lady Mary frowned. She preferred a more dignified acknowledgement. I held up my hands, "There remains, before we eat and enjoy the fine beef whose smell has my stomach aching, one more task. We need to appoint two squires." Only a handful of people knew who it would be: my brothers, Sir Richard, my wife and my mother. "Step forward, Henry of Hartburn and Geoffrey of Hartburn." The shock on their faces almost made me smile. "Captain Joseph of Aylesbury has begun to make men of you. My sons will now continue that work. Geoffrey, you will be the squire of Sir Samuel. Kneel and swear fealty."

He looked around as though he was seeking flight. My son said, "Come, cuz, I will do my part to help you achieve what I have this day." His gentle voice must have worked for Geoffrey knelt.

Sir Richard's son looked up at me, "I know not what to say, my lord."

"Swear that you will serve Sir Samuel as a loyal and faithful squire." He nodded and I held the hilt of my sword. "And do so whilst holding this sword."

His hands came out as though he feared the hilt was hot to the touch, "I swear I will serve Sir Samuel as a loyal and faithful squire."

Samuel reached down to raise him up. "This will be an adventure cuz. Embrace the moment."

It was easier with Henry and Alfred for the precedent had been set. The cheer when Henry rose made both Sir Richard's sons flush with embarrassment rather than anger. It was a start.

The Ripples of Rebellion

"And now, Edgar, clear the hall and fetch in the food."

The apparent confusion as servants moved tables and benches from the side soon became more organised. Edgar handled this sort of event well. My uncle and aunt had trained him well. Eirwen and I, along with the others on the top table, had chairs while the rest had benches. There was a hierarchy. Eirwen and I were in the centre. On Eirwen's right were my mother and aunt, along with my daughters, Myfanwy and Eleanor. On my left were Samuel, Alfred and William. On my aunt's right were Dick and his wife. Next to them were Thomas and Lady Anne, along with Isabelle, Thomas' mother. Sitting to William's left were Alfred, Eleanor and his children.

My mother and Eirwen had arranged the feast and there would be ten courses. No food would be wasted for whatever the squires, pages and servants did not eat would be given to the poor of Stockton. It was rich fare but then again one did not knight two sons every day. We had fine wine from the manor in Anjou, La Flèche. We did not have as much contact with the manor first given to Sir Leofric, but the ties remained.

I smiled as I heard Roger gently badgering the two new squires. I think they found it harder than Joseph's training.

Samuel and Alfred could not stop smiling. They were desperate to don their new spurs and wield their new swords but, at the same time, they enjoyed the comments from their uncles, cousins and matriarchs of the family. The wine and ale flowed and the platters were brought in and then cleared. It was late in the afternoon by the time we had reached the desserts. I did not bother with those. Instead, I ate the tray of cheese brought in by Edgar. The steward knew my likes and dislikes.

Eirwen leaned in and said, in my ear, "You said the right words, my husband, and everyone is pleased."

"And the food that you and my mother devised was faultless. Would that every day could be as perfect as this one."

Just then Roger appeared at my shoulder, waiting for me to stop speaking. Behind him, I saw Henry and Geoffrey looking exhausted. "Yes, Roger?"

"Service has finished, my lord, the squires would know if they can now eat."

"Of course." I waved to Henry and Geoffrey. "You did well. When you have eaten fetch your belongings from the warrior hall. Roger will show you the chambers of Sir Samuel and Sir Alfred. Tomorrow, Geoffrey, you and your new master will go to your manor. The real work begins then."

They both bowed, "Yes, my lord." They chorused together.

The Ripples of Rebellion

I wondered if it was my imagination or the wine but the two seemed different already. Time alone would tell.

Normally the household would retire when the Lord of the Manor did so but I knew that this occasion was different. My mother and the senior ladies retired relatively early, not long we had finished the food. Many of those from the town also left early so that it was a younger group of the family who lit the candles and revelled until it was so late that even I felt weary. It was Eirwen who brought proceedings to a close. She wagged a finger at our sons, "You two have had a long and arduous day. With no sleep last night, you need your beds."

They stood, somewhat unsteadily. It could have been exhaustion, the drink they had consumed or a combination of both. They bowed and Samuel said, "Thank you, Mother, Father. This has been the greatest day of our lives. There may be better ones ahead but I cannot see it now."

My brother Alfred laughed, "You cannot see much at the moment, nephew, but believe me, as great as this day is, the day you marry will be greater and that will only be surpassed when you become a father."

There was a cheer but I saw that my brother William looked pensive.

Alfred said, "My children are now abed and I shall join them. Thank you, brother. Today has been a fine one."

That was the signal for all to depart and when most had gone Eirwen said, "I will retire. Do not be long, husband."

William was still seated and I nodded to Eirwen, "Leave a candle burning and I will try not to disturb you." Left alone with my bachelor brother I said, "Alfred can sometimes be a little thoughtless, brother. He means nothing by it."

"You mean the comment about taking a wife?" I nodded, "That does not worry me. It is my choice and I do not feel the need to spill my seed. Does that make me strange?"

"It makes you William and I am grateful for all that you do."

"Besides, I feel that all the women in the castle are like sisters, and I am comfortable with that. As for children…I was as proud today as any. Samuel and Alfred are your children but I think I have contributed to their education."

"You have."

"And now I have another task, the education of Henry and Geoffrey."

"I have made that hard for you by giving Redmarshal to Samuel."

"No, brother, for Samuel asked me, while his mind still functioned, to visit Redmarshal and cast my eye over it. He wants advice."

"And you are happy to do that?"

"I will never be a lord of the manor but this gives me the chance to try out some ideas I have." He stood, "Goodnight, brother, and now I hope that we have a time of peace. You deserve it."

"Goodnight." I was left alone in the hall. Edgar and the servants would be hovering close by but I wanted a few moments alone. William was right and yet he was wrong in the same breath. The land needed peace but Alfred and Geoffrey needed war to temper them. Had I known the problems Henry and Geoffrey had caused then I regret not taking them in hand sooner. Hindsight is a wonderful thing for you see everything perfectly.

I stood, "Edgar, I will retire. All did well and I thank you."

"You are welcome, my lord. It was a pleasure."

Ireshopeburn Stanhope
    Daddry Shield   Wolsingham

                            Bedburn

N

2 miles

               Barnard Castle

          Bowes Castle

The land around Barnard Castle 1271

Chapter 8

Henry Samuel
Dervorguilla of Galloway

The next time I saw Geoffrey was at the funeral of his father. It was shortly before Christmas and my best friend had been steadily deteriorating. Henry had seen the decline in his father's health more recently for Alfred had brought him with me when I had visited. Geoffrey had changed while he had been in the charge of Samuel but the death of his father changed him even more. His remorse at the grave was such that he dropped to his knees and sobbed. His mother went to put an arm on his shoulder as did my son. It was a wet day when he was buried, not in the chapel, for he was not of the blood of the Warlord, but in the small cemetery adjacent to it. There he would lie in honourable company, for many of those who had served the Warlord and the ones who followed lay there.

We retired to the hall. I saw my mother looking sadder than most. This was not a death of her generation. She was used to those. This was a death of the next generation and that aged her. Richard was her only son-in-law and I knew that it had hurt. She spent a long time in conversation with Eleanor and her grandsons. The funeral was not a day for the young men to be squires but to be sons who mourned their father and supported their mother. Henry and Geoffrey looked in as much shock as anything.

I was silent for most of the time. I did not eat a large amount and I drank sparingly for I had much on my mind. When my brother William spoke, I jumped. "You have as much to mourn as his family, brother."

"What?"

"You and Richard were brothers in arms. You were the one who introduced him to our sister, Eleanor. You and he faced the enemy at Otterburn. You will miss him more than most."

He was right and this was a time to unburden myself, "I missed him before but I did not spend as much time with him as I should have. He was sick and…" I shook my head, "Had he been hale and hearty I would have visited every week and we would have hunted and sparred but he was wasting away."

"Do not be sad, brother, but be grateful for your health." He nodded towards Henry and Geoffrey, "See, they have changed and that is down to you and your sons. You swore an oath to Richard and whilst they are not yet completely redeemed, they are growing and changing. We had seen it in Henry for we see him every day but Samuel has worked a miracle with Geoffrey. Your friend is now in heaven and he is thanking you."

My brother was right but it did not stop me from thinking of my own mortality. My melancholy was interrupted when my mother and Eleanor approached, "My son, let us retire to your solar for Eleanor would have a word with you."

"Of course." Eirwen saw me leave and I nodded to her. She would play the hostess in my absence.

There were just two chairs in my solar and I stood. It was a chilly room and one I did not use as much in the winter. The chimney passed along one wall and I stood with my back to that. My mother nodded to Eleanor who straightened her back and began to speak, "My lord, Henry Samuel, brother, I wish to thank you for all that you have done for me and my family. You are a great lord." She sighed, "Hartburn has been my home these many years but now it is a place of ghosts; my husband and my son's. It is a good manor and the people there are hard working. They need more than a sad widow who mopes and weeps. When I left the manor to come here I swore that I would not return. There would be too many sad memories. I want to live here. Henry lives in the castle and if I live here I can see him each day." She smiled, "I can see that he has changed. I know not how this change was effected but I am grateful. Appoint another to be lord of Hartburn. Mother has told me that she and her ladies will find a place for me here and I would like that."

My mother gave a firm smile and a nod.

"Of course, but would your sons not expect to inherit the manor?"

"After you took them, I spoke often with Richard. We had more time. We did not have two wild cats to watch. Richard believed that the boys," she smiled, "to us, they will always be boys, naughty boys but boys nonetheless, would have to earn whatever they were due. He did not want them to be given the manor. He always said that he won Hartburn fighting for Sir Thomas and that was a good thing. Let another be Lord of Hartburn."

I took her hands, raised them and kissed their backs, "Then I shall follow the wishes of my oldest friend. You shall come to live here but I must speak with your sons. I want no ill feeling from this."

"I will fetch them, brother."

They stood. Eleanor left and my mother put her arm around me and said, "Your grandfather and father would be proud of you, Henry Samuel."

The Ripples of Rebellion

I felt myself growing with pride at her words.

I sat on the chair vacated by my mother. There was a knock on the door, "Come."

"You wished to see us, my lord?" It was Geoffrey who spoke and it was a different Geoffrey from the one I had encountered on the day of the hawking.

"Your mother wishes to come here to live."

Henry smiled, "That is good, my lord, for she would be lonely at Hartburn, and I shall see her every day."

"You know, however, that this means I must appoint a lord to the manor."

They looked at each other and nodded. Geoffrey spoke, "You found two who were lower than bandits in the forest for at least bandits have an excuse for their behaviour. We did not. We have spoken on the occasions that Sir Alfred and Sir Samuel were together, and we can now see what we were. Then we did not. Today is a sad one for me as I now know that I let my father down. I was a disappointment to him. Perhaps had my brother lived it might have been different, I know not. It could be that his father's illness stopped him from training us but the seed within us, within me, was turning me bad. Your son is a patient man, my lord, and a kind one. It has taken time but since he was knighted and I became his squire I have learned to like myself a little more. I would be a knight." He shook his head, "If I had been told that in the spring then I would have laughed but I can see the future now. It is a little foggy and far off but it is there." He turned to Henry, "Perhaps we fed off each other, Henry. I miss you, but I think that apart we are better than together."

"As do I."

I liked their words and their attitude but I gave a word of caution, "But, think on this, if the knights of the valley go to war then you two will have to be together."

Henry smiled, "There is no war yet, my lord, and we change every day. The wild young pup grows into a dog that does not worry the sheep but guards them. We will make that journey."

The air cleared, we rejoined the others and I waved over Dick. Edgar brought us wine and he said, "What have you been up to, my lord? This is a funeral but I see smiles creeping across faces that I thought would be sad."

"Sir Richard is mourned but in his death there is hope," I told him what had happened and he looked genuinely pleased.

"That is good. My wife will make Lady Eleanor welcome here and the babe that is shortly to be born will help her, I think."

The Ripples of Rebellion

"She will not be here, nor will you, Dick. I would give you Hartburn." His face looked shocked. "Come, cuz, surely you knew that I could not let you languish here enjoying a lazy life. That is not what our grandfather would have wished."

"You are right but this was always my home."

"I know but our blood means that pleasure has to be forgotten, for duty is all."

He sighed, "You are right."

"They are good people there and the land is fertile. It is a good place to bring up your child."

He smiled, "It is and Stockton is not far away. I will be a good lord of the manor for you, my lord."

By Christmas, there was a new lord of the manor in Hartburn and Dick had a son. William was born on Christmas Eve. The mother and child were healthy and the birth was witnessed by my mother, Lady Mary and Eleanor, Richard's widow. It meant we had much to celebrate at Christmas. That proved a good thing as we had snow and ice for a month after. I worked with my men at arms and archers, as well as Alfred and Henry, as we cleared the snow from the bailey.

Alfred shook his head, "We freeze here and Matthew will be enjoying the hot sun of Africa."

I stopped, mid-shovelling, "And he would swap duties in a heartbeat, Alfred. We have a little snow to move but he will be facing death on a daily basis."

"Sorry, you are right, Father, but Henry and I yearn for action."

"And that will come but for now let us sweat a little and clear this snow, eh?"

The rider who came to the gates at the end of February, not long before noon, looked chilled to the bone. I did not recognise the livery but the rider was an older man. Edgar came to me, "My lord, we have an emissary from Barnard Castle. He has a missive from Lady Dervorguilla of Galloway."

"Then fetch him to my solar and ask Sir Alfred to join us."

The Balliol family lived to the west of us and were a most powerful family. The baron had died a couple of years earlier. The new baron, Alexander, had not been at Northampton and I did not know him. What I did know was that Lady Dervorguilla of Galloway was in line for the Scottish throne should anything happen to King Alexander. As he had yet to sire an heir, that made Lady Dervorguilla of Galloway a most important person.

Alfred arrived before the emissary. Roger and Henry were with him. "You two can wait without."

Alfred asked, "What is it, Father?"

"I know not but an emissary from Barnard Castle is not a trivial event."

Roger put his head around the door of the solar, "My lord, your visitor."

"Bring him in and some refreshment for our guests. The ride from Barnard is a hard one at this time of year."

The door opened and the visitor smiled, "At any time of year, my lord. It is good to see you. I am Miles Longstaff, gentleman, and I bring this from Lady Dervorguilla of Galloway."

"If you stand close to the chimney you will gain a little warmth until the mulled ale comes."

I took the letter and used my dagger to slice through the wax seal.

My son gave a nod and said, "I am Sir Alfred, the earl's son."

"A pleasure, my lord."

The letter was penned in a strong hand. I had heard the matriarch of the Balliol family was a formidable woman and her hand showed that.

Earl Henry Samuel,

I write to you as the one knight in the north who can be relied upon to do the right thing. King Alexander has spoken of the service you have done for him and I am writing to you to implore some aid.

The forests close to my sons' home are not a safe place and are infested by those who would plague Balliol land. Circumstances mean that my children are not the knights to scour my family's land of bandits. That task is best appointed to your men. I heard what you did for King Henry in Chesterfield and would have you do the same for my sons' lands. I wish you to bring your men at arms and archers and to make this part of England safe. You and your men will be recompensed.

The Ripples of Rebellion

My emissary, Miles Longstaff, Gentleman, can give more details of the problem. If you cannot aid me then I know not to whom I can turn.
Yours
Dervorguilla of Galloway

I folded the letter and placed it on the table. The door opened and Edgar, aided by Roger and Henry, brought in honeyed ale heated with a poker and toasted oat cakes. I smiled, "Eat, and when you are warmed, we will talk more. Edgar, have a chamber made ready for this gentleman."

"Yes, my lord."

I waited until the colour came back to the emissary's face and he looked a little warmer. I held up the letter, "I am guessing that you know the contents of this letter."

"Yes, my lord."

"The forests where these bandits congregate, I do not know them. Tell me more."

"There are many forests, my lord. Over the years bandits and brigands from both sides of the border have gathered there. They are like a plague and take from the villagers. They raid the roads so that merchants are attacked and murdered. Trade from Penrith and Carlisle has dried to a trickle. Even Lady Dervorguilla's people need to ride armed and protected."

"There is no lord there to keep order?"

He sighed, "It is Balliol land now, my lord."

"And that does not answer my question." He looked from me to Alfred, and I said, "My son is discreet and besides, if we are to aid you then we need to know all."

"My lady had four sons. Sir Hugh and Alan died before their time. Sir Alexander was given the title and his spurs when his brothers died. He is not a warrior for he had no training, my lord, and his younger brother, John, is a studious youth."

"The Balliols cannot defend their own family's lands."

He flushed, "My lord, that is unfair."

"What is unfair is that I am expected to risk the lives of my family and my men because the Balliols cannot defend their own land."

"My lord, many merchants have been butchered. Isolated farms have been raided, ransacked, robbed and buildings burnt. The bandits intimidate those who would give us information and they have become

The Ripples of Rebellion

bold of late. They attacked one merchant not far from Bowes Castle." He said, weakly, "There will be payment."

"Dead men cannot spend gold, Master Miles." I opened the letter again and read it. "What men are there in Barnard Castle that could be used?"

"We have twenty sergeants and fourteen archers."

I snorted, "On what is the Balliol money spent?"

"The baron, before he died, had a land dispute with the last Bishop of Durham, Walter Kirkham. His lordship lost the case and was tasked with founding a college for the poor at the University of Oxford. It was and is expensive."

I began to feel some sympathy with the family. Our own family had suffered at the hands of the Bishop of Durham. I turned to Alfred, "What think you, my son?"

"What would the payment be, Master Miles?" My son had grown since his knighthood.

"Two shillings a day for knights, a shilling for sergeants, squires and archers. Six pennies for each spearman."

I shook my head, "It would be cheaper to hire your own men."

"May I speak frankly, my lord?"

"Of course."

"Your men are trained. We have all heard of your exploits at both Evesham and Chesterfield. We were surprised when you did not take the cross with The Lord Edward. Trained men that are ready to fight are better than those yet to be trained."

"If we do accept this commission then there are conditions."

"Of course, my lord."

"We would serve for, at the most, one month and that includes travelling to and from the bandits' lair." He nodded. "This will be a unique event. I will not bring my men a second time. It is incumbent upon you to train your own men and clear up your own lands."

"Of course, my lord. It is what I have been advocating."

"And Sir Alexander and John Balliol will accompany us along with the men of Barnard." I saw the doubt on his face. "The last condition is most important. If we are to risk our lives then I want the lords of Barnard to do the same."

"I shall make the case with you, my lord."

I stood, "Roger."

My squire entered, "Yes, my lord."

"Take this gentleman to his chambers and then fetch Joseph of Aylesbury and Robert the Fletcher."

"Thank you, my lord."

"Will you be with us, Master Miles?"

"I will, my lord, for I am a warrior."

Left alone with Alfred I said, "Would you and Henry like to come with me or would you rather watch Stockton?"

He laughed, "Stay here and watch women sew? Henry and I relish the opportunity."

"He will need a good horse."

"Osgar has one. His mother paid for it."

"Good."

"What of my brother, Samuel?"

"Samuel has a manor to run. No, we will just take two knights and our captains can advise on the rest."

When they arrived I told my captain of sergeants and my captain of archers what was needed. "We will have to leave a garrison here but with Elton, Hartburn, Norton and Redmarshal now with knights then it should be safe enough."

"Then, my lord, we have seventeen sergeants, including myself."

I looked at Robert and he stroked his beard, "There are three of my archers who recently became fathers and I would leave them here." I nodded. "Then, with me, there are eighteen of us."

"Good, we leave tomorrow."

All three were shocked. Alfred said, "That is hasty, Father."

I shook my head, "The sooner we get there then the sooner we can quash this threat. In all of this, the people of the lands close to Barnard Castle are forgotten. If we are to scour the forests, as we did at Chesterfield, then let us do so now. This time they are not rebels but the lowest of all, brigands."

They bowed and Alfred said, "Then let us make haste."

When I told my wife and my mother both understood the need. Like me, however, my mother was cross that they could not defend themselves. "Thanks to the fortune the Balliols received from the marriage to Galloway they should have an army the size of the Earl of Gloucester. Even the founding of a college would be as but a drop in the ocean. It is good that you go, Henry Samuel, for the good of the innocents, but I am less than happy."

I would not have time to tell the other knights of the valley personally about the commission and I left that to William. He had a lot of information to give me about the land. He had read of the wars on the borders in the time of Matilda and King Stephen. "When I have spoken to the others I will make copies of the maps that you will need."

"Thank you, brother."

The Ripples of Rebellion

The rest of the afternoon was spent preparing for the journey. My mail had to be cleaned and weapons sharpened. We would not need lances but I had Roger find some good spears. We would not need food for that would be provided by Barnard Castle. I would ride the gift of the Scottish king, Duncan, but Roger also took a spare courser, Brutus. He had his own horse, a gift from his father and it, too, was a courser. His father was a farmer but he knew horses and had bought this one from Abel. We had a sumpter for our weapons. We were lucky in that all my archers could be mounted. Osric and Osgar kept us well-supplied with horses. The horse farm was a wise investment for us.

We dined in the Great Hall. It was not a special feast but I knew that we would not enjoy such fine fare again until we returned. We retired early and Eirwen cuddled in closely, "Take care, husband. The cause might be a worthy one but it is not worth your death."

She was right. The rebellion against King Henry was not yet over. The knights of the valley would be needed to defend England again.

Even though we lay on the same river as Barnard Castle we did not follow the river. The bends and meanders would add days and besides, there were few roads alongside the river. Instead, we headed due west to pass through Sadberge, Great Burdon, Piercebridge and Gainford. It was less than thirty miles and while Miles had done it in a hard morning's ride, we were leading sumpters and would need to conserve our horses for the trial ahead. It would take us more than five hours.

I rode at the fore with my son, Joseph and Miles. Robert and half of his archers rode half a mile ahead of us and the rest brought up the rear with the baggage. They were our eyes and ears although we were in the valley, and I did not fear an ambush. Once we passed Barnard Castle then we would be in danger. As we rode, I questioned Miles about the bandits.

"Has anyone done anything about the brigands?"

"Yes, my lord, men were sent into the forests to try to find their camps."

"And?"

"Ten men were lost and four wounded by arrows from the trees."

"Who led the men? Sir Alexander?"

He shook his head, "No my lord, it was me. It was my failure."

We rode in silence for a while and I said, "It takes a brave man to admit to failure. What did you learn from your failure?"

"That the forest is like a wooden fortress."

Alfred said, "Father, you and the others took many men in the forests of Chesterfield. Surely this will be easy for you."

The Ripples of Rebellion

Joseph sighed, "Sir Alfred, the men we fought in the Chesterfield campaign were soldiers. They were rebels and when they were defeated they surrendered to take their punishment. None fought beyond the time when all hope had gone. The men we fight are not made of the same metal. These are men who choose to live in the wild, beyond the law. They are outlaws and men who choose such lives know that they will be punished by death. They will do all that they can to defeat us. We will have to watch for knives in the night. Our archers will need to find the traps that are prepared for us and, when we fight them, we will need to be as ruthless as they are."

Alfred looked at me, "Ruthless, Father?"

"Joseph is speaking the truth. When you strike one of our enemies you do so to kill. He may not be wearing mail but you must strike as though he is. If you do not, if you hesitate then you doom not only yourself but also your squire and, perhaps, the men that you lead. There will be no surrender from us for they will not take ransom. They will kill any who asks for quarter. Do not ask for it." My sombre words ended the conversation.

Behind us, I heard Henry and Roger speaking, "And us, Roger? Will we not be watching the horses?"

"Perhaps but what if they attack the baggage? If I was a bandit I would seek to take from those I saw as being weak, the squires. I would take the horses. Horses can be eaten and by taking our supplies they shorten the campaign against them. Make no mistake, Henry, every man we take will have to fight."

Barnard Castle was a mighty edifice. It was built on a cliff making one side of the castle impregnable. Inside the castle, there was a mighty dry moat that protected the huge keep. There was a double wall. The town lay within the outer wall in what was called the town ward and the rest of the castle, the stables, warrior hall, kitchens, workshops and servants quarters lay inside the second. Any attack on the castle had to negotiate three walls and would be doomed to failure. The townsfolk looked up as we clattered through the gate and their town. My blue livery with the yellow gryphon was known and I saw smiles. The knights of the valley had a well-deserved reputation.

We dismounted in the outer bailey. Miles said to Joseph, "The warrior hall is over there. His lordship and Sir Alfred will be accommodated in the keep. Ralph of Bowes is the captain there. He is expecting you."

We dismounted and led our horses through the gate and over the wooden bridge to the mighty keep. Roger and Henry spied the stables and headed for them. Miles took Alfred and me towards the donjon.

The Ripples of Rebellion

Whilst this was a fortress it was also a palace for Lady Dervorguilla was used to luxury. She had many residences but this one was the Balliol family home and she had made it reflect her money and her power. That she did not greet us was unsurprising. Her sons waited for us in the hall but neither looked like warriors. My son, Alfred, was young and yet he carried himself like a soldier. I did not know how Sir Alexander had gained his spurs, perhaps it was through inheritance, but I could see, as he offered me a pudgy hand, that he would be of little use to us as a warrior.

"Earl, we thank you for coming in our hour of need." He looked beyond Alfred, "Are there more knights coming, Sir Henry?"

I shook my head, "My son and I lead men at arms and archers. We do not come to find an invading army."

The younger brother John, spoke. He was softly spoken and had the soft hands of a scholar, "They are savages. Our father should have wiped them from the face of the earth."

"Yet he did not." I looked around the hall. It was festooned with tapestries showing battles past, "We will need to clean the sweat and dirt from our clothes before we meet your mother."

Miles nodded, "Follow me, my lord."

They had been expecting more knights and four rooms had been allocated to us. Alfred and I would each have our own chamber and our squires had paillasses. We would only need them for a short time. I knew that there had to be spies in the town who would have seen the arrival of the Earl of Cleveland with his warriors. Already the bandits would know we were coming and I wanted them to have as little time as possible to prepare. I took off my mail and travelling tunic. I washed myself in the warm water provided.

Roger arrived with our bags and he took out my better clothes. The clean tunic still smelled of rosemary and would not offend the nose of Lady Dervorguilla. I took my comb and used it on my beard and hair. I did not oil it as some did. Roger arranged his own bed and then changed into his better clothes. He and Henry would be serving us.

"Well, Roger?"

He was my eyes and ears, "Ours are the best horses in the stables, my lord. There is a courser but he looks old and fat. Sir Alexander's squire is not a young man and his paunch suggests to me that he eats better than he fights."

"The sentries?"

"They look to be of reasonable quality. They dress like soldiers but how they will fight, my lord…?"

The Ripples of Rebellion

"You and Henry need to keep your wits about you in the kitchens. From what Miles told me the bandits knew he and his men were coming and ambushed them. There may be a spy here. Play as though you and Henry are simpletons with more muscles than brains. If there is a spy, then they may slip up."

"Yes, my lord."

"How is Henry doing?"

"He still has a long journey ahead of him, my lord, but this is not the same youth you had to fetch back when he ran off. There are edges that need to be smoothed but he has the blood of your family and it will out."

"Good."

There was a knock on the door and a liveried servant stood there, "Sir Henry, Lady Dervorguilla awaits you."

"Tell her that we will be down shortly." He frowned as though the mistress was used to her orders being obeyed instantly. "We will come in good time." My stare told the man to leave. We went to Alfred's room and I opened the door. "Let us descend but, before we do, you need to be aware that there may be a spy in the castle. When Miles took men to find the bandits he was ambushed. Say nothing to anyone. Henry, you and Roger have a most important task to perform. Play simple poltroons who know nothing and listen. Alfred, the only one who knows my plans is me. Those ideas are in my head. When we leave this castle I will tell you, Joseph, Robert and Miles what they are. Until then they are locked in my mind." All three nodded. The journey west had been a fruitful one. I knew where the danger lay and I had my plans ready. My grandfather had told me that when he had been a sword for hire, and that was what we were, he had rarely confided in any other. Only Birger Persson had been privy to his plans and only then when it was necessary.

The frown on the face of the dowager countess told me that she was displeased with our tardy arrival. "This is not what I expect of my guests, Earl Henry."

I bowed, "I thought that we were here to do a job of work and not bend and scrape. We are here because the Balliol family cannot control their own lands."

Had I slapped them then Sir Alexander, John and their mother could not have looked more shocked. Lady Dervorguilla reacted first, "How dare you. Do you know who I am? My grandfather was the brother of William the Lion."

"And my grandsire, the first Earl of Cleveland, was the one who captured William the Lion. I am unsure of the point that you are making?" I would not back down. This was a battle I had to win. "You have asked for my help. I am giving that help but it is reluctantly given for, unlike the Balliol family, my knights served King Henry in the recent rebellion and we thought to enjoy a time of peace. If we offend you then I apologise and I will take my men back to Stockton on the morrow."

The look on the face of the countess told me that I had won. "Do not be hasty, my lord. We are pleased that you have come to our aid but my sons and I are disappointed that you have brought but one knight."

"It will be enough. We recently aided Lord Henry of Almain in scouring the forests of Chesterfield of rebels. We know our business."

"And how will you do it?"

I looked at Sir Alexander who had asked the question, "And will you be riding with us, Sir Alexander?"

"I do not ride. I have a condition."

I said, bluntly, "That does not please me. Your sons will have to take over when we leave. How will they learn to be knights if they do not watch my son and I?"

She shook her head, "I have lost two sons. Alexander and John are destined for greater things than being a man with a sword."

"You do not make my task easier, my lady." I sighed, "You will pay my men for one month of work. We will try to perform the miracle in that time but if not…"

Sir Alexander persisted in trying to delve into my mind, "And what are your plans, Earl?"

"You need not know my plans." The two brothers stared at me as though I had insulted them. I had no time for them. "Master Miles has told me that the forests where the bandits have their strongholds are to the north of us. Stanhope Castle is manned by the men of the Palatinate and that marks the northern boundary of the bandits. I will make my plans accordingly."

Silence fell until the steward asked, "Should I serve the food, my lady?"

I had confused her, and she waved an airy hand, "Yes, of course."

We sat at a table that had the other guests already waiting. I was seated between Sir Alexander and his mother. Alfred was next to Sir Alexander and John Balliol. Grace was spoken and then the food was brought in. It was good food and well cooked but I had plans to finalise and to do that I needed more information.

"How many men will I be leading?" I looked at Sir Alexander, who shrugged. I knew the answer for Miles had already told me but I was trying to work out if more could be found.

The Ripples of Rebellion

His mother spoke, "Master Miles, how many men?"

"Twenty sergeants and fourteen archers, my lady."

I shook my head, "You told me that on the way here and it is not enough. What of Bowes Castle? It belongs to the Earl of Richmond, I believe. Could he not send men?"

The countess said, "We asked for help from Richmond, but Count Peter died two years since and the lands now belong to his niece, Eleanor of Provence. It is a skeletal garrison they keep there."

Eleanor was the wife of the king. This was a tangled web.

"Thirty-four men is not enough, I want at least fifty men from this manor."

My steely tone made her nod, "You shall have them. Master Miles, see to it."

I knew that the extra men would not be of the best quality but I needed numbers. I wanted men who could guard horses. They did not need to be good warriors. From what Miles had told me the thirty-four men he commanded were good ones. Even more worryingly the extra men would delay the start of our mission.

We ate in relative silence for a while. The only conversation was about the food. Eventually, Sir Alexander asked, "Where will you start?"

I sighed, "Where do the bandits strike?"

"Why, on the road from Penrith and Carlisle and the road from Durham."

"So, they must live in the forests to the north of those roads."

"Of course."

"Then that is where we will start." I had already told them that I would head north. Sir Alexander seemed remarkably inept. My answer seemed to satisfy him, confirming my opinion but I had other plans as well that I wished to remain in my head.

"Will you be staying here in the castle?"

"No, my lady. When we leave we will not return here until either our work is done or the month is up."

That surprised all three of them. Perhaps they had not believed me when I had stated it earlier. "You mean that you would leave with the task unfinished?"

"Lady Dervorguilla, I can afford to spend no more than a month here. I have my own lands to watch but if we have not scoured the land in less than that time then the problem will remain that of the Balliol family."

The Ripples of Rebellion

I knew that I had not pleased them but I did not care. I doubted that either King Henry or his sons would be overly concerned about bandits when there were still isolated bands of rebels further south.

Chapter 9

Henry Samuel

The Spy

Thanks to my request we could not leave as quickly as I had planned. It took two days to assemble the men that I would lead. I chafed at the delay for every day gave our prey more time to prepare. They would know that I had arrived and could be preparing a welcome for us, similar to the one given to Miles Longstaff. There was a buzz in the town as the townsfolk gossiped about our arrival. It was on the day after our arrival that Roger showed that he and Henry had obeyed my orders and observed those in the castle. It was late in the afternoon and Alfred and I had just met with Miles to finalise the number of men we would take. He had spent the morning riding the land to issue orders on behalf of the baron. We supped wine in the Great Hall as he told me of the men who would be joining us and I set the time of departure.

"My lord, we need to speak to you." Roger's tone left me in no doubt about the seriousness of the request. Alfred and I walked to the fighting platform and found a quiet place where we would not be overheard. "We have found a spy. It was Henry's sharp eyes that noticed Ethelbert, the wine steward. We saw him leave the castle last night after putting a young servant in charge of the wine. He was gone for an hour. I saw him just now when Master Miles returned and spoke to you. He has left the castle again."

Henry pointed, "See, my lord, there he is. He is wrapped in a cloak with a beaver hat upon his head." I saw the man, cloaked against the cold, he was hurrying towards the stand of homes that lay beyond the castle. There were a few houses outside the castle. All were mean dwellings made of wattle and daub. They lined the road we had followed from Gainford. Some of them had small hedges to protect the few crops that they grew. In places, there were two or three of them together.

"Can you two follow him and see where he goes? Do not stop him or let him know that you follow but see who he meets."

The two, eager to be of use, fairly raced down the stairs and out of the gate. The wine steward had disappeared between two of the dwellings by the time they reached the point where we had last seen him. Roger was resourceful and he looked back to the castle.

The Ripples of Rebellion

Alfred said, "I think he went between the two houses close to Roger."

I pointed and Roger nodded and headed to the place I had indicated. He and Henry disappeared too. Alfred said, "As you have not yet divulged your plans this does not matter much. All that they know is our numbers."

"What I fear is that they might either move from their camp or ambush us or both. I do not wish to lose any men. A perfect campaign for me is one where I lose not a man and the enemies we fight are totally vanquished."

It did not take long for the man to reappear and when I saw Henry following him I was relieved. If there was a bandit in the village and they were discovered then he would not have hesitated to slit our squires' throats. We descended and, as the man stepped through the gate, I put my hand to arrest his progress.

"Ethelbert is it not?"

"It is, my lord." He made to move but I barred his passage. "My lord, I have work to attend to."

Just then our squires arrived and he looked behind him. Seeing them his shoulders slumped, "And yet you have the time to leave the castle and visit those mean houses beyond the castle. Let me see if you can convince me of the innocence of your errand."

"Innocence, my lord? There is no crime in visiting an old friend,"

Roger said, "An old friend who mounted his horse and rode north as soon as you had left."

"You will come with us and explain to your lord and master why you left the castle and conspired with others."

Roger and Henry prevented any chance of flight and we headed back to the donjon. Sir Alexander and his brother John were seated at the table drinking wine. Miles was speaking to them. I nodded to Roger and Alfred along with Henry and I approached the table. Roger would wait by the door in case the man tried to flee.

Miles was speaking to Sir Alexander, "So that will give fourteen men to guard the castle."

"It is not enough."

"But Sir Alexander, it will have to do."

They all looked up as I approached, "Do you rule here Earl Henry or do I?"

I gestured behind me with my thumb. "We have just seen this man leave the castle, speak to one who lived outside the walls and then return. His co-conspirator left on a horse. I think that Ethelbert is a spy."

The Ripples of Rebellion

Miles turned in shock and anger, "Now it makes sense. Do you remember, my lord, when I planned the raid on the bandits, Ethelred was most solicitous about the wine and waited throughout the conversation?"

"He was a servant. I do not worry about servants."

"My lord," I tried to be as patient as I could but I was becoming annoyed, "The man has told a confederate of the numbers of men we intend to take. They may well be waiting for us. I need every man I can take and I need surprise."

"But he is a wine steward."

"Who is like a tapestry on a wall, my lord. You said yourself that you did not notice them. Do you watch what you say when they are close?"

His flushed face told me that he did not. "And what should I do with him?"

"I know what I would do but this would not happen in my household. He should be incarcerated. For my part, I would have him punished, and hanged as an example to the rest of the servants."

"But he is a wine steward!"

"If he is not locked up then I take my men this night and return to Stockton."

He sighed, "Very well. Miles…"

Miles strode over to the man who cowered at the soldier's approach. Miles grabbed him by the shoulder and banged his face into the door. Roger opened it and the spy was marched away. Miles had lost men in that ambush and he would not be gentle with Ethelbert.

"What now, Sir Henry?"

"Now? We will dine this night and on the morrow do that for which your mother is paying us by scouring the forests of those who hold the roads to ransom." We left the hall. "Roger, you and Henry return to the house. I want to know how many men lived there. If there are others still living there then return for help."

Alfred said, "But you do not think that there will be."

I shook my head, "More than a couple of men who do not work and sit in a house all day would arouse suspicion."

"Yes, my lord."

"Alfred, send Joseph and Robert to me. I will be on the north wall." I headed through the businesses that lay close to the north wall and climbed the steps to the fighting platform. One of the sentries approached and I said, "Give me space, I wish to speak to my men."

"Yes, my lord."

The Ripples of Rebellion

I pulled the cloak up. It was sunny but it was a cold wind that tore in from the north and east. My two captains and Alfred joined me. "We leave tomorrow." They nodded and my captains waited expectantly. They knew me well. "I have a plan. I need you to decide which men will be used and to organise them."

They said, in unison, "Yes, my lord."

I told them the plan and after asking me a couple of questions for clarification they left. Alfred and I descended more slowly. I knew my son would have questions and he did. I explained to him, much as my grandfather had with me, the reasoning behind my plan. We had just crossed the bridge and were heading for the Inner Ward when I saw Miles leaving a tower that lay to the south of the Great Hall. We waited for him.

I saw that his knuckles were bloody and I waited for him to speak. "That is the Prison Tower. He is guarded."

I gave him a wry smile, "And you fell and hurt yourself on the steps."

He shook his head, "I questioned the man. He is a soft coward who told all. The men he reported to are bandits. He is paid by them for information. He is in a privileged position and as you said to Sir Alexander, privy to much that should be secret."

Just then our squires ran to meet us. "Well?"

"The dwelling is empty. There were beakers and platters suggesting two men and the mean stable had seen two animals there recently."

Miles nodded, "And that concurs with what Ethelred told me. He spoke the truth."

"Then that confirms my plan to leave on the morrow but we will leave before dawn. I want the men roused and ready by Lauds. Miles, do not give warning to your men. There may be other spies but by leaving then we avoid close scrutiny. Who is the captain of the guard this night, Master Miles?"

"That will be John of Boldron. He will command the men during our absence."

"Then send him to me. Alfred, take our squires and ensure that all the horses are ready for the morrow."

I was left alone again in the middle of the Inner Ward. My thoughts naturally drifted to Matthew. He would now be baking in the hot sun of the Holy Land. Whatever dangers we faced they would be as nothing to those that he would have to deal with. I prayed that he was watched over by God.

"Yes, my lord."

The Ripples of Rebellion

Miles and John of Boldron stood behind me. "Thank you, Master Miles. I would speak with John alone." If Miles was put out to be excluded from my plans I did not care. If my secrecy saved one life then it would be worth it. "When we leave you are to command?"

"Yes, my lord."

"And tonight, you are also in command of the night watch?"

"Yes, my lord."

"Then here are my orders," I told him and when I had finished, he looked around, Miles had left us. "John of Boldron, I command here. Obey me."

"Yes, my lord."

I softened my harsh words with a smile, "What I do will make this land safer and your lives easier in the future."

"Yes, my lord."

I had clearly upset Sir Alexander and that had annoyed his mother. That evening, as we ate, it was a chilly atmosphere at the table and as soon as we had finished I rose and said that we were to retire, it became icy. The countess liked things done her way and to control her home. My actions and words had upset the rigid order of things. I rose at Matins. The bells from the nearby Egglestone Abbey tolling woke me. John of Boldron had obeyed my orders. The countess would be upset as the captain of the night guard had woken the servants to begin preparing food early. It was simple enough fare but we ate bread, cheese and ham before clattering out of the gates. Those in the Town Ward would be awakened. You cannot mask the hooves of a column of horses. I cared not. We rode north and took the road to Stanhope.

When dawn broke it was Miles who saw that we had missing men, "My lord, half of your men are not here."

I nodded, "I know."

"Where are they then, my lord?"

"I know where they are as do my two captains. That is all you need to know."

He said, flatly, "You do not trust me."

I sighed, "Miles, I believe you are a good warrior but if I tell you here and now then my words, our words, may be overheard. Until all the elements of my plan come together then we need secrecy." I pointed ahead. "The village of Bedburn lies ahead, does it not?"

"It does."

"The villagers there, have they been attacked?"

I saw him frown, "Well no, but it is just seven miles from Barnard Castle."

The Ripples of Rebellion

"And as such within easy travelling from the castle... if you were a spy who needed to report to your masters. When you tried to find their camps you came from the other side of the forest, the north?"

"Yes."

"We will try from the south but I will leave four of the men we brought to watch the village."

I had studied the maps given to me by William. The river was a barrier and there were few bridges. The attacks had been on the road that ran from Penrith to Barnard Castle and yet the bandits had managed to evade capture. They had simply disappeared. The waterfall at High Force was a barrier and that meant there had to be a ford that they used west of the falls. I calculated that their base would have to be between Bedburn and the track that led west.

I sent two archers ahead of us and across country. Miles frowned as they left and disappeared into the trees. When we reached Bedburn we stopped to water the horses. We dismounted and tightened girths. The handful of houses disgorged people who came to smile and fawn at us. I was not fooled. When my two archers rode in with a youth between them, I saw the faces of those in the village change from smiles to scowls.

Bob the Archer grinned, "We found this one, my lord, just as you predicted. He came as soon as your horses approached the village."

I walked to the youth who was about twelve summers old. "So, son, where were you going in such a hurry?"

A man strode forward, "What gives you the right to question my son, my lord?" There was a slight Scottish burr to his voice. It was not unusual in these parts.

I turned, "I am Earl Henry Samuel of Stockton and King Henry has charged me with scouring the land of bandits. There are bandits living in the forest are there not?"

He shrugged, "We do not know."

I strode next to him and put my face close to his, "You lie and your son was sent to tell the bandits of our approach." He backed away, clearly frightened. I was not Sir Alexander and he knew it. I turned back to the boy. "Where is the bandit camp?"

He stood defiantly, "I will not tell you!"

His father rolled his eyes for his son, whilst bravely facing up to me had confirmed that he was heading for the bandit camp and as he was afoot then it had to be within a few miles of us. "Master Miles, assign four men to guard the village. No one leaves and we will deal with the conspirators when we return." I stared at the headman, "And if any do try to leave they are to be shackled."

The Ripples of Rebellion

"Aye, my lord. James, Hob, Erik and Wilson, you heard the earl."

"Yes, my lord." The four men were the soldiers without mail. These were not warriors but armed with a spear and wearing a helmet they would easily control the handful of men.

"Captain Robert."

"Aye, my lord. Tether your horses, string your bows. Today we go to work." Roger and Henry tied our spare horses with the archers' mounts and armed themselves with spears taken from the sumpter.

The archers of both Barnard and Stockton did as they were commanded. My archers looked more professional. They had their bows strung in half the time of the Barnard ones and they each chose three arrows to hold in their left hand. Captain Robert shook his head at the tardiness of the Barnard men. The captain led them off down the path where they had found the boy. It might not lead to the enemy camp but it was a start. We followed in a mounted column of twos with Joseph and myself at the fore and Miles just behind. Alfred and the squires brought up the rear. Alfred had objected to the task at first until I explained that I needed him and the squires to guard the rear. The rest of the Barnard men were there and they needed a strong leader. We rode with drawn swords but our shields hung from our cantles. I was counting on surprise.

This was not like the forest at Chesterfield. Here there were more pine trees, The needles made the path different from those we were used to. It was also darker and more Stygian. I trusted my archers who were not just on the path but spread out like beaters at a hunt. The path climbed and then dropped, it twisted and turned as it followed the contours of the land. This was a hunter's trail or, in this case, a bandit's path. We had travelled just three miles or so when I heard the shout of pain and then heard Captain Robert shout, "Loose!"

"Spread into a line."

My sergeants quickly obeyed but I heard Alfred having to encourage the Barnard men to obey the command. Miles, Joseph and I had the easier path as the others had to negotiate trees. It made us the point of an arrow. When I saw the backs of my archers I slowed. I could not see their enemies but arrows were coming towards my archers. It was an uneven contest. The bandits were just that, outlaws who did not train every day. They were not blessed with the finest yew bows and the best of arrows that were well-fletched. Even as we neared Robert I saw a bandit fall, his chest pierced by an arrow.

"Their camp is just ahead, my lord. These men are trying to slow us to aid the escape of the others."

"Charge!"

The Ripples of Rebellion

I counted on a number of things. They were unlikely to have bodkin arrows. They would be facing mailed men on big horses. They had been surprised. Duncan was the best of horses and he took off down the path leaving Joseph and Miles behind. One bandit, braver than the rest, stood to face me and released an arrow. It was aimed at my chest but the speed of Duncan meant that by the time the arrow was sent, I was closer and it clanked off the side of my helmet. He paid for his courage with his life. As Duncan knocked him to the side I slashed down at his shoulder with my sword and it cut deeply. He would bleed out. The charging horses had an immediate effect and the remaining bandits fled. It was a vain attempt to escape us. Horses could travel faster than men and the archers were racing through the trees to take any who tried to hide. When we reached the clearing that they had used as a camp I was surprised at how spacious and organised it was. The few who made it to the clearing were soon slain by my archers.

"Master Miles, have your men dismount. I want the wood they used to build their hovels piling in the middle and burning. Collect all their weapons. See if they have stored any loot or food, I want them left with nothing."

"My lord, should we not keep pursuing them?"

"I will, Master Miles."

"But there will be too few of you."

From ahead of us I heard screams of alarm and shouts, "Not when we are joined by my other archers and sergeants. Do as I command and await me here."

Released from their duty of watching the Barnard men, Alfred and the squires joined me. Alfred asked, "Our men?"

I nodded, "They left in the middle of the night and entered the forest from the west. Some bandits will have escaped and will take time to capture but I am hoping that we have broken the bandits' backs this day. You squires, use your spears. This is a hunt and you keep your distance from our prey."

We followed the noise of combat until we found Rafe and the rest of my men. They were removing weapons from the dead. "I have sent Wilfred back for the archers' horses my lord." He pointed north. "The survivors fled that way."

I turned in the saddle, "Robert, take all the archers back to the clearing and help Sir Miles. The rest of you come with me. Spread out in a long line. We will harry them until it is time to return to Bedburn. Roger and Henry, stay behind Sir Alfred and me."

I had not seen all the bodies but the ones I had passed told me that we had slain upwards of forty bandits. There would be more than that but we had hurt them already. We now took a steady pace through the trees. We did not have the eyes and ears of our archers but, most of the time, our horses gave us sufficient warning. The bandit who came at me from my left side had cleverly hidden behind the bole of a large and ancient tree. He had an old sword and he was swinging it at my side as he emerged. Duncan had not reacted and I had no warning but luckily for me Roger had his wits about him and he urged his horse forward to skewer the man in his back with his spear. I nodded my thanks and took the opportunity to pull up my shield. The arrow that came at Alfred flew from the gloom ahead. The sound of the snapped string and the noise of the flight alerted my son and having lifted his shield, instinctively, he was able to flick it up and deflect the arrow. I did not see the archer but I saw the tree from where the arrow had appeared. It was clear ground and I spurred Duncan. The archer had been nocking another arrow and was aiming at Alfred when the noise of my horse's hooves as well as his snorting head alerted him. He switched targets to me but by the time he released, I was so close that the arrow missed me completely. I hacked through his skull. The noise of death filled the forest and we worked our way up the ridge. The trees were thinner at the top. A storm had taken some out. I could see that the forest continued to the north. I reined in.

I turned, "Roger, sound the horn. Gather the men here."

He put the horn to his lips and gave three blasts, a pause and then a fourth. As men arrived, I looked to see if there were wounds. Jack of Egglesclif had a cut to his leg. It was not a major one but it bled. His comrades tended to him. The rest had bloody swords and dents in shields but we had avoided a tragedy. Joseph placed his horse next to mine. "A good start, my lord."

Before I could answer Henry said, "Surely it is done. They are destroyed."

I shook my head, "The rats' nest has been destroyed but not all the rats. They will have more camps that they use. Joseph was right, we have made a good start but tomorrow we have to spread out and search this vast forest. We need to spend as long as it takes seeking enemies. If nothing else that will stop them from feeding themselves and starving men will leave this area. They may find other places to raid but that will take time. As long as we stop them from taking harvests we weaken them."

"Yes, my lord, but rats with no place to run can be harder to kill."

"Aye, Joseph, the easy part is over. Are we all here?"

"They are."

"Then let us return to the clearing and then the village."

The Ripples of Rebellion

As we headed back down the slope Joseph said, "I wonder how Sir Matthew and my boy are doing? His mother misses him, my lord."

"As I miss my cousin, but this is an adventure for them and the experiences will last them a lifetime."

"It is certainly a more noble occupation than hunting those who prey on travellers."

We saw the smoke from the pyre long before we reached the clearing. If nothing else, we had identified one of their camps. We had not passed a better location in our pursuit of them and that boded well. Miles was speaking to one of his men as we approached. He turned, "How goes it, Earl?"

"We slew many and lost none. How many do you estimate were living here?"

"There had to be more than a hundred and fifty from the hovels and shelters we destroyed. There were footprints from children and women so not all were warriors."

"We saw no children, nor women. You would have expected them to be easier to find." Alfred's observation showed that he was learning and listening.

"They may have been sent hence as soon as our archers found them. That might explain the rearguard who slowed us down. They would have hidden and we could have passed them without even knowing. There is still a large number for us to find. It is a good start. Come with me, Miles, and we will return to Bedburn. Joseph, bring the rest of the men when all is safe. I want no woodland fires. Douse the embers before you leave."

It was late in the afternoon when we reached the village. We had eaten a little in the clearing but we were ravenous by the time we arrived. I waved over the man charged with watching the villagers, "James, have they behaved?"

"Yes, my lord, but I trust not one of them. They are a shifty lot."

We had brought supplies with us and I said, "Light a fire and confiscate some large pots. We will get some food prepared for the men." I hung my helmet on my cantle and dropped my coif to my shoulders. It felt much better. I slipped my mail mittens from my hands. "Roger and Henry, unsaddle the horses. Water and feed them. Miles and Alfred come with me." We wandered over to the open space between the two largest houses. The men and the boy who had led us to the bandits were gathered in a huddle. There were four men and the youth. I pointed to the man whose son had been key to our success. "You, come here." He walked sulkily toward me. His son followed. "What is your name?"

The Ripples of Rebellion

"David of Crook."

"We found the bandit camp. You knew of it." He said nothing. "Men were attacked and killed by those bandits and you protected them."

"We did not."

I turned to Miles, "Master Miles, did any men from this village come to the castle after you were attacked to tell them of the nest of bandits who lived close to their village?"

"No, my lord."

"Then all of you are guilty of aiding bandits."

"You cannot prove it."

I smiled, "I do not need to. When we leave this village we will burn it to the ground. Bandits will not be given succour here any longer. You may stay and continue to farm the land but you will be punished. Consider this lenient. The men could be hanged."

"You cannot do this."

I walked up to him, "I can and I will."

"We will appeal to his lordship."

I pointed south, "The road lies there. If you take it now, you can be there before they close the gates." He glowered hatefully at me but backed down. "Tonight, you will all be confined to your houses. If any tries to leave, man, woman or child, they will be punished. Tomorrow, we will leave and you may do as you wish."

The men I led camped around the houses. I had each group set their own sentries. They knew that there were survivors left alive and that any lack of vigilance would result in death. We would be safe. I sat with Miles and Alfred. We ate the hunter's stew we had made and dunked day-old bread in the juices. When we had finished Miles asked, "And your plans for the morning, my lord?"

"I will make three columns. You, Joseph and Robert will each lead one. They will be made up of a mixture of my archers, my sergeants and the men of Barnard." I used my hands to illustrate. "They will leave here and one will go due west, one north-west and one southwest. Each one will continue until they reach the edge of the forest and then return here."

"The forest is large, my lord."

I sighed, "Then use common sense. If it has passed noon then start your return. I do not want men risking the forest at night; the bandits know it and we do not. I will leave the same four men to watch the spare horses and our belongings."

"And you, my lord?"

"There is a task which I must do. I will take just Alfred and our squires."

The Ripples of Rebellion

"Is that not dangerous with bandits still abroad, my lord?"

"I have weighed up the dangers and consider the risks manageable. We hurt them today and I believe that it will take them at least one day to start to reorganise. Your three patrols will push them further west and north."

Alfred said, "Towards Scotland."

I nodded, "Towards Scotland. They may well have friends there and they may try to embroil them in a further fight. If I do not return here tonight, do not fear. The day after we repeat the patrols."

"But the bandits will know what we are doing."

"And that second day will be the harder one. It is why each column will have some of my archers. They will ensure that we are not surprised."

Miles was silent, "Had I been in command I would have done none of this."

I smiled, "I am a border knight. We have fought in battles and acquitted ourselves well but fighting in unfamiliar terrain and hidden enemies is something we are also used to. You, Master Miles, will either learn to adapt or spend your life fearing such men as these bandits. They killed your men and hurt your pride when you were ambushed. Learn from it and do not let it defeat you. The men I shall give you will be good ones. Do not be afraid to seek their advice. They may not be nobles but they are all warriors and that is what is needed."

I rose and went to speak to Joseph and Robert. I gave them their instructions. They had fewer questions. That night I stood a watch as did Alfred. I could see that it surprised Miles. From what I had seen he was a good warrior but he had much to learn about leadership. Having seen Sir Alexander and his brother John, I could see the reason. He had no one on which to model himself.

Chapter 10

Henry Samuel

The nest of vipers

I waited until my three patrols had left before we mounted. I gave James and his men their instructions and then took the road north. Alfred waited until we were a mile north before he asked me, "So, where do we go then, Father?"

"Stanhope. The Bishop of Durham has a castle there and men. The castellan needs to know what we have done. If I can, I will use the men of Weardale to aid us. They can close the back door on the bandits."

"You are driving them north and west?"

"Did you not hear the accents of the men? The ones in the village and the ones in the forest all had Scottish twangs to their voices. They are incomers and settled here from Scotland; King Henry might welcome genuine settlers but these seem to me to be remnants of warbands from times past."

"And that is why you plan on burning the village."

"It is. If they do wish to settle here then they must work for it. The connection with the bandits must be severed. We have just another three weeks or so to make this land safe. I must be draconian or risk failure."

The road went north until Wolsingham. The town had no castle and existed just to provide food for the Palatinate. We watered our horses in the trough there. I noticed that the accents of the people who spoke to us were north country rather than Scottish. It was a safe place to rest. The road then followed the River Wear up to Stanhope. We reached the small castle before noon. The motte and bailey castle dominated the tiny town. While the donjon was made of locally quarried stone, the walls were still wooden. There were just four men in the castle when we rode in, our hooves clattering on the stone.

I dismounted and a mailed man came from the donjon. He saw my spurs and bowed, "Good day, my lord. I am Alan of Stanhope, the castellan and the Bishop's law in these parts."

"And I am Earl Henry Samuel of Stockton."

At the use of my name, he beamed, "Then we are honoured to have the hero of Otterburn in the Bishop's castle. Come within and take refreshment. Ketil, take their horses."

As we followed him I said, "Ketil? That is a Viking name is it not?"

The Ripples of Rebellion

He nodded, "Many Danes and Vikings settled here when they finished raiding. Ketil's family keeps the same names. He has the blood of the Vikings and wants to be a warrior."

The hall did not justify the name 'great'. It was a small one and barely eight people could have used it. It reflected the diminutive size of the castle. Alan shouted, "We have guests. Food and ale." Alfred and I sat. Alan said, "Can your squires be permitted to sit, my lord?"

"Of course." They sat.

"Now, before my wife brings us food, what brings an earl here to this remote part of the Palatinate? The Bishop normally warns me when men wish to hunt and you do not seem as though that is your intention."

I shook my head, "We do come here on a hunt but not for animals. We hunt men. We had a skirmish in the forest south of here yesterday and destroyed a bandit camp."

His wife came in and put a jug of ale and four beakers on the table. My squires took out their coistrels. There were two loaves, they were yeoman's bread, as well as some cheese, apples and spring onions. I said, "Thank you, Mistress. This is a feast."

"You are welcome, my lord. Had we known we would be visited then better fare would have been readied."

"This will suffice."

She left and we began to eat. Alan spoke as I ate. "It will take more than one skirmish to rid the land of them."

"You know of them?"

"Aye, but they do not worry us here."

Alfred asked, "Why not, Castellan?"

"The baron of Tynedale has a castle at Langley and he scours his land of all such men. The road from Hexham and Corbridge is kept safe by him and the men of Prudhoe. Those castles deter such practice."

"But not Barnard Castle."

He looked at me and shook his head, "Old Baron Balliol just liked to accumulate land. It brought him into conflict with the Bishop of Durham. He was unconcerned by the attacks."

"But Wolsingham and Stanhope, do they not suffer?"

"The bandits fear the Bishop of Durham. They know that Auckland and the Bishop's palace are not far from here. If the bandits caused mischief in Weardale then the Bishop would do as you seem to be trying to do and rid the land of them."

I had finished the bread and cheese. I wiped my mouth on my cloth and said, "I had hoped that we might be able to use the men of Weardale to end this threat."

He shook his head, "I have ten men, my lord. We are barely enough to defend the walls should the bandits think to attack us."

I rose, "Then I thank you and I will return to Bedburn."

He started, "That is a nest of vipers my lord."

"What makes you say that?"

"There used to be just two houses at Bedburn and then, about four years ago the two families disappeared and the village suddenly grew. The ones who came did not sound like local men. It was about that time we heard of attacks on the road from Penrith. I have no proof but I think that the men of the village are in league with the bandits. The bandits may even be run from Bedburn. They need to be watched."

We had left just four men to watch the village and I had threatened to burn it. "Thank you, Alan of Stanhope. We will leave now and make all haste."

Once mounted I said to the others, "We ride hard for Bedburn. I would be there in an hour."

"Why?"

"Alan of Stanhope has a good head on his shoulders and, I am guessing, a nose for such things. I did not like the headman at Bedburn and now I fear that I have underestimated him. We left four men and our horses at Bedburn…"

We rode as though we were going to war. The road to the hamlet twisted through trees and we were galloping. It was hard to hear anything above the hooves of our horses but when we were just four hundred paces from the village I saw four men fall upon Wilson as he lounged against the bole of the tree. He was not looking at the village but up the road for he had heard our hooves and it cost him his life. The wood axes chopped him to pieces. I did hear his death cry and I saw James, Erik and Hob run from the horse lines. After slaying Wilson the killers turned their attention to the three Barnard men raving towards them.

I stood in my stirrups with a drawn sword and shouted, "Draw swords. Show no mercy for they will show you none."

The sight of the butchered body of Wilson would steel the hearts of our squires and my son. Even as we neared the men attacking the three survivors, I saw Erik fall as he was run through with a spear. James and Hob stood back-to-back but they were outnumbered. It was the youth who had tried to warn the bandits that first day who gave the alarm. He pointed to us and gave a shout. It saved the lives of Hob and James but doomed the bandits to a deserved death. The youth took off like a greyhound and ran into the forest. This was no time for fine strokes and chivalrous gestures. I leaned from the saddle to sweep my sword across the neck of one of the axemen who had killed Wilson. I veered Duncan to the left and reached over to smash my sword into the skull of a second. James and Hob were now in a position to have vengeance for the deaths of their friends and with Alfred and our squires wielding swords, those who stood were soon overwhelmed. I had the luxury of watching Henry kill his first bandit. He was a huge man with an axe wielded two handed. Henry showed that the lessons with Joseph and Alfred had paid off. He jerked the reins of his horse to one side so that the off-balance axeman struck air. Henry wheeled his horse and hacked into the back of the man's skull. The others disappeared towards the forest.

Roger and Henry went to follow but I said, "Hold. Our horses have ridden hard. Let us see to our fallen." We dismounted and I said, "Roger and Henry, attend to the horses. Alfred, go and see if any remain in the houses. Be careful. Strike first and ask questions later."

I knelt by Erik. He had bled out and was dead but at least he had not been butchered like Wilson. I stood. James and Hob, with shocked and angry faces, walked towards me. Their tunics were covered in a sea of blood. It was mainly their enemies' and Erik's but I saw that they had wounds. "Go to the squires and ask for honey and vinegar. Those wounds need to be attended to."

They both nodded. Before he turned to obey me James said, "I am sorry, my lord. We let you down. We were not vigilant enough."

I pointed to Erik, "They are the ones who need your apology for they died as a result. It is in the past. If you learn from it, then it will not be a waste. When our men return, we will bury our dead. I want them to see what we face."

They left and I went to the dead bandits. They had weapons I had not seen before. The wood axes were just tools but the spear, swords and long daggers had been hidden from us. I mentally berated myself for not having searched the houses. That would all be remedied when we burnt down the village. Alfred came back, "There are none left alive, Father. The houses have been emptied of cooking pots and food."

I nodded, "Then they will have gone to join the others. It confirms what I thought. This village was the heart of the bandits. They were hiding in plain sight. A clever plan. I am guessing that when Miles came the first time, he warned the villagers to be wary of bandits. He might as well have trumpeted his intention to find the bandits. I am just surprised that he did not suffer more losses."

By the time Robert and his patrol returned the bodies of the dead villagers were burning on a pyre. We had built it so that the wind would blow the smoke into the forest. The bandits would have to endure the smell of burning flesh. Robert saw the cloak-covered bodies and shook his head. He lifted the cloaks to see who they were, "Our first losses. It is sad." I saw the men of Barnard looking in horror at the butchered body of Wilson.

"Did you find any more today?"

"We picked up the trail of a dozen or so. They headed up the ridge and took paths our horses could not climb. They descended to the other side. We saw signs, as we neared the village, of flight north and west."

"They would be the women and children. They must have gone when our watchers were distracted."

"How did this happen?"

I shook my head, "I have yet to question them. James knows that it was their fault but I take some of the blame. I underestimated the villagers." I explained to him my theory and he nodded his agreement.

The other two patrols arrived back, and they had enjoyed a little more success. Six more bandits had been accounted for but the trails of the survivors all led to the same place; over the ridge and to the north and west. We also had a warning. One of my men at arms had almost been taken out by a deadfall. The bandits had laid a trap. Had he not been wearing a helmet then his skull would have been crushed. As it was, he was angry at having his helmet dented.

"When we have eaten we will look at the map but now that you are all here we can bury our dead."

In a perfect world, I would have sent them back to Barnard Castle for a burial but we had too few men for that. I would need every man to end this task. The men of Barnard dug deep graves and the bodies were well wrapped in blankets we had found. Their bodies were covered with stones and then soil. I spoke words over them. I had buried enough men to know the right thing to say. When it was done, we stood around the graves.

Miles looked pensive. These were his men. My men had suffered scratches but he had lost two men and added to those he had lost in the first ambush, it weighed heavily upon him. James and Hob had their heads together and before we headed back to the fires where our food was cooking James said, "My lord, this was our fault. I was in charge so it lies on my head. I was taken in by smiles and the offer of fresh cooked food. They said that they did not blame us but you were a Southerner and were persecuting them. I did not believe them but the women made me feel sympathetic, my lord. I felt sorry for them."

I nodded, "I understand but that is how they work. They play on the sympathy of good men like you. They have black hearts, and they are cruel. Wilson was hacked to death. They were chopping his body after

The Ripples of Rebellion

he was already dead. We forget that now." I raised my voice, "Tomorrow we burn this nest of wrongdoers to the ground. I intend to seek the survivors before they can regroup. Eat and rest. Tomorrow, when I have looked at a map, we will have a hard day of riding."

The sun had not yet set and the light from the fire enabled me to read William's map. It was not an original but a copy. There were gaps on the map and I had already used charcoal from the fire to add detail. When we returned to Stockton the master map would be updated. Roger and Henry fetched us food and I sat with Alfred, my captains and Miles.

"We clearly cannot ascend the high ground and that means we must take a long ride around it. Here I can see a road of sorts that heads due west."

Miles pointed to Stanhope, marked as a castle, "This would be the shorter route, my lord."

"I know and the one they would expect us to take. By taking this longer loop to the west and then the north we may well avoid detection. I think that they will have a second camp towards the northwest of this land. The fact that they have all fled north and west attests to that. They crossed the high ridge where our horses would struggle. See, they can still raid the Penrith Road as well as the road to Stanhope. The Stanhope garrison is too small to be an effective deterrent. This village, marked with a house what is it?"

"It has no name that I know of. There are a couple of tiny settlements along the road. The chapel of ease of St John is used by the people who live there. They are hardy folk who eke out a living."

Luke, one of Miles' men, had just brought food and he said, "Some houses are called Ireshopeburn because of the beck there and on the other side of the chapel of ease are two houses called Daddry Shield."

"The people there, are they loyal?"

"They are Durham men, my lord, and all those who live there go back generations. It is said that their forebears lived here in the time of King Coel, if you can believe that."

"Thank you, Luke."

"Then all begins to make sense. They chose this village because they wanted to be nearer to Barnard Castle. Their spies could give them information. There is nothing north and west of these two isolated communities until Alston and that is too far away. If God smiles on us then we can rid the land of these bandits and be back in Barnard Castle within a week or so."

The plan settled, we ate. I saw that Henry was picking at his food. I assumed he did not like the taste, "As a squire, Henry, you learn to eat whatever there is before you as you do not know when more food will be forthcoming."

"I am sorry, my lord, the food is fine but my mind is distracted." We were all silent. If he wished to unburden himself then we would listen but warriors never pried into the minds of another. "I killed a man today. I struck his head and my sword grated on his bone." He pointed to his breeks, "That is his blood. As he fell, he turned and his eyes saw me. Will his ghost come for me?"

I shook my head, "I should have realised. Sorry, Henry, the killing of a man, especially the first time, is something that will live with you forever. The man was a killer. Wilson and Erik are a testament to that. If you had not killed him he would have tried to kill you. He would have taken your horse, your sword, your helmet and your leather jack. He would have been stronger then and he might have killed Roger too. What you did was commanded by me and there is no sin. If his spirit comes back then do not fear it for you have God on your side." I took out my sword and held it like a crucifix. "We are lucky, we carry our own crosses with us. If you fear a ghost then when we pass a church pay a priest to use holy water and bless your sword."

He was silent and Roger said, "I felt the same when I killed my first man, Henry. It passes but you will always live with that memory. It will be part of you."

Joseph sighed and put his arm around Henry's shoulders, "And the day that you care not about those that you kill is the time to hang up your sword. For those who feel no remorse in the taking of a life become bandits. You will kill only to save your own life or because you are ordered to do so by a knight. My son Robert had never killed a man before he went on the Crusade with Sir Matthew. Even now he may be worrying about the death of a Turk or a Saracen. What he does is for God. What we do is for the innocents who live in this land and live in fear of the bandits."

He nodded and began to eat. I sheathed my sword and said, "And that is another reason I pray each night. I beg forgiveness for taking a life."

I arranged watches but made sure that Henry had the same watch as Joseph and that it was one of the first ones. Joseph could continue to counsel the youth. He was a father and there was too much history between Henry and me to allow intimacy, at least, at the moment. It was Henry who woke me, just before dawn. He had some ale and it had been warmed with a hot dagger and infused with honey. "Thank you. Did you manage to sleep?"

"I did. Joseph is wise, is he not?"

"He is and that wisdom has been earned in battles and combats."

"Yet he is not a knight."

"But his son shall be and that makes Joseph a proud man." He nodded, "Listen, Henry, you may have to kill again. If you hesitate and you debate the stroke then you may be the one to die. It is better not to think about the blow when you fight. It is the survivors who can reflect on such things."

"Do not worry, Earl, I am not the same wild child you wished to spank. I have changed. The killing has also changed me but I will not let down my shield brothers. I now feel like a warrior. It is just sad that my father can never know this."

I gestured to the sky, "He is in heaven, Henry, and he knows. More than that he was my best friend and I know that he would be proud of you."

"Even though I was so horrible."

"That was not you and your heritage will out. You are of the Warlord's blood and it is a powerful force."

Chapter 11

Henry Samuel
Ending the Threat of the Bandits

We had twenty-five miles to ride. We kept the same formation as before but the difference now was that Alfred and our squires did not need to chivvy and chase as much. The men of Barnard had suffered deaths and knew that the squires and Alfred had saved at least two of their number. We passed houses and farms. More than half of them were burnt-out ruins but, after Eggleston, we saw no settlements and our local expert, Luke, assured us that the families who greeted us had lived here for a long time. I could not see how they made a living. The ground was very rough and they could not plough. The Weardale Valley lay not too far to the north and that was where the cereal crops were grown. The people we passed kept a few sheep and goats. They appeared to subsist on small strips of land and what they could forage in the river and forests. Luke told us that many of them quarried stone. They sold it at the market in Stanhope and that brought an income. I admired their resilience. It was no wonder the bandits had left them alone. There was little to take from them.

The road on which we travelled was little more than a widened track. There were few ruts and my archers had to use their short swords to hack at the branches that threatened to sweep us from our horses. It meant that the trees were perilously close to us. All conversation stopped as we listened for sounds from our right. The lack of a stone surface helped to dull the noise of our horses' hooves and I was confident that my sharp-eared archers would detect any noise. In the end, it was not noise that alerted us to their presence but smoke. The same wind that had swept the stink of burning flesh from our camp now blew the smell of woodsmoke towards us. To the east of us lay forest and it was highly likely that any fire would be lit by bandits. Robert signalled for one of his younger archers, Darwin, to climb a tree. Using his horse's back to make a start he scampered up the tree like a squirrel. He disappeared from sight. When he descended, he pointed to the north and east. We had a starting point. There was no really well-defined trail. We would be moving through virgin forest. That would make life difficult for us but I hoped that it would not be an expected route and that we might take them by surprise. If they were watching or laying traps and deadfalls, then it would be along the paths. Our route was harder but safer.

I waved Joseph, Miles and Robert closer, "Let us head into the forest. Robert, have your archers dismount and form a skirmish line ahead of us. Joseph, we will follow up with our sergeants. Miles have your archers join Robert and your men can lead the horses of the archers as well as the sumpters with the supplies. They will be our third line. If we need them to fight then I will have the horn sounded three times and they can release the horses."

They nodded and left to instruct their men. I saw them either speak quietly or use hand signals. I turned and waved to Alfred and our squires. I saw Henry hand the reins of our sumpter to a Barnard man. I pointed to the space next to me and Alfred moved his horse there. I pointed behind us. Roger and Henry already had their spears at the ready and they raised their shields as they obeyed me. I knew that, in our valley, we asked squires to do more than the squires of the lords who did not live near the borders. It put them in peril but I believed it made better knights. We did not have the luxury of an excess or warriors. Every blade was needed.

Once the line was ready I nodded to Robert. He signalled to his archers and they moved forward, each with a loosely nocked war arrow. I saw that he had placed the Stockton archers in the centre. When we struck, they would be a powerful weapon. I gave them a head start and then pointed my sword. Duncan picked his way over the uneven ground. My line of sergeants looked pitifully small but we were all mailed and I trusted all of them. This time there was no ambush waiting for us. The women who had fled to join them would have given them a warning but they could not have expected us from this side of the ridge. I guessed that would be where they would have the watchers facing the east, the sentries who would sound the alarm to the camp. The smell of woodsmoke grew stronger. Horses' hooves are muffled in forests by leaves and such on the ground. The noise that we made was the brushing of branches and I think that the noise of the camp disguised that.

When Robert stopped and held up his hand I did the same. The line of horsemen stopped. A heartbeat later the line behind stopped too. I saw through the trees a lighter patch of ground. It was flatter. I could see that from the evenness of my line of archers. Robert did not give a command but I saw him draw his bow and the others emulated him. We had caught the camp unawares. There would be women and children in the camp but Robert and his archers would not be releasing blindly. Every arrow would be aimed. He knew that his task was to kill as many men as he could. Survivors would run east, towards the ridge, but I was prepared for that.

The sound of the arrows seemed like a flock of birds taking to the air. I could not see but I imagined that the ones in the camp would look to the skies. When the arrows dropped like deadly rain drops then they would know but by then a second and a third flight would be in the air. The shouts and screams told me when the arrows had descended. I waited patiently but I could feel the horses of Roger and Henry as they moved them forward in anticipation of our attack.

"This will not be a wild charge. We will ride swiftly but carefully to the camp. The ground is uneven here. We can take prisoners of the women and the children but strike carefully and ensure that the men are dead. This will be their last stand and they will try to take as many of us with them as they can."

They both said, "Yes, my lord."

I was eager to move as was Duncan, but I waited until Robert turned and waved to me. I shouted, "Sergeants, follow me!"

The trees meant that the gap between each rider was about ten paces. The archers turned and pressed themselves against the trees to facilitate our passing. Once we had passed then they would follow. They could use swords as well as any sergeant at arms. I saw that this was as big a camp as the other one and just as organised. They had felled trees to make crude lodges and I saw women and children fleeing into them. The ground around the campfire was littered with arrow-stuck bodies. Robert had caught the bandits either eating or having a conference of some kind. The men who had survived were now grabbing weapons. I saw two men running, not towards us but to two horses tethered to the north of the lodges. I spurred Duncan. He was a big warhorse but he had clever hooves and he picked his way through the bodies. I was aware that Alfred was with me but as the two men who were trying to flee were not mailed I was confident in my ability to take them.

The horses had no saddles and the men would not have time to saddle them. They both used logs to stand upon and launch themselves onto the backs of the horses. After untying the beasts, they used the flat of their swords to encourage them to move. They were heading along a trail that led north. When we reached the trail then Duncan's hooves thundered, and I heard hooves behind. Someone, probably Alfred, was following me. I was gaining on the two bandits with every step we took. I shouted, "Yield, for you cannot escape."

The one at the rear turned and shouted, "Never!"

His bravado was a mistake for his companion turned at the shout and both horses slowed. I veered Duncan to the left and held my sword at head height. The two bandits also turned. They both came at me. The difference was that while all three of us held a sword, I was supported by the cantle of my saddle and when I swung I would not risk falling. I had my mail mittens on and when I swung my sword to block one blow I used my mittened hand to block the strike from the other. His lack of a saddle meant that while it numbed my hand it did not break the mail. I stood in my stirrups and swung my sword at the first bandit. He tried to block it but such was his unsteady grip on his reins that when the blow connected he was knocked from the saddle. The other bandit lunged at my middle. His sword scored a line across my cantle and then grated across my mail. My surcoat was cut but the mail was unbroken. His lunge was his undoing and I hacked across his neck. I almost severed his head and his corpse slipped from his saddle. I whipped Duncan around to deal with the fallen bandit but there was no need. Roger had skewered him.

"Thank you, Roger, that was well done."

He dismounted to retrieve his spear, "It would not have been needed, my lord, you had them in hand."

"Load the bodies onto the horses and fetch them along. I will head back."

By the time I reached the camp, it was over. My men were finishing off wounded men and Miles Longstaff had the women and children in one place surrounded by a wall of spears. I estimated that there were no more than twenty all told. I waved over Henry who had a bloody sword, "Fetch the rest and our baggage. This will be our camp."

"Yes, my lord." It was a more confident warrior-like Henry who mounted his horse and rode off. At least one of Sir Richard's sons had turned a corner.

"Robert, take my archers and head to the ridge. Joseph, send four men at arms with them. Hunt the survivors. There will be watchers on the ridge."

"Yes, my lord."

"Miles, this will be our camp for the night. I want the women guarded. This is your land. You can speak to the women."

"And say what, my lord?"

I sighed, my task had been to rid the land of bandits and I was now confident that we had done so. Was I supposed to do everything for the men of Barnard? "What do you wish to happen to them?"

It was as though the thought had not occurred to him. He looked at them, "They should be punished."

"And the children?"

The Ripples of Rebellion

He chewed his lip and then shook his head, "We will take them back to Barnard Castle. I will let the baron make that decision."

"Then tell the women that. I can see from their faces that they fear our wrath. They are used to cruel men and we have defeated their men. Reassure them that they will be unharmed. I trust that none of your men will think to abuse them. I know mine will not."

He turned and headed to them. I dismounted. Alfred and Henry approached. Alfred pointed to a body on the ground close by. It was the youth who had tried to warn the bandits that first day, the son of the headman of Bedburn, the man I now believed was the bandit leader. "He fought to the end. It was Joseph who slew him."

I was just pleased that it was not Henry. To kill a youth would have been hard. Roger rode in with the two bodies and the horses. I heard a wail from the women as they recognised them. The return of the two dead men ended all hope for the bandits. The threat to travellers was gone.

Robert and his hunters returned just before dark. They had with them the weapons they had taken. "I think just two men escaped, my lord. They headed east. I am sorry."

"Do not be. You have done more than could have been expected, we all did. The threat is gone. Tomorrow, we spend the day destroying this camp and then, on the day after, we will head to Stanhope. We will let Alan of Stanhope know what we found. This will be safer ground for the bishop to use for hunting."

The bandits had food and we discovered new items of clothing. I had Miles question the women and, after some dire threats using my name, he discovered that some merchants heading to Penrith had been attacked, robbed and murdered. It explained the two horses. We had not seen evidence of horses at the first camp. The news hardened the hearts of even the most sympathetic soldier. The women might not have robbed and murdered but they had colluded with the men and supported them. The camp had not been used for some time and there was grass on which the horses grazed. I sent out the Barnard men to search the nearby woods for any bandits we may have missed. They returned at dusk with the news that there were none.

The next morning, with the women and children in the centre, we set off on the trail north. We deduced it led to the road to Stanhope. Before we left, we demolished the buildings and piled the logs in the centre of the clearing. We lit the pyre and leaving four men to watch it we left. We moved at the pace of the women. They were constantly looking for ways to escape and had to be watched closely. It was the middle of the afternoon when we reached Stanhope. Alan of Stanhope was happy to cooperate with us and the prisoners were housed beneath the donjon in the place normally reserved for horses. It was warm and dry but, most importantly, it meant that they could not escape. We camped in the outer bailey.

My leaders and Alfred dined with the castellan and his wife. We told them all and I saw that they approved. Alan of Stanhope had not been in a position to rid the land of bandits but now that it was done it would be a safer world. "They will return, in the fullness of time, my lord. There are always outlaws. Men break laws, rob, commit murder and flee. The Palatinate is a lawful place and their only refuge is the forest."

Miles said, "And we are so close to the border that most of those who come are from Scotland. The Scottish lords have no jurisdiction in England and Scottish outlaws feel safe here. They are close enough to return to see their families."

The time spent in Stanhope was useful. I had thought that as it was in the Palatinate it was a safe place to live. I now saw that it was not. We left the next morning for the long journey back to Barnard Castle. It was twenty-two miles and took us past the burnt-out village of Bedburn. I saw the effect the blackened skeletal timbers had on the women. Their refuge was gone.

Miles sent a rider ahead to warn the baron of our return. It was getting on for dusk when the weary women and children trudged through the North Gate and into the Town Ward. They were taken across the bridge to the inner ward. Miles took it upon himself to place them all in the prison tower. I cared not what happened to them. We had done our part and taken them. As we entered the castle I discovered that Lady Dervorguilla and her ladies had left the castle with her son John and were travelling to London. The cynic in me wondered if they were trying to gain favour with the ailing king that was King Henry while his son was at the Crusades. She would be given short shrift for Richard of Cornwall was not easily taken in.

Sir Alexander almost baulked at paying us what was owed. I felt sorry for Miles who squirmed as the baron made out that it had been an easy task. I was ready when he quibbled with me.

"Baron, you commissioned me to rid your land of bandits and your mother offered me a fair payment. We have done all that was asked. Now if you wish me to go to court, as your father did, and ask the Bishop of Durham to arbitrate…"

I let the sentence hang in the air and I saw him pale, "No, Earl, we shall pay you for the land is now safer. We thank you."

We dined with the baron but he was excluded from our conversation. Miles and Alfred had got on well. As we prepared to head to our chambers, Alfred said, "Is there not a place for Miles in Stockton, Father? He is a good warrior."

I shook my head, "There is always a place for good warriors but he is the captain of the baron's guards. It would offend both the baron and his mother if we took him. What I will say, Miles Longstaff, is that should you ever be released from this service then come to Stockton. There you will have a chance of spurs."

I said the last loud enough so that the baron heard. He jerked his head around and said, "Captain Miles, we need you here and this last campaign has expunged the disgrace of your earlier loss."

Miles coloured and I leapt to his defence, "He was betrayed by spies, my lord. What has happened to the spy? The wine steward, has he been punished?"

The baron looked down at the table, "He escaped two days after you left. There were accomplices."

"Then, Baron, you need to look to yourself and your security, sooner rather than later. Your mother and you have used up all the favours you are likely to get from me."

We left as soon as the gates were opened. I was happy to get away. We had our pay and had gained two horses. The soldiers we had led honoured us with a guard of honour on the way to the North Gate. We had grown close in the short time we had been with them.

Chapter 12

Henry Samuel Montfort's Revenge

We had not been away for as long as our families had expected but that did not stop them from giving us a good welcome. Richard's son had been born before Christmas but Thomas' wife, Anne, had given birth even as we were heading back from Barnard Castle. There was a joyful air in the castle. We had not been away as long as had been anticipated and with no losses my wife and mother ordered a feast. Samuel and Geoffrey attended, as did all the knights except for Thomas who stayed by his wife's side. Both my son and his squire noticed a difference in Henry immediately. He did not swagger but he moved with a confidence that even Geoffrey did not possess. I gave our squires permission to sit at the table and the three of them were like hens pecking at grain as their heads darted forward and they told each other all that had transpired.

Samuel looked at his brother, "How was it managed, brother? I thought that I had done well for Geoffrey is a better man now than he was, but compared with Henry he is still raw clay."

Alfred shrugged, "This was not war, brother, but there was danger. Henry could have lost his life and he did not. He killed and now knows what it is to be a warrior. I think that the two boys had too long a childhood. That was because their mother nursed their father and their elder brother was dead. There was no one to control them and they fed off each other." He grinned, "Our mother and father would never have allowed us to become as bad."

I smiled, "And I made another good decision when I made them your squires."

"But there will be no war for Geoffrey and I, will there, Father?"

"You wish for war?"

Samuel shook his head, "No but Alfred and Henry now understand what it is to be a warrior. The training of Henry will be easier."

"I think that war will come again to this land. Rebellion simmers beneath the surface. We are lucky in the north for we were, in the main, loyal to the king. De Vescy was the exception and that rebel took the cross with the king's sons. There are others, further south, who are still supporters of de Montfort. There are those who lost lands and wish

The Ripples of Rebellion

them back. Until the stone that was Evesham has stopped sending ripples to the shore then no one can be sure that there will be peace."

"Have we heard how the Crusaders fare, Father?"

"The last I heard was that they had reached the Mediterranean and were sailing to Africa."

"Africa? I thought that their destination was the Holy Land."

"As did I but remember that Egypt lies in Africa and it could be that King Louis and the other leaders think that they can win that way." I shrugged, "I confess that it has confused me. We will hear more news soon enough."

I was trying to put a brave face on it but I had expected more information. News had to come from London and through York. It was a long journey The shortest way to Durham was across my ferry. Messengers sent to Durham often rested at the castle and it was in that way that we learned news of the world beyond the valley.

The next day began our normal lives as knights and mine as lord of the manor. Samuel was right and Henry threw himself into his training. He had natural skills and even Joseph was impressed with the change in attitude. I only heard of the changes for I was busy hearing cases that had gathered in my absence. There were disputes over land that I had to settle. There were crimes that needed to be punished. None were of the magnitude of the bandits in the forests but they needed to be handled well. My grandfather had taught me that those duties, while less glamorous than going to war, were just as important. When that was done, I had to meet with my steward and my reeve. This was the time of planting. We had to decide if we needed new animals. When all that was done I met with the town council. The town was growing and was prosperous. We had to plan for new roads and houses that lay outside the town walls. The Warlord who had first organised the layout of the new town had come from Constantinople and he liked order and cleanliness. Houses did not just erupt, they were planned along roads that were straight. They did not crowd on one another but there was space. The Warlord had known that building too close together invited disease and conflict. It took as long for me to work with the council as hearing the cases and organising the farmers.

By the time all was done, it was May Day. Whilst not a true Holy Day, it had been celebrated since the time of the Romans. It was a good tradition as it marked the ending of the planting and brought the hope of a good crop. I am not sure if it was pagan in origin but as the priests did not object neither did I. It was a time for girls and young women to put on their finest clothes, attach flowers to their hair and dance and sing.

The Ripples of Rebellion

They paraded through Stockton and ended their dance at St John's Well where they sang.

Sing a song of May-time.
Sing a song of Spring.
Flowers are in their beauty.
Birds are on the wing.
May time, play time.
God has given us May time.
Thank Him for His gifts of love.
Sing a song of Spring.

It was traditional for those who could afford it to give them pennies. As lord of the manor, I gave them each a silver sixpence. This was the day when many maidens would catch the eye of a young man and, often, courtship followed. My generosity was to add to the dowry that the young women would bring to the marriage. Some of the girls had been given, over the years, four or five sixpences. The wise maidens would now have silver to bring to the marriage.

We held a feast in the Great Hall and as Thomas and Anne came with their son, Henry, and Richard and Margery brought William it was a chance to celebrate the newest members of the family. We used the opportunity to have both babies christened in the family chapel. It was crowded but cosy and we left the chapel to walk the short way to the Great Hall. We were all dressed in our best and the sun shone. Eirwen gripped my arm tighter and said, quietly, "A perfect May Day."

"You are right, my love, God smiles on us."

Being a May Day feast meant it began earlier than normal. That was partly because Lady Mary and my mother, Lady Matilda, were no longer young. They liked to retire earlier than they once had. The young mothers, too, would need to be abed earlier.

We had just finished the beef course when I saw Joseph appear at the door. He was captain of the guard and looked agitated. I said to Eirwen, "I will see what has upset Joseph." As I left the table I speculated that it was probably some young buck who had enjoyed too much ale in the hot sun and needed to be warned about his behaviour by the lord of the manor.

Joseph, seeing my approach, waited without. When I reached him, he closed the doors and led me to the inner bailey. When we were outside and the castle was bathed in the last light of the day, I asked, "What is it, Joseph?"

"My lord, a messenger passed through on the ferry. He was heading for Durham. I knew the man and he told me his news." I saw the pain on his face and waited. "My lord, Henry of Almain and his squire have been murdered in Italy. They were in a church while he prayed. Two of the de Montforts did the deed."

"Matthew and Robert?"

He shook his head, "Ralph did not know. The Regent, Richard of Cornwall, is said to be angry beyond words. He has ordered every Montfortian nest to be scoured." He shook his head, "The murder was in March. The north, it seems, is one of the last places to hear of the act."

"We have no Montfortians close by so that is good. As for the delay…It would take at least ten days or more to get the word to England and if the seas were against them then even longer. If I was the regent, I would want some time to mourn my son. Who knows, he may even have disbelieved the news and waited for confirmation." I put my arm around his shoulder. I knew that his thoughts, like mine, were dark ones. Matthew was a household knight, and he took his duties seriously. I could not see him standing idly by while his master was murdered. "Let us not jump to conclusions, Joseph. We will wait for more news." He nodded. "And what of the Crusade?"

"Ralph said that The Lord Edward still planned on sailing to the Holy Land. Henry of Almain was on his way to Gascony to take command of that land for his cousin."

That did alleviate my fears a little. He would not have gone alone. Perhaps he had more than a handful of knights with him. Even as the thought flitted across my mind it begged the question of how the murder had taken place.

"My lord, I need to tell Robert's mother the news. If…"

"Of course. Let your deputy take command. You and your family are all that is important now." I put my hand on his shoulder. "But just your wife, eh? I will tell the others later."

"Of course, my lord."

Before I opened the door, I adopted a smiling face. I would not spoil the celebrations. I would give the news on the morrow. I did not want others to have the dire dreams that I knew I would have to endure. I was relieved that my mother and aunt had both retired. I sat next to Eirwen. "Husband, what is it?"

"Nothing."

She shook her head, "That false smile may fool others but not me."

"I cannot tell you here but when we retire then I will."

I was distracted and I was just happy that the younger ones were too busy dancing to wonder why the earl had adopted such a serious face on a day of celebration.

The Ripples of Rebellion

Once the door to our bedchamber was closed Eirwen led me to the bed, and we sat. She held my hands. "Now, tell me all."

I gave her the facts. Eirwen was clever and although I had not mentioned Matthew, like me she knew that if Lord Henry was dead then Matthew might have suffered a wound or even death.

"Lady Mary will be distraught. She was joyous this day seeing her first grandson. The news will break her heart." I nodded, "Tell your mother first. She can advise you."

"I cannot expect my mother to do that which is my duty. It is my fault that Matthew went on Crusade. If anything has happened to him then it is laid at my door and no other." She squeezed my hand, "I will ask my mother's advice but I shall be the bearer of the sinister news."

As I had expected my dreams were not pleasant ones. I was a soldier and knew the perils of enemies who would attack regardless of any rules or thoughts of chivalry. The bandits we had slain were nobles in comparison with such men as the de Montforts.

I rose early and, with Eirwen, went to breakfast. My mother was an early riser. She had attended chapel and was now helping the servants to lay the table with freshly baked bread, ham, cheese, strawberries and honey cakes. My mother was perceptive and as we approached her said, "What is amiss, my son?" Eirwen waved the servants away and I told her. She made the sign of the cross and shook her head, "Mary will take this badly. Would you like me to tell her?"

I shook my head, "It is a duty appointed to the Lord of the Manor and the head of the family."

The others in the castle descended to join us. It was clear from our serious faces that something was wrong but none would dare to question my mother. Lady Mary had been to the chapel too and it meant that she was one of the last to arrive. Little William made her morning by giggling and gurgling as she tickled his chin. This was not the moment.

Dick had one of the shorter journeys but he was keen to get back to his new manor. He had made many improvements in the short time he had been the master. His mother pleaded with him to stay longer, "Must you go, my son? I have barely seen my grandson."

"Then come and stay with us for a while. There is no Matthew to divert you and you know that we would make you more than welcome."

"Perhaps I will."

Thomas and Samuel had the same need to get home. I could see that my sister, Geoffrey's mother, was also torn. If she stayed in Stockton then she would see her son, Henry, every day.

The Ripples of Rebellion

Alfred said, "Come, Henry, we will make up for the day of leisure that was the May Day. Let us work on your horse skills. St John's Well and the green were well flattened yesterday, we shall use that."

We were almost alone, William had stayed.

"Roger, join Alfred this morning and help to train young Henry."

He gave me a curious look but said, "Yes, my lord."

Eirwen said to the servants, "Leave us awhile. You can clear when we have vacated the hall."

I looked at my mother who nodded, "Lady Mary, there is no easy way to say this but Lord Henry of Almain was murdered in a church in Italy."

I saw the confusion on her face and then realisation dawned. I saw her eyes widen. She managed to say, "My son..." and then a strange thing happened. It was as though her face slipped and then her legs would not hold her. Her eyes were open but she fell as though poleaxed. I was close enough to her to arrest her fall. There was little else that she could do.

Eirwen shouted, "Edgar, send for the doctor."

William knelt next to her. He shook his head, "I have read of this but we will wait until the doctor confirms it. There is something that has gone wrong in her brain. See how the side of her face is frozen. Lady Mary, can you speak?"

My aunt's eyes were open and I saw her trying to speak but it was a babble and white drool came from the side of her mouth.

William nodded, "That is a symptom."

Dick and the others had heard the noise and came down. Richard saw his mother and knelt next to her. "Mother..." Alfred, Henry and Roger had rushed back in too.

My cousin looked at William who said, "She suffered this attack when my brother told her of the murder of Henry of Almain."

Before more could be said the doctor arrived. We stood to allow him to attend to her. Even as he did so I noticed that her breathing was becoming more laboured. "She will live, will she not?" My cousin was clearly in shock.

He asked the question of William. William was the wise one in the family. My brother said, "I am doubtful but I am not the doctor."

Doctor Erasmus stood, "Sir Richard, your mother has little time on this earth. If you have aught you wish to say then now is the time. She needs a priest."

My mother said, "Like me, she has been to the chapel already. She has made her peace with God." She made the sign of the cross.

"Thomas, fetch the priest."

The Ripples of Rebellion

"Yes, Earl."

Richard knelt, "Mother, it is your son, Dick. Do not leave us, I beg of you." I was above him and I could see the dying woman's eyes as she tried to speak. No words came from her mouth but I think I saw some in her eyes. "I love you. Mother." His sister Margaret was shocked beyond words and my wife had her arm around her.

Suddenly the light went from Lady Mary's eyes. They were still open but Lady Mary was now dead. Dick looked up at the doctor who knelt to close her eyelids. That done he rose and shook his head. "She is with God and the earl now."

We were all stunned and it was my mother who took charge. She was still the matriarch of the family but her generation was becoming fewer, "Thomas, Dick, Alfred and Samuel, carry Lady Mary to her chamber. Eirwen, Eleanor, come with me and we will prepare her for the funeral. This is women's work." She nodded to William who went to comfort Margaret.

When the four knights returned, I had Edgar fetch in strong wine. We needed our spirits bolstering. I told them all the news that I had heard. Dick shook his head, "You should have told us last night, Earl. We had a right to know."

I spoke gently for I understood his anger, "And the result of that might have been your mother's death last night and you, the same night I had; one filled with dire dreams. We do not know if Matthew is alive or dead. Either way, we can do little about it. We just have to wait until news reaches us. Italy is a long way from here. I did what I felt was right, Dick. It is all any man can do." I saw that Roger and my daughters were now giving comfort to Margaret who was sobbing.

William put his arm around Dick, "Henry Samuel is right. There is no point in speculating. From what Joseph was told only the Regent's son and his squire were killed."

Samuel had been listening, "The word my father used was murdered. We all know Matthew; he is of the blood of the Warlord. He would not stand idly by while his lord was murdered."

"Samuel, we wait and we pray. We owe it to the family to be strong. I know that all of you have courage on the battlefield but here you must show a different kind of courage. Whatever doubts and fears you have must be kept within you. Know that the door to my solar is always open. You can unburden your thoughts to me. Before the rest we are stoic." I looked at Henry and Geoffrey, "This is all part of your training, not to be knights but to be men."

They both stood a little taller and nodded. The transformation from the wild boys was complete.

The Ripples of Rebellion

Lady Mary was buried two days later. We had left space in the chapel next to my uncle. The stone mason would, in the fullness of time, make an effigy. Dick had come to realise that I had been right to do what I had done. As he said to me, at the funeral feast, "She had one last night of joy when her world was complete. Now we must wait and wonder at the fate of my brother."

"I have thought about that, Dick, and in here," I patted my chest, "I do not believe he is dead."

He shook his head, "You are in the land of witches and fantasy now, cousin. How can you know?"

I shrugged, "I do not know, I believe, and in that is a world of difference."

William nodded his agreement, "I am a man of letters, Dick, and not war. I do not have the bond with Matthew that you and my brother do. Let me ask you, do you think he is dead?"

"I do not know."

"Close your eyes and try to see him in your mind."

He did as William had suggested. He opened his eyes, "I do not see him dead."

"Nor does the man who trained him. Until we hear more news then let us believe that he lives."

It was good advice, not only for Dick but the rest of us. It did not do to simply wait. We had our lives to live and all of us threw ourselves into making our world as good as it could be. If he was dead then the stronger manors would be a memorial for him and if he lived then he would return to a better world. William and I had dismissed the idea that he would have gone to the Holy Land with The Lord Edward. He had sworn an oath to Henry of Almain. He would have kept his word. Of course, he might be wounded or incapacitated too. What we did know was that the body of Henry of Almain would be returned to England and when that day came we would know one way or another. When Joseph's old friend Ralph returned south we wrote a letter for him to take to Richard of Cornwall. If he knew anything then he would tell us. He was a good man. We waited.

Chapter 13

Henry Samuel

Back from the dead

After the funeral, each evening as the last ferry was crossing the river, I had taken to standing alone on the gatehouse by the river gate to peer south. In the days since the funeral, I had been restless. I had thrown myself into being the lord of the manor but I hated not knowing what was going on further south. I think I went to the river to look for a liveried messenger. The letter would not have even reached the regent yet but I hoped beyond hope that word would come soon. Dick and I had already decided that if he was wounded and still in Italy we would sail there and bring him home. The same would be true if we heard that the worst had happened. It would not be like Sir Thomas' father, Sir Samuel, he would not be buried abroad. He would lie in the chapel.

Joseph joined me one evening a few days after the funeral.

I turned as he ascended the stairs, "How goes it, Joseph?"

"My wife is taking it hard, my lord. I keep telling her that we know nothing yet but she weeps and touches the old clothes he left behind." I nodded. "I have watched you come here, my lord, and wondered why."

"Ralph, when he brought you the news, came on the last ferry for it is a long way from York and I hope that the news, when it comes, will also arrive by the last ferry. Besides, this is a good place to reflect on the parlous nature of our lives." I pointed south. "Sir Geoffrey Fitzurse and his sons perished there and Thornaby is now a land of ghosts. When my grandfather returned from the Holy Land it was to find a devastated manor and a desecrated tomb. I think that standing here helps me to see things more clearly."

He nodded. It was a quiet night. The ferry with Hob and Rafe, the ferrymen, was on the south side of the river. They had a fishing line over the side. As soon as the sun dropped below the western horizon they would return to this bank, secure the ferry and go to their home. If they had caught fish then it was seen as a gift from the river. The salmon in the river were of good quality and a whole salmon was a treat. As we watched we heard hooves descending the trail, across the river, through the trees.

The Ripples of Rebellion

"That is more than one horse, my lord." I knew what Joseph meant. It was not a messenger. It might be merchants heading for the inns in the town before carrying on to Durham. We had many such visitors.

"It is." We saw three riders approach and they were all cloaked and cowled. They led horses. I saw at least three warhorses. That suggested knights but only one looked to have the build of a knight. "Let us go down and greet our visitors."

We entered the gatehouse and went down the ladders to the barbican. The brands in the sconces had not yet been lit and it was dark, like descending into a tomb. Even though it was the place an enemy would be least likely to attack we had a portcullis we could drop. The gate itself was small. A rider had to dismount to enter. The sentry who stood there was coming to the end of his duty. When the ferrymen entered, he would lock and bar the gate and lower the portcullis.

"Visitors eh, my lord?"

"Aye, James, go to the castle and warn Edgar and her ladyship that we have visitors."

"Yes, my lord."

With the lord of the manor and the captain of sergeants on guard, there would be little threat to the castle. The path wound down to the river and Hob and Rafe were already making good progress. Their cousin, Nate, waited on our side to help with the securing of the ferry. The horses were at the fore and I saw that two of the passengers were helping to pull on the ropes that drew the ferry back and forth. My hopes rose that this might be news of Matthew.

The sun had dipped below the horizon and the fading light obscured the faces but when I heard, "Father!" and then, a heartbeat later, "Henry Samuel!" My spirits soared like Erasmus my falcon. The two men pulling on the ropes pushed their way to the front rail and dropped their cowls. It was Matthew and Robert. Nate deftly secured the ferry as Robert and Matthew lifted the bar. There was no ceremony and they both threw themselves in our arms. No words were spoken and we hugged each other hard. The three ferrymen were mindful of the moment and they began to walk the horses ashore. James the sentry had returned and, placing his spear next to the wall, he came down to help.

I released Matthew and said, "You cannot know the pain we have endured not knowing if you lived or died."

"We came as soon as we could, my lord. It is many leagues from London and we rode as though the devil was chasing us. Now we are here and my home never looked as welcoming." He suddenly turned and, like a magician revealed the third passenger, "And this is

The Ripples of Rebellion

Thomasina, I intend to seek your permission and that of my mother to marry her."

I confess that my breath was taken away. She was a beautiful young woman. I could see that even in the gloom. I also knew that I had some bad news to impart but the riverbank was not the place. I took Thomasina's hand and kissed the back of it. "You are welcome, Mistress Thomasina, and as for my permission, Matthew, you are a man and a knight. You make your own decisions."

"I hope, Earl, that you will think me worthy enough for your illustrious family. Matthew has told me all about them on the way north." She had an accent but she spoke well.

"Come, let us get to the hall. Your arrival will make what has been a gloomy place, cheerful once more."

Joseph said, "You can leave the horses with my son and I, Sir Henry. We have much to say and this night is a time for families."

My cousin said, "Thank you, Robert. We both know that I would not have made it back without you. I shall not need you until the morrow. See your mother, as I shall see mine."

Thomasina had her arm linked through Matthew's and she clung to him. We walked through the river gate and headed across the bailey. The door to the hall was ajar and the cobbles were bathed in soft warm light. I saw Edgar waiting. As soon as he recognised Matthew his face lit up in a huge smile. He had been the steward while Matthew was growing up. He had missed him as much as any.

"Sir Matthew, our prayers have been answered and we thank God. It is a pity your poor mother…" I shook my head too late to stop the outpouring of bad news and Edgar realised his mistake. "I am sorry, my lord."

We stopped and Matthew searched my face. I shook my head, "Your mother died a short time ago, Matthew, I am sorry."

The look on my nephew's face almost broke my heart. Thomasina hugged him and I saw then that they were meant for each other. Eirwen and Alfred appeared behind Edgar and Alfred let out a whoop. He could not have known that I had just given Matthew bad news.

Putting my arms behind the couple I gently propelled them into the hall, "Come, let us go within. My mother has also missed you. Edgar, Joseph has their bags, bring them."

"Yes, my lord." As Eirwen led the couple inside he added, "I am sorry, my lord, I did not think and…"

"It is no one's fault, Edgar. The news had to come out soon enough."

The arrival of the couple rippled through the hall. The widows of the valley all made for the Great Hall as did the squires. Matthew's grief

The Ripples of Rebellion

would have to take second place as he was assaulted by questions and hugs. I took off my cloak and hung it from the peg on the wall. When I entered the Great Hall I clapped my hands and said, "Let us have some silence, eh?" I saw my mother, along with Eleanor, Isabelle and Rebekah, nodding their approval. "Matthew has returned home and has just been given the sad news about his mother. Let us respect his needs. He has also brought Mistress Thomasina whom he intends to marry, let us make her welcome, too, but gently. Seara, fetch food and wine."

My words had taken everyone by surprise. I saw joy on my mother's face. Her marriage had been cut short by a murderer but she valued marriage more than most. She would want Matthew to marry. She held her arms out, "Come, Thomasina, I am Lady Matilda, let me welcome you to the family." The hug was warm and my mother led Thomasina to the cushioned chairs that were close to the fire. "Sit here and tell me and my ladies all about yourself. We have a wedding to plan and that is work for ladies and not steel-clad warriors."

Matthew said, "Where is my mother's grave?"

"Where you would expect it to be. She is next to your father in the chapel."

"I would visit her, now, my lord."

"I will come with you."

We slipped from the hall leaving Alfred and the squires in a buzz of conversation as they took in the arrival. I said nothing as we walked across the dark bailey to the chapel. A candle burned in the chapel. No words were spoken. None were needed and I was there only to give comfort. Matthew was a man but at times like these, a father figure was needed. My mother and Eirwen would take on the role of foster mother but Matthew had been my squire. We entered and I stood back as he prostrated himself across the tomb.

He wept and this was the place for such tears. I watched. Eventually, he raised his head, "I am sorry we did not arrive home in time for you to see my bride, Mother, but I had news to deliver and I did my duty to my lord. It was a long journey. Thomasina will make a good wife and I love her. I hope that you would have approved of her and I will try to be as good a husband as my father was to you. I know that you will be reunited with my father now and that is the only good to come from this dire news." He bowed his head and then turned.

It was as he turned and walked towards me that I saw a slight limp, "You were wounded?"

He nodded, "I was too late to stop the murder but I did my best and suffered a wound for my pains. The heirs of de Montfort were excommunicated but they live and if I get the chance they will die by my hand."

We walked across the bailey, "And the other household knights?"

"I was the only one. There were just four of us on the journey although we travelled with two kings and their men." He shook his head, "He was murdered in church whilst on his knees. He was killed in revenge for the death of Simon de Montfort at Evesham but Henry of Almain was not even at the battle."

We were nearing the donjon and I said, "A startled snake snaps at anything, Matthew. The family is evil but their punishment now lies with God. Let us talk about this another time. For tonight put on a smile and let us make your bride to be welcome."

He smiled, "She is lovely is she not?" I nodded, "She is not noble born."

I laughed, "And when has that ever been a problem to this family? You love her and that is enough. You can return to Redmarshal when…"

We had reached the entrance hall and he said, "I have been given a manor. Richard of Cornwall gave me Egglesclif."

"A kingly gift."

"He had lost a son and was making up for what his father did to this family. I fear that there will be much work involved for he said there has been no lord for fifty years."

I nodded, "More. My grandfather never spoke of a lord of Egglesclif. We can visit when the women plan the wedding." We paused outside the hall where the laughter of women could be heard. "You wish for a marriage sooner rather than later?"

He grinned, "I would have wed her before we left Italy but she wanted to wait until we reached here. She is not sure that she is good enough for this family."

"Then she knows us not. I look forward to getting to know this remarkable young woman."

In the time we had been away, Edgar had set the servants to prepare the hall for food. I was able to stand back and watch my family welcome the knight we thought might have died and his betrothed. Alfred and the squires crowded around Matthew. William sidled next to me. "Here is another tale for me to record, eh brother?"

"And it is a most interesting one. It was Simon and Guy de Montfort who did the murderous deed and Matthew was wounded for his pains. He is to be lord of Egglesclif."

It was rare that I could surprise my younger brother but I succeeded, "I had almost forgotten that manor. It was never in the family. Even when the Warlord was the earl it belonged to..." I saw him trying to think.

"The king."

"Of course. Then it will need much work."

"I thought to ride there tomorrow with Matthew. If you can tear your inky fingers from parchment and ride then you can come with us."

He smiled, "I have not left the castle since I helped Samuel to organise Redmarshal. It will be good to ride under a warm sun."

My mother came over and put her arms around us both, "What are you two conspiring about?"

"Matthew has a manor, Egglesclif, we will visit it tomorrow."

"Good, for we have much to plan with Thomasina. She is just what this family needs. She is a delight but I fear that Mary," she made the sign of the cross and lowered her voice, "would have disapproved. Mary was very proper. She would have wished for a marriage to a noble family. It is better that she never knew."

William could not help but roll his eyes. I loved my mother's honesty. She had known Lady Mary better than any. They were as close as two women could be. She knew her faults and still loved her. When my mother, Isabelle and Rebekah passed it would be the end of an era.

Eirwen and I were able to talk at the table. All the attention was on the young couple. "And one day our sons will bring a bride to Stockton, Husband. Will they be as fortunate as Matthew?"

"Fortunate?"

"She has a sound mind and from what she has told us endured great danger both on the road and at sea. She and Matthew are clearly in love and yet she told him that she would not wed unless his family approved. This bodes well for she is sensible."

"Our sons will marry well and it will be like us, for love. That day is not yet here."

"We said that about Thomas and yet he found a bride in the most unlikely of places."

"Matthew would be married as soon as he could."

"And that is what we need after the sadness of his mother's death. It will be a wedding on Midsummer's Day. That gives us time to prepare well and for you to make certain that his new manor is a suitable one."

My mother ensured that the bride-to-be was cosseted and cared for as though she was a royal princess. For her part, Thomasina looked to be overwhelmed by it all. I am not sure what she expected but it was not this.

The next morning we all breakfasted together and then Matthew, William and I, along with our squires rode towards Egglesclif. Alfred

The Ripples of Rebellion

and Henry had the task of informing the rest of the family of the joyful news. We were the ones to deliver it to my brother, Alfred, at Elton and to Matthew's brother at Hartburn. Dick was overjoyed not only that his brother was alive but that he had also returned with a bride. The news about the manor was also pleasing. It was not far from Hartburn. The delivery of the news delayed us and it was not until almost noon that we rode into the run-down manor of Egglesclif.

I had warned Matthew not to expect much but even I was appalled at what greeted us. Jack of Egglesclif came from the hamlet but he had said little when we questioned him about his former home before we left. His face had clouded over and he was not forthcoming. I did not press him on the matter.

The manor house was a ruin. The walls could be made out but the roof had collapsed inside. I saw a small church but it was more of a chapel of ease. It was, however, built of stone. There looked to be two inhabited dwellings around the green. From what I could see there had to have been, perhaps, a dozen or so houses originally but they had fallen into disrepair and over the years reclaimed by the soil. I saw little evidence of tilling. One of the two inhabited houses had a goat tethered outside. We reined in and I said, "Richard of Cornwall's gift looks like a poisoned chalice now, Matthew."

"He could not have known it was like this. We lived just a few miles away and we knew nothing."

William said, "There is no reason for men to travel here although the river looks like it could be bridged."

I shook my head, "The last thing we need is to give enemies a back door to our lands."

"Do not forget, my lord, that this land will now have a lord of the manor. If there was a bridge then I could guard it."

"You and Robert?"

"Give us time and we can make it a good place to live. The river is handy and it teems with fish. It is true that there is little tilled land but we can change that. The first thing we need is for me to meet these," he pointed to the handful of people who had emerged from the two houses, "my people."

William said, "And you cannot bring Thomasina here yet. You need a home."

My cousin was in a positive frame of mind, "And what better than to have a house which we have built? It will be ours and not an inherited one. This is all good, my lord."

William smiled at me, "He has the right attitude. Our grandfather would have been proud of him."

The Ripples of Rebellion

We dismounted and handed our reins to our squires. They walked our horses to the houses and it allowed William, Matthew and me to study the village. We had the chance to see who lived in the hamlet. I saw a man who could have been in his late twenties and a greybeard with him. There was one old woman and a younger woman. I counted four children. As manors go it was the smallest one I had seen.

They recognised our spurs and, as we neared, the old man bowed and said, "Good day, my lord. How can we help you?"

I looked at the young man, "Have I seen you at bow practice on a Sunday morning?"

He shook his head, "No, my lord. We worship in the church." It was an evasive answer.

I looked at Matthew who nodded to me and then spoke, "I am Sir Matthew of Stockton and Richard of Cornwall has given me this manor. You are?"

The old man said, "Walter of Egglesclif and this is my son Ralph. This is his wife, Elizabeth, and they are his children."

"And you?"

The older woman said, "I am Gammer Greystone. Walter is my brother."

"Why are there not more people here?"

It was the greybeard who spoke, "There were. We have had no lord, well since before I was born. There is no one to look after us."

I frowned, "Surely having no lord means you can do as you wish. Do you pay taxes?"

The old man looked at the ground, "None has come to collect any. Not for twenty years or more."

"Then you should be rich." I did not like this man.

"We have little in the way of land that we can farm. It is why others left. The house my sister Megan uses was lived in by John of Egglesclif and his family. When he and his wife died, his son Jack left."

I would question Jack when we returned to the castle. "And the other people?"

"Some died of disease. Others left. The village has been dying since I was a boy."

"Yet you stay," Matthew said, pointedly.

"Where else would I go?"

I snapped, "You are too lazy, eh?"

"That is unfair, my lord."

"Things will change now. We intend to build a home for my knight and his bride. I will give land to those in Stockton who would relish the chance to have land to work and a place to call their own. We will see the Bishop of Durham and have a priest appointed. Every Sunday will see the men of the village practise weapon skills."

The young man laughed, "That is just me!"

Matthew said, quietly, "No it is not. There are two boys that I can see. Perhaps giving them good habits will result in more pride than I can see." He looked at me, "This is more urgent than I thought, my lord. When can we start?"

I looked at William who had the kind of logical mind that enjoyed such puzzles. He rubbed his chin, "The crops are in and that means there will be spare men in all the manors. If we ask for two men from each manor as well as the knights and the squires then we can make a start. I know of at least two poor families in Stockton who would appreciate the gift of land." He paused, "And there is Jack of Egglesclif."

Matthew asked, "Jack of Egglesclif?"

"A man at arms and a good soldier. It is clear that he left this village. He serves me and Joseph of Aylesbury. He would make a good Sergeant for you and the start of your own retinue. We will speak to him. You are right in one respect, Matthew, this manor has fallen so far that the only way is up. It cannot become any worse." I turned, "Farewell. We will return in the morning."

Chapter 14

Henry Samuel

The Bishop of Durham and the found men

We spoke, as we rode back to Stockton, about all the problems in the gift of the regent. It was William who brightened the mood. The road from Egglesclif to Hartburn had made us all see a task that would be difficult for even Hercules. "But, Matthew, summer is approaching, and your return will make all the men in the valley willing to help you. As well as the two poor families who will relish the chance to work the land and have a home, there are others who might choose to make a living there. The ferrymen might see an opportunity to improve their business. Most importantly we have the chance to make a home for you and Thomasina that will be the envy of the other ladies in the manor."

I saw Matthew smile at the thought and I asked, "Tell me how you two met."

William nodded, "I would that I had my wax tablet so that I could scribe the words but I shall use my memory instead."

As Matthew told me the story I realised that luck and fate had much to do with it. The death of Thomasina's grandfather enabled the couple to make their decision. I wondered if the old man, whom I did not know, had chosen to die. I had seen it before when men and women tired of life. They wished to shed the weariness. If her grandfather was an old soldier then death would not have frightened him.

"Her father was an Italian soldier and her mother was English. How did they meet?"

"Her mother served in an alehouse in Bordeaux. She was the daughter of an English archer killed in a border fight in Gascony. When the King of Naples passed through her father was billeted in the inn and the rest, as they say, is history. Her mother would not have had much of a life in the inn and from what Thomasina said, the couple were in love. She followed him back to Italy and that was where Thomasina was born. He left her in Viterbo with his parents while he followed King Manfred to war. He died in battle and Thomasina barely knew him."

We were nearing Hartburn and William said, "She has barely a trace of an accent."

"She insisted on speaking English from the moment we met. It has improved. She still calls Robert, Roberto."

From behind us, his squire laughed, "I like it, my lord."

We stopped at Dick's hall to water our horses. We had spoken briefly on our way to Egglesclif and now Dick and Margery came out of the house with a jug of ale for us. We held out our coistrels and Dick said, "Well, little brother, you have seen your manor. Do you still wish it? I passed there once and thought it was deserted."

He nodded, "It is a place that can be rebuilt and in that building will be parts of Thomasina and me. This is a fine manor, Dick, but you did not build it."

"A good attitude and if there is anything that I can do then please ask."

"There is, I intend to ask every lord in the valley to send men to help us transform the manor. The women will be busy planning the wedding."

William added, "And knowing our mother, Henry Samuel, she will have furniture made. We may not think of such things but women do."

"And if there are families who do not have enough land to work, brother, I have plenty."

On the last part of the journey, I said, "I will ride to the Bishop of Durham. You will need to be on hand at the manor and I can be the one to ask for a priest."

I sent for Jack of Egglesclif and Joseph as soon as I returned. William went to write up what he had discovered and to draw up some plans for a hall. The final design would only be decided upon when Thomasina had the chance to see the new manor. William could plan the basics for no matter what the couple decided the hall would need foundations and strong walls.

Jack looked a little apprehensive when he entered my solar. It was my sanctuary and my men at arms rarely visited. I had Roger watch the door while the four of us spoke. I let Matthew do most of the talking. "We have just seen your former home Jack, would you like to tell us more about it?"

He nodded, "Was Walter of Egglesclif there?" Matthew nodded. "He is the reason I left. After my family died, I was alone and he offered me no help. I confess, my lord, that I am no farmer. You have seen the land. Without an animal to pull the plough, it is almost impossible to make a living. I left and almost before I had packed my belongings his sister had moved into my family home."

"Thank you for your honesty. As his family are the only occupants of the manor then I can hardly evict them."

The Ripples of Rebellion

"He drove others out, my lord. He is a vindictive old man. His son is not so bad but a little simple and easily dominated by his father. Walter is evil."

"I was going to ask you to come with me and be my Sergeant at Arms but I can see that would not work."

Jack looked up, "You would make me Sergeant at Arms?"

"That was my intention. The earl gave me permission to ask you but..."

Joseph said, quietly, "Think about this, Jack. There are others ahead of you here. My son, Robert, will need someone to help him and I can think of no better man than you. One more thing, there is Annie."

I asked, "Annie?"

Joseph nodded, "The daughter of Peter the Potman. Jack has been courting her this last year. If he was at Egglesclif, my lord, he could have a home and be wed." Peter the Potman was a potter who made and sold pots made from Stockton clay. He lived on the north side of town, just outside the town walls.

"Well, Jack, does that make a difference?"

"Yes, Sir Matthew. Annie and I wish to be wed and her father is happy that we wish to do so. Their home is small, and he has four daughters. One being wed makes life easier for him."

Joseph said, "Aye, and you would have a good set of pots made as a dowry, eh?"

"One thing, Jack."

He looked at me, "Yes, my lord?"

"You would have to deal with Walter. Can you do that?"

"For a new life and a home of my own? Aye, my lord, but I will never like the man."

"You need not do that. I have barely met him and dislike him intensely. Just treat him fairly is all we ask."

I went with Matthew to the two families whose names had been given to me by William. They lived in two hovels not far from St John's Well. They had come to Stockton earlier in the year when the plague had ravaged the rest of their village. It had been close to the Wear and they had come as far south as they could to escape the disease. They eked out a living fishing in the river and foraging along the riverbank. My townsfolk were kind and the two families were often given bread and vegetables that could be spared.

Matthew was gentle when he spoke to them. He said that he could offer them houses and land to farm. They would need to help him to build the manor but, in return, they would be given seeds to plant and supported until their farms produced. Their answer was clear. The hovels in which they dwelt would not offer protection when winter came and a roof along with the promise of the chance of a new life made them jump at the opportunity.

I rode to Durham, the next day, just with Roger. I had sent half of my men to the manor with Matthew. He had always been popular as my squire and they looked forward to the task. It was something different to their usual routine.

Robert Stitchill was the Bishop of Durham and I liked him. He had overcome illegitimate birth to become one of the most powerful men in England. Added to that he was a religious man and no warrior prince. He allowed his knights and lords of the manor to ensure the Palatinate was safe. He also did good works. He had recently invested in a hospital at Greatham, to the north of Norton. He appreciated what we did as knights of the valley and I was accorded an interview as soon as I arrived. I left Roger with the horses. We would not be staying.

"Alan of Stanhope sent me word of what you did, Earl, and you should know that I am grateful. That bandits could cause such problems this close to my palace at Auckland is worrying. How may I help you?"

I told him of the gift of the manor from Richard of Cornwall. He frowned, "I do not object to the gift, my lord, but as the manor belongs to the Palatinate then it should have come from me."

"Bishop, the Regent had just lost his son, murdered in the most despicable way imaginable. I think that it can be forgiven."

"Of course," he made the sign of the cross, "and the murderers are now excommunicated and beyond God's grace. Tell Sir Matthew that he has my blessing. I will ensure that the legalities are dealt with." He looked to the monk with the wax tablet who had been listening to all our words. "Brother John, see to it."

"Yes, Your Excellency." The cleric scratched something on the tablet.

"There is a church but no priest, Your Excellency."

He smiled as he rubbed his chin, "And there I can help you. I have a monk, Oswald, who is not suited to a life of study and contemplation. He likes to be active. I have been looking for an opportunity to satisfy him and this seems the perfect opportunity." He turned to the monk, "Find Oswald and fetch him here."

Brother John rose, "Yes, Your Excellency."

When he had gone the Bishop said, "While we are alone I must tell you of unrest that abounds in the land. Those who were dispossessed by the King after Evesham are conspiring. We have many travellers who pass through the Palatinate and they tell me of plots and plans to unseat the king."

The Ripples of Rebellion

"You have told the regent?"

"Of course, but the king is not well. I fear that the grief caused to Richard of Cornwall will distract him. While the heir to the throne is serving God in the Holy Land, those who wish their lands back may take advantage."

"Surely there are none in the north."

"Sadly, there are. The Neville family gained land but it was at the expense of those who supported Simon de Montfort. Gainford, Sadberge and Great Burdon are three such manors and all lie close to you. The Nevilles have yet to appoint lords of the manor as they are busy consolidating their newly acquired lands in Yorkshire. I tell you this for you need to be on your guard."

We could say no more for the door opened and Brother John brought in the monk, Oswald. I saw immediately what the Bishop meant for he was a huge man with hands like shovels. I could not imagine him copying down holy texts and scribing delicate pictures.

"Oswald, this is the Earl of Cleveland. He has a church but no priest. He is happy to offer it to you."

His face lit up. When he spoke he had a deep and resonating voice, "I would be honoured, my lord."

I thought it as well to offer a word of warning, "I need to tell you, Oswald, that the manor has been neglected for fifty years. My cousin, the lord of the manor, will need help to build the village. There will be less than twenty people for you to minister to."

His smile grew, "Better and better, my lord, for whatever comes will be from these hands and his lordship."

I could see that his answer pleased the bishop who said, "If you wish, Oswald, you may leave with Sir Henry or do you need time to gather your belongings?"

"I can be ready as soon as you need me, my lord. I am not a worldly man and have few belongings."

"Brother John, find a horse for Father Oswald." I saw the smile grow larger as the monk was given the title.

"My squire, Roger, is outside with my horses. When you are ready, then join him."

After they had gone the bishop said, "And there is something that you can do for me, Earl, if you would."

"If it is in my power, then I shall do so, Your Excellency."

"There are two brothers who serve me as archers. Edward and Edmund Williamsons are good men, but they have fallen out with the captain of archers." He shook his head. "I know not the details but there is disorder amongst the ranks. They need cohesion and the brothers are popular with some of the younger archers. I did not think it was right to dismiss them out of hand but if you could offer them a position?"

I did not need to think twice. Matthew would need archers. "Of course, Your Excellency, but I only want willing men. Pressed men are of little value."

He stood, "Then let us go and ask them."

The archers were on the green loosing at the mark. I saw as soon as I spied them that there was division. The majority of archers were on one side. There looked to be six who stood apart. "The brothers are there?"

We stood close to the smaller group. "Aye, now do you see what I mean?"

The bishop waved over one of those from the larger group, "Captain Waleran, a word if you please."

As the man came over, I identified the two brothers who were with the smaller group. It was not just that they looked similar but their hands tightened on their yew bows as the captain approached.

"This is the Earl of Cleveland."

The captain beamed, "I have heard of you, Earl. You were the saviour of Otterburn and, I hear, have scoured rebels and bandits from two forests. They are mighty deeds."

"Thank you. I have a new manor to man and I need men."

"I am loath to lose any men."

The bishop said, gently, "Waleran, I know of the chaos that is being caused by your dispute with two of your archers. Bloody noses and knuckles cannot be hidden."

His demeanour changed in an instant and he snarled, "If you mean these two curs then it is because they cannot obey orders."

One of them, I later learned it was the elder, Edward, who snapped the reply, "Your orders caused a man to be hurt so badly that he cannot draw a bow again."

The bishop said, "Peace. Edward and Edmund, would you be willing to serve Sir Matthew of Egglesclif as his archers?"

"And leave this reptile? In a heartbeat but I would ask one thing first, Earl."

I frowned, "I am not used to being given ultimatums."

"It is not that. The man who was maimed, David of Dunelm, was an archer and can no longer ply his trade. He can fletch and he is a hard worker. Could he be offered a place too? We would come in any case but without work then what is to become of our friend?"

"We would care for him, Edward."

"Bishop, charity is not for the likes of David. He is a proud man and needs the opportunity to work."

"Then I will happily offer him a place. We leave as soon as you can return here. Is your friend handily placed?"

"He waits without the walls. My brother will fetch him. I promise you, my lord, you will not regret this."

Somehow, I did not think I would. The enmity between the captain and the brothers was such that the bishop pointedly stood between them so that they could not come to blows.

We headed back towards Roger, Oswald and the horses. The bishop said, "Now I know why there was such anger. David was a good archer. All that I knew was there was an accident, and he could no longer draw a bow."

"You will still have a problem, Bishop Stitchill, for the ones who were with the brothers looked to be less than happy."

"Then I will send them to Stanhope. Alan of Stanhope needs more men. It might be best for all."

I did not say it, but it seemed to me that the problem lay with the captain and not the men.

Father Oswald and Roger were clearly getting on. I heard their laughter as I approached. "We have three men to take back to Matthew."

The priest grinned, "My flock is growing."

It did not take long for the archers to find their friend. I could see that he had the build of an archer and I saw no physical impairment but I knew from my own archers that any weakness in an archer's right side caused problems that prevented the drawing of a bow.

The fletcher bowed, "Thank you for this opportunity, my lord. I swear I shall not let you down and you will find that despite my injury I will work as hard as three men."

"What happened?"

The three of them all looked over to the captain of archers who was standing and watching us but was beyond earshot. David explained, "I was tardy one day. I had eaten bad fish. The captain punished me by making me hold a block above my head. Something snapped in my shoulder. It has healed and I can use my right arm, but I cannot draw a bow."

"Can you use a sword?"

"Every archer can use a sword, my lord, but why do you ask?"

"The work of a fletcher is useful, but my cousin needs men at arms. Even a maimed archer can be made into a good swordsman."

The three looked happy at my words. I turned to the bishop, "I will bid you farewell, Bishop Stitchill, and if you have other men you think would serve us then send them down the road. Stockton welcomes warriors." We mounted. The three men hefted their belongings onto their backs. I said, "Ride double with us. It is not far to Stockton, and we will make better time. David, ride behind me." He looked reluctant and I smiled, "You will learn that in the valley we share what we have and if that is the back of a horse then so be it. Come."

We left the castle and headed down the road to Stockton. David was quiet but I heard the other four chattering like magpies. It felt good to give men the chance of a new life. The manor deserved it too.

We reached Stockton just before sunset. Our horses were weary but it was worth it to arrive back in time to eat. The three men were taken to the warrior hall and Father Oswald to the castle. The sooner he met Sir Matthew the better.

That night as Eirwen lay in my arms I told her all that had happened. What worried her the most was the news about the potential unrest. I tried to dismiss it. "Richard of Cornwall is still the Regent. The grief for his son will pass and he will assert his authority again. In the meantime, I will visit these manors and see if there is a problem."

Chapter 15

Henry Samuel

The making of a manor

I had sent to my other lords who promised to supply workers for Egglesclif. The ladies of the manor were quite happy to stay and to plan the wedding. Eirwen had pointed out that Thomasina had arrived with only one change of clothes. She would be a lady and needed to be dressed appropriately. They called upon the services of the seamstress from Stockton, and we left them busily sewing. Carl the Carpenter had been warned that he would be needed to make furniture for the new hall and that he should begin to source the wood that he would need.

Thanks to the Regent's gift of Henry of Almain's horses we had enough animals to carry not only the new men and priest but also supplies. While the rest of us would return home to our halls Matthew and his small band would stay at the manor. Matthew had already decided that Walter's sister, Megan, could vacate what had been Jack's house and he and his men would use that. It was an important decision as it would put his stamp of authority on the village. I would have been happy to work alongside the men but Matthew was insistent that I need not do so. I would be able to watch them work.

We left for Egglesclif. Little visible work had been done while I was in Durham. William and Matthew had merely pegged out the lines for the foundations of the new manor house. When we reached the manor I was disappointed that I saw no evidence of Walter of Egglesclif having done anything. His son was toiling in the vegetable plot but that was all. We dismounted and tethered the horses on what had been the green and common grazing land but was now overgrown. The animals would crop it and make it look tidier. William and Matthew pointed to the lines they had drawn and the men, led by my knights, stripped off to dig the ditches that would be the foundations. I went with Matthew to the houses. Walter was seated outside the house he shared with his son. Megan was next to him. Matthew frowned when he saw that Walter made no effort to rise. It was not in our way to exercise our authority aggressively but Walter was clearly showing disrespect.

"Walter, do you not rise when your lord approaches?"

He struggled to his feet, "I am sorry, my lord, but I am an old man."

I said, "I would have said a lazy and insolent one."

The Ripples of Rebellion

Matthew used a gentler tone than did I, "We have spoken to Jack of Egglesclif and he told us that the house you occupy was his, Gammer Greystone."

"It was, my lord, but it is a fine house and it seemed a shame to let it go to waste."

"And I thank you for being a caretaker. Now it is needed for my men and me. I will live there until my hall is built and then it will revert to the house of Jack of Egglesclif."

"You would evict a widow?"

Matthew smiled, "No, I would return an old lady to the bosom of her family where she will be welcomed and loved. You have until noon to vacate it." She nodded but hatred burned in her eyes. "And Ralph, when you have tended your plot I want you and your sons to help me build my hall. You, Walter, can come now."

"I am old, my lord."

"And I can find work for old men." Matthew stared at Walter and said, quietly, "This manor now has a lord and I will manage the land and the people as I see fit." Just then the two families who would be living in the village arrived having walked the four miles from Stockton. "Here are two new families and we will be erecting their houses at the same time as mine. Any who do not wish me as their lord can leave…with my blessing."

Ralph said, "We will come now, my lord." He glared at his father, "I for one look forward to this village being a place of growth once more."

His wife, Elizabeth, nodded firmly, "As do I."

"Good."

I said to Matthew, as we headed to the two families, "You will have trouble with Walter."

"I know and I will deal with him."

The two families were young. Will son of Will had a wife who looked to be less than fifteen summers old and she had a nursing babe. Leif Egilsson had two young sons. I guessed, from his name and blond hair that Leif had Viking blood in him.

"Welcome." Matthew spread his arm around the shells of buildings that remained. "You may choose any plot you like. We have not yet cleared the land for I wanted you to have some choice in the selection. When you have chosen there will be men to help you. My uncle and I do not expect you to work alone."

"We are more than happy to. This gift of land is unexpected. When you have lived in a hovel for more than a month this seems like a palace already."

The Ripples of Rebellion

I said, "The gift, Will, is of a roof. The land that you will work on is Sir Matthew's. He is a fair lord but the profit from the land will be shared equitably."

His wife, Nanna, said, "And I promise that we will increase the yield year on year. My father was a good farmer until the plague took him. I am just happy that there is a church. We can have Thomas christened."

"You could have had him christened in Stockton."

"My lord, we lived outside the walls and did not feel part of the manor. How could we ask the priest to christen our son?"

Her words humbled me and made me feel guilty. I had not even known that there were such people in Stockton, William had and I would listen to my brother more.

Roger joined the men in digging and I was able to explore the land. The manor was on a good site. It was on a hill and could be easily defended. When the manor house was built Matthew could build a wall. I made my way down the slope to the river. It was far narrower here than at Stockton. I estimated it to be no more than forty paces wide. However, the steepness of the slope meant that any bridge that might be built would have to be more than seventy paces wide. We would have to make do with a ferry. I saw that the current was fast and the water looked deep. Fording would be an impossibility. I had heard that when the river froze it could be crossed and there were local legends of a drought that had allowed the fording of the river back in the days of Uhtred the Bold. I could not see it. As I headed up through the trees and brush, I saw deer hoofprints. Matthew could hunt. I wondered if Walter had taken deer. I guessed he had. Perhaps that was why he resented the arrival of Matthew. There would be order and he would no longer enjoy the licence he once had.

We had brought food from Stockton and at noon I commanded that all take rest and eat. I sat with William, Matthew, Dick, my brother Alfred and my sons. I smiled as I saw Father Oswald playing with the baby of Will and Nanna. The babe was giggling. It was a good start.

I nodded over to Walter, "Has he done much?"

Dick said, "As little as possible. To be fair his son and grandsons have toiled hard, as had his wife." He turned to his brother, "You have the makings of a good manor here. The three men and the priest you brought from Durham have worked as though their lives depended on it and Will and Leif have dug until their hands bled."

I said to William, "It is you who is the master mason here, is all going as you expect it to?"

The Ripples of Rebellion

"It is. The two men chose dwellings that were far enough from the hall and church so that they can plough the land and we have sufficient stone already to make the hall two-storied."

"Can you make a staircase?" My brother Alfred was curious as was I.

William shrugged, "I will bring Carl the Carpenter to help me for I can make the plans but these hands were meant for ink and not woodwork."

I waved my hand in a circle, "There should be a wall around it. I doubt that the king would sanction a castle but a wall with a fighting platform, allied to the steep slope would make this a hard place to take."

My brother Alfred nodded, "I remember when Elton was assaulted, we needed a steep slope then."

William said, "The priority will be the houses of Will and Leif. Midsummer is still some time away. Even if the hall is not ready then the bride and groom can stay at Stockton but the families need homes. We can build a pair of wattle and daub dwellings in a week."

We ate and felt the warmth of the early summer sun on our heads. "We should bring our oxen here to plough. This land has not been turned for fifty years. It will take a few turns with the oxen and a good ploughman. If we leave them here for a week then we can plough more than we need to use now and their dung will enrich the soil." I was no farmer but as lord of the manor I had learned much.

William nodded, "They can plant a crop of beans and then when they are harvested, oats and barley. The roots of the beans will feed the soil."

I pointed to the river, "There are deer."

Matthew brightened, "Then I can send out the two archers at dusk one night and we can feast royally."

By the end of the day, as the majority of us left for our homes, they were exhausted but still smiling at the progress that had been made. Matthew chose to stay in his manor and I knew that the bonding over the campfire they had built would make them one body. Father Oswald had spent the day, along with the women, cleaning the church. Nanna had asked if he would christen the baby and that was planned for Sunday. We would observe God's day of rest and it would be an opportunity for Matthew to see the worth of his archers.

Of course, the absence of Matthew when I returned necessitated a shower of questions. Remarkably the calmest appeared to be Thomasina. Since her arrival I had seen the least of her. After I had washed and we were seated at the table I asked her to sit between Eirwen and me so that I could speak to her. I could see that she was nervous as did Eirwen. My wife leaned in and said, "He might have the title of earl but Henry Samuel is still just a man. A good one, I grant you, but a man with all the attendant traits and faults." She glanced at me, "He snores."

That made Thomasina giggle.

"I do not."

Thomasina nodded, "Then he is a man for my grandfather said the same and he sounded like an angry hive of bees."

Her statement allowed me to ask her about her family. She added details that she had not told Matthew. I knew that I would have liked her grandfather had I met him. He was like my men at arms, a warrior. There are two types of warriors. There are the ones who enjoy the violence and the fighting. They tend to have short but glorious lives and then there were those like Joseph. They were men who were good at their trade but saw it simply as that. A way to earn a living and raise a family. Thomasina's grandfather had been like that. Sometimes when she spoke of him she lapsed into Italian as she struggled to find the English words. It sounded beautiful and although I did not understand the actual words her tone and her eyes gave me the sense of it. Eirwen had seen more of her and it was she who guided Thomasina and helped her when she struggled.

She grew more confident and easy in our company, "And how is my new home coming along, my lord?"

I gestured with my knife as I sliced some venison, "Ask my brother, the architect."

He was seated on the other side of Eirwen and had heard the question, "We have laid out the land and begun to dig the foundations."

I smiled, "William did more of the pointing and the rest more of the digging."

William held up his hands, "These are the hands of a writer and a planner. Besides, I would just have got in the way. You will have an entrance hall which faces west. It means we can build a double door. That will make it warmer. In any case, it will be warmer than this stone edifice. We will build a chimney on one wall in the hall you will use to eat. It will back on to the kitchen. There will be a drawing room which also faces south and west. The kitchen will have a buttery, pantry, beer and wine cellar."

"Cellars? They will be below ground?"

"I am using the slope so that the cellars will be below ground but you shall be able to get to them from outside. There will be a hog bog."

"Hog bog?" I smiled at her pronunciation of a word she had never heard.

"A place for the pigs and the chickens. It will be at the back door and means your servants can just throw out the kitchen waste."

"Servants? We have none."

Eirwen nodded, "But you shall. I have spoken with Annie, Jack's intended. She is young and hard-working, and she can cook. If it is agreeable to you then she would be able to help you to cook."

I said, "There is also the wife of Ralph, Elizabeth. She is unlike her father-in-law and is hard working."

"I can cook."

"But, Thomasina, you will be able to choose when you cook. Believe me, when you have children the support of someone who can cook and help you is something you will come to appreciate. You will be the lady of the manor and there are duties and tasks with which you are unfamiliar. We will help you with those. My daughters and Matthew's sister, Margaret, can help you,"

It was clear that she had not thought that far ahead. I think that the rest of the plans went over her head and she was distracted. She did not hear about the rooms on the ground floor and the three bed chambers on the second storey. She did not hear about the stable and the barns nor the wall around the hall and the strong gates that would be built. She could not visualise the hall.

Eirwen saw her distraction and said, quietly, "You have much to take in, Thomasina. Just take it one step at a time. It will be like the journey here. You did not manage that in one day, did you?" She shook her head, "And every day saw you learn something new about Matthew."

Her face lit up, "Every day was like a new adventure."

"Then it will be the same here. Once William has the walls built a little we shall ride to visit your new home. It is not far."

I added, "And Matthew will not spend every night at Egglesclif. He will return here."

"Good, for this is the first night since I met him that I have not seen him. I miss him."

I took our oxen the next day. I realised that the other derelict houses were not only an eyesore, they were taking up valuable land that could be used to grow things and be used for grazing. Matthew had a chance to plan his village. There would be just five houses at first and while there would be others in the future, he had the opportunity to plan how it would look. The Warlord had planned well in Stockton and it was only now, more than a century and a half since he had built, that we were moving beyond the town walls.

The Ripples of Rebellion

I let the others get on ahead of me and I rode with Roger and the ploughman, Egbert. He worked for me and cared for the two oxen. He had a plot of land to the north of St John's Well and his was the best ploughed land in the valley. He did not need much for every farmer whose land he ploughed gave him some of the crop that was grown. He was looking forward to spending some time on what was almost virgin land. His son Ethelred was with him. Egbert was training his son to take over when he gave up the plough. We arrived almost an hour after the others and William had them working already. Roger's father and brothers were farmers and while Roger had left because he wished to be a warrior, he had learned much at Whorlton. He and Egbert chatted like old friends.

When we arrived, Will and Leif were covered in daub. Matthew must have had them working after we had left for the two new houses had posts in the ground and the willow was in place. They were covering it with daub. It was not a complicated task but a messy one. It would take time to dry but it meant that within a week the two families would have a roof over their heads. There was a cheer when the two oxen arrived. The turning of sod was a significant event. Although work did not stop for long it ceased long enough for Father Oswald to bless the plough, the oxen and the land. William pointed to the fields that would be tilled. The division of the fields would come later. They would be divided into hides and Matthew would decide who would get what. There were now more farmers than hitherto and Matthew would have his first real decision to make as lord of the manor. Ralph, Jack, Will, Leif, Edward, Edmund and David, not to mention Father Oswald, would all need to be given strips of land. Each farmer would know his own plot and at first, all would look the same. However, every farmer would choose their own crops.

As the oxen began to make the green earth into brown so the birds descended to devour the wildlife that was exposed. I saw a bold kestrel plunge down to take the mouse that had lost his home. At the moment there was just one goat on the common land, the green, but soon there would be more. Matthew had money. He had been frugal on the journey back from Italy and the Regent had been generous. My nephew would need to invest some in animals. His manor would need at least one milk cow and the common land was big enough for a small flock of sheep. The women of Egglesclif would all share in the bounty of sheared wool and would spin it. The milk would make the cheese.

I saw that the willows by the river had already been heavily copsed. While they were supple the women were making fish traps. The only woman not doing so was Gammer Greystone. She and her brother just squatted like toads on the old tree stumps. Matthew would have to deal with those two human pieces of grit. They would be like the stones in buskins. They would irritate until they were removed.

By noon half of the future fields were turned. While the oxen rested and Egbert and Ethelbert ate their meal I spoke to them. Egbert waved a hand at the field they had turned, "My lord, I would stay here another day. We have turned them once but another turning will do no harm and if Sir Matthew would move his horses to the exposed land then their dung, in addition to my two oxen, will make the land more fertile. The next ploughing will mix it well." He pointed, "The next ploughing will be at right angles to the first."

He was a good ploughman and took pride in his work. I waved over Matthew who was delighted at the advice, "This is all new to me. My father was no farmer and knew nothing of this."

I shook my head, "We are all warriors, Matthew, when you have ascertained the worth of your farmers then you will choose one as Reeve and Bailiff. You are the lord of the manor and part of that responsibility is to choose men wisely."

I did not attend on Sunday. I wanted Matthew to enjoy the day with his people. Eirwen and Thomasina did ride there and Roger went with them along with Margaret and my daughters. They attended the christening and saw the first evidence of walls. I had seen the first signs of stone on Saturday night before I left and whilst not yet impressive, they rose but the height of a man's knee, they were a sign of the future. They were made of stone and mortared. Will and Leif had roofs over their heads and it was now a village risen like a phoenix. It had yet to gain all its plumage but the progress could be seen.

When Eirwen, Margaret, my daughters, Matthew, Thomasina and Roger returned that Sunday night all of them were as joyous as though they had drunk a firkin of ale. My daughters and Margaret were particularly giddy. Perhaps it was the rare excursion from Stockton that had invigorated them. It was good to see Margaret smiling. The death of her mother had upset her and she had withdrawn into herself. The table was filled with chatter that was of hope and the future. Lady Mary, Henry of Almain, Karl and Thomasina's grandfather were dead but not forgotten. They were named in the prayers before we ate, however, their deaths were now a distant memory and were replaced by hopeful dreams of the future.

Chapter 16

Henry Samuel

The Green Shoots of Growth

The weddings, for Jack and Annie were to be married at the same time, would take place in the parish church in Stockton. As much as we all wanted to use the church at Egglesclif, it was impractical. It was too small and the hall, whilst finished, was largely unfurnished. There was a bed built in the bed chamber by our carpenter and a table with two chairs, but despite our best efforts, it was not yet a home. In spite of that Matthew and Thomasina were determined to live in what can only be described as spartan conditions.

The weddings were seen as propitious. Midsummer Eve was also known as St John's Eve and as we had the well of St John the people of Stockton traditionally held a parade and a service at the well. With two brides the ceremony had added significance and while not all the town was invited to the wedding feast in my castle, all participated in the parade and the two brides-to-be were showered with flowers as they walked back from the well to church. The church was packed. Peter the Potman gave away Annie and I was given the honour of giving away Thomasina. My own daughters looked enviously at the Italian bride coming into the family. They would not be long behind…once they had found a husband. Matthew's sister, Margaret, was also a spinster and she was older than my two daughters. I saw the three of them looking enviously at Thomasina as I led her to the altar. Since their return from Egglesclif, the three had been more than distracted. Peter the Potman led Annie down the aisle after Thomasina and Matthew were married and the two couples left the church to tumultuous cheers from all those, and there were a great many, who could not fit into the church which, although larger than my chapel, was not big enough to accommodate everyone who wished to attend.

It was a lovely feast but there were ghosts there. I could feel the recently departed Lady Mary and my Uncle William. I also thought about my dear friend, Richard. This was not his family but he was part of my retinue and had helped me to train Matthew. When I had knighted Matthew, it had been the start of a journey. He had returned from his quest, won a bride and was now about to become a lord of the manor. Those thoughts compensated a little for the sad ones.

The Ripples of Rebellion

The couple had decided that they wanted their first night as man and wife, lord and lady, to be in their new home. Accordingly, the wedding was in the morning and the feast in the afternoon. The knights of the valley would be their guard of honour on the short journey to their new home. Gifts were given and they would be sent the next day by wagon. Matthew and Jack each rode a horse with their brides before them. With knights and squires flanking them and dressed in our finery we made a fine sight as we rode the few miles to Egglesclif. There were farms and houses along the route. Many people had been to Stockton for the Midsummer festival and had walked back to their homes while we feasted. They now waved a second time. It was that second welcome that made Thomasina feel as though she was home. The warmth from ordinary people touched her.

The others who lived in Egglesclif, Father Oswald apart, had not attended the service and, instead, the house in which Jack and Annie would celebrate their first night had been thoughtfully decorated by the villagers with flowers. Edward, Edmund and David would sleep in the open on the shortest night of the year. Annie and Jack would have just one night alone before the other three returned to their cramped quarters. There would be a hall built for the warriors of the village but that had to wait until the hall was built. All of them understood that. Will and Leif's families cheered along with Ralph and his. The exceptions were Gammer Greystone and Walter who were conspicuous by their absence.

The two men dismounted and, taking their brides in their arms, crossed the thresholds. It was a symbolic gesture and when the knights all cheered it seemed to confirm Matthew as Lord of Egglesclif. The doors closed and the horses stabled, Robert returned with us to Stockton so that the bride and groom could enjoy the new hall alone on their wedding night. The feast was not over. There would be more celebrations at night. Eirwen had engaged some musicians to play and there would be a dance. The absence of the couples would not detract from the joy of their day.

The rest of Stockton was celebrating too. The alewives had made plenty of ale and tables had been placed in the street. Every household had provided food and Peter the Potman and his wife had paid for a pig to be slaughtered. It had been cooking since the rise of the sun and, as we entered my castle, the smell of roasting pork made me hungry once more. The celebration of Midsummer was also the chance for the squires to enjoy themselves. Henry and Geoffrey showed the change in their personalities by making a real fuss of their mother. It was the right thing to do and the tears my sister shed were of joy at redeemed sons.

The Ripples of Rebellion

The tables in the Great Hall were arranged around the side so that there could be dancing. The travelling musicians were more used to a minstrels' gallery than being seated close to the dancers but they had been paid well and there was the promise of food. Such itinerant musicians never refused food.

Eirwen and my mother had left a space for me, and I sat between them. My mother took my hand, squeezed it and kissed it, "This was well done, my son."

"I had little to do with it."

"I saw you lead a bride to the altar and it made me proud. You are the head of this family. I do not wish to speak ill of the dead, but everyone says that you are an inspiring leader. Your poor Uncle William never was. He lived in the shadow of Alfred his brother, then his own father, Sir Thomas, and, finally, in yours."

I did not like to speak of such things and so I changed the subject. I pointed to the young people who had chosen to sit at one table. My daughters and sons were there along with the squires and Margaret, Matthew's sister. Like all young people at such parties, they were happy and they were loud. I saw my sister Eleanor frown. I suspect she was worried that her sons might be reverting to their wilder side. I had no such doubts. My squire, Roger, was there along with Robert and as he demonstrated to Matthew whilst in Italy, Robert had a sensible head on his shoulders. The two of them would manage the younger ones. I looked down the table and saw my sons looking enviously at the younger ones. Now they were knights and had to behave differently. Matthew's marriage had also shown them that they were ready to become family men themselves.

While others had always enjoyed feasts and parties as a chance to be loud and exuberant, I preferred to sit and watch. William was the same. My brother Alfred enjoyed both singing and dancing. Eirwen had long ago given up on persuading me to dance. It was Alfred and his Gascon wife, Eleanor, who led the dancing. Eleanor was vivacious and full of life. It was they made more people dance. I wondered if Matthew and Thomasina would have danced. As more people took to the floor so those of us watching began to smile. My father had been like me and watched rather than participated. My mother was well used to watching.

It was she who turned to Eirwen and said, "I see that Roger is a good dancer. Look he has made the delicate flower that is Margaret take to the floor and see, how she blooms."

Margaret was the quiet one. She barely spoke in any case but since her mother had died so suddenly, she had almost become dumb. Roger was a smiler. He had come to me to become a knight and he had embraced the world of Stockton completely. As my squire, he was my contact with the castle and the town. He was immensely popular and I liked that he had taken it upon himself to dance with Margaret. I saw then that she had dancing skills. As a young lady, her mother had ensured that she had been taught to dance, as had my girls, but she looked to be a natural. My mother was right, Margaret looked like she had been a bud but as she was whirled around the floor by Roger of Whorlton, she blossomed.

I was so bemused by the dancing that I had eyes for nothing else and it was sharp-eyed William who leaned over and said, "I have never seen Myfanwy look so radiant and Matthew's squire looks to have gained much from his foray into Italy."

My daughter and the son of Joseph, my captain of sergeants, were dancing on the opposite side of the floor and I had not seen them. They, too, were smiling but there was more. They looked to be dancing closer than the other couples. It was verging on the unseemly. The dances were all well prescribed with a series of steps and arm movements. It looked to me as though Robert and Myfanwy were subverting them.

William knew me well and he sensed my disquiet, "Brother, this is not the time for a lecture. It is a feast and these weddings and the fine food will expunge all the deaths we have endured of late. See how your other daughter Eleanor is dancing with her cousin Geoffrey and they, too, are not following the traditions of the dance. They are young, let them enjoy themselves."

I turned, "We were never like that."

"No, brother, but our bold brother Alfred was and he has set the tone. You have raised your children well. See how Alfred and Samuel are smiling and enjoying the dances. They see nothing untoward."

Had William not drawn my attention to Myfanwy then I would have seen nothing. I suspected that he regretted telling me. He was in the favourable position of being the favourite uncle of all the children in the family. He had always enjoyed all the pleasures without any of the pain. It did not spoil the evening but it made me stop drinking and Eirwen noticed.

"What is amiss, husband?"

"Robert and Myfanwy, are they not dancing too close?"

"Have you no eyes, my husband? When Matthew was away in Italy did you not notice the tears shed by our daughter?"

"I thought it was a concern for her cousin or some ailment of young women."

She laughed and placed a soft hand on mine, "In the world of war you are the master but all else is a mystery to you. Since the return of young Robert, she has smiled more. She made as many preparations for this wedding as Annie and Thomasina. I think that they are in love. When we visited Egglesclif I saw the closeness of the two of them."

I shook my head, "Pah! What nonsense! She barely knows him."

She sighed, "When you were away and Myfanwy was younger, we lived here at Stockton and she and Eleanor played with Robert and the other children. They were friends. I do not know when it began but something changed and they became close. When Matthew was given Redmarshal Myfanwy began to take more care of the clothes that she wore and how she looked. Whenever Matthew came to the castle she visibly brightened and it was not for her cousin but his squire."

It all made sense and explained the closeness I saw before me but I could not believe that I had been so blind as to miss it. If this had been war then men would have died because of my lack of vigilance. I shook my head. My reaction was one of pride. Robert was a good squire. Matthew had told me of the courage he had shown in Italy and on the ship home. His father was a good man. Yet Robert was a squire. He could not marry and he was not close to knighthood. My wife did not understand such things. I could not and would not oppose the liaison but it would pose problems for me.

Now that I was aware of what was before my eyes, I saw that when they returned to the table for refreshment their hands touched longer than the other dancers. When they sat, they were as close as two warriors in a shield wall.

I turned to Eirwen, "I see that you are right and your words are true but Robert is a squire, and a young one at that. Roger is closer to knighthood than Robert."

She laughed, "See, husband, your squire is a man and Margaret is a woman. Marriage is infectious. Today, in church, you were so concerned with Thomasina and Matthew that you saw nothing else. Our daughter and Margaret saw, today, that they have a chance of marriage and happiness."

"Roger? Margaret?" Had someone made me temporarily blind? Why had I not seen these things?

"When you were away Margaret was sad."

"I thought that was because her father died and then her mother. She pined for her brother."

"All of that is partly true but, while you were fighting the bandits, she confided in me that her heart was set on Roger."

"You said nothing."

"I am saying it now. I did not want to take away from the marriage of Matthew and Thomasina. You know Roger is ready for spurs."

"He is but I thought another year and then…"

"Husband, I know why you procrastinate. You will need another squire and Roger is familiar. You hate change but this is right."

"You may be wrong."

"Then tomorrow, ask Roger his intentions. Let us see who is right and who is wrong." I hated when my wife spoke so confidently; it meant that she was right.

"And what of Myfanwy and Robert?"

She smiled, "You have glowered and glared for an hour, my husband. Others have seen it and both the couples, whilst they have eyes for one another will have seen it. Clear the air if only to stop you from dwelling on such matters."

She was right. I needed to clear the air. I was sure that this was just the effect of too much wine and the party. I did not sleep well and I slipped out of bed when I heard the first cock crow. The shortness of the night meant that it was just past Matins but the sun was peering over the eastern horizon. I dressed in my plainer, more comfortable clothes. The only ones awake in the castle were the night watch and the bakers who were beginning their task of baking bread for the castle. It was a monumental task. By mid-morning they would have finished baking and would start on the next day's dough. It was a comforting circle. Even Edgar was still abed. I left the castle and walked across the bailey. I saw the faces of the sentries as they peered down at me. I ascended the town gate. Here was where the watch would gather each night between their patrols. There was a brazier for warmth. Even in summer, there could be a chill to the night air.

It was Garth of Rus' Worthy who was in command. They all stood when I entered, "Good morning, my lord, yesterday went well. Sir Matthew has won a beautiful bride."

"That he has." Garth's words, whilst well-meaning, did nothing to put my mind at rest.

I went to the door that led to the fighting platform. "You are up early, my lord, is there a problem?"

I smiled, "No Garth, probably too much food. I will walk alone around the walls." My tone told them to give me space. I left the guardroom and felt the chill from the early morning. I wrapped my cloak tightly about myself and went to the river gate.

The water was black and still. There was a current but it barely rippled the water. A movement on the south bank told me that a creature was hunting. It was probably a fox. In the woods on the other side of the river, I heard the shriek of an owl as it ended the life of some creature. Life went on. The men in the guardhouse cared not who danced with whom. They had their own problems. I cared for all my men but such was the parlous nature of life in the borderlands that they could be called to war at any time and death would be just a mistake away. What did it really matter who my daughter married so long as she was happy? I was not Lady Mary. I did not give as much thought to rank. The grandsire of our family, so William told me, had been a lowly warrior who was elevated to be a housecarl and given Norton by King Henry. I had to judge a man by his actions and not his blood. Robert was a good man. My wife was right, Roger was ready for his spurs. I would just have to find another squire and if I did not then I had men at arms enough to take on that role. Whorlton was one of my manors and Sir Geoffrey, Roger's father, was a farmer and not a warrior. I would knight Roger but I would first ask him his intentions. I felt a little aggrieved that he had not spoken to me.

I returned to the hall and as I entered smelled the fresh bread. Edgar was in the hall, and he looked up in surprise when I came in cloaked. "My lord, is aught amiss?"

"No, Edgar. I just needed air. Tell the servants that I am pleased with their efforts yesterday. All went well and that is good."

"They enjoyed it, my lord. It was the finest of Midsummer feasts that any can remember and the women-folk all like a good wedding. Yesterday they had two. When they are happy men are happy. Weddings are good for the manor, my lord." He smiled, "I will fetch you food. The beef was good yesterday and there are some choice cuts left. I will bring you some with the first of the bread."

My steward was pointing me in the same direction as my wife. I sat at the table. The servants brought in platters with cold meats, cheese and, of course, freshly baked bread. Maud, one of the older servants said, "Would you like some ham to be fried, my lord?"

"No, Maud, Edgar is bringing me some beef."

"The brides looked lovely yesterday, my lord. Sir Matthew has done well and we are all happy for Jack and Annie. We shall miss them, but they have a chance of a new life and that is good for the young, is it not?"

Everything I heard was clarifying my thoughts. When the beef came, I sliced a hunk of manchet and smeared it with butter. The bread was almost hot and the butter soaked into the bread. I put some thick slices of beef on the bread and then topped it with a spoonful of hot mustard. Edgar knew I liked it. I had enjoyed the food at the feast but this simple fare was just as good and it put me in a better mood.

The Ripples of Rebellion

The hall filled. Dick, William, Alfred and my sons were followed by their squires. Roger raced in as they were filling their platters, "I am sorry I am late, Earl, I was late abed and…"

"No matter, Roger, I have already eaten. Find food yourself and then you and I can speak." I saw his face cloud but he nodded and headed for the ale.

Even had Eirwen not said anything the manner of the entrance of Myfanwy would have told me something was in the air. She was always a late riser but she entered hot on the heels of Robert. Both were oblivious to my scrutiny but they were laughing and smiling. It was as though they had not a care in the world. My knights sat close to me and the conversation was about Egglesclif. The day would see them all return to their manors but the next day they would return to the task of growing a manor. Matthew was popular. He always had been. My sons saw their future in his. While Samuel had Redmarshal he had yet to win a wife and Alfred was waiting for his manor. They were happy to work knowing that they would be given as much help in the future.

William was the one who put a damper on the mood, "I hear that the king is unwell." We looked at him and he smiled, "I make a point of speaking to every visitor. Peter the Potman has an uncle who is a sailor. He told Peter the Potman of the illness and he told me. We need the heir to the throne back in England."

Robert had joined us, "We have the Regent. Richard of Cornwall holds the reins of the kingdom."

William said, "He has lost his son. That has to have an effect." He looked at Henry and Geoffrey who were laughing with my daughter and Margaret. The effect of a dead family member had changed their lives.

When I finished, I rose and Roger had clearly been watching me. He stood and followed as I headed for my solar. When I reached it, I said, "Come and sit."

He did so but looked nervous, "What have I done to offend you, my lord?"

I smiled, "Nothing." His eyes told me that he did not believe me. "First, let me say that you have done all that was required of you as a squire." The fear on his face was that he was going to be dismissed. "I promised that I would make you a knight and you are ready. I will give you your spurs at summer's end."

He beamed, "Thank you, my lord. I feared…"

"You feared what, Roger?"

He shook his head, "It matters not, my lord."

"Now I will speak to you as head of this family, the Warlord's family. Now that you are to be a knight what are your intentions?"

"Intentions, my lord?"

I sighed, "We have fought together, and shed blood. There should be no secrets. You know of what I speak."

He sighed, "Margaret." I nodded. "We were afraid to speak before."

"Why, am I such an ogre?"

"No, my lord, but…Margaret is the daughter of an earl."

"And?"

He looked dumbfounded, "I thought it made a difference."

"Then you have not learned much about this family. Does my cousin reciprocate your feelings?"

He smiled, "Aye, she does. We have grown close and my time on campaign has confirmed her feelings."

"Then one step at a time. I shall knight you at summer's end. That will give you the chance to pass all your tests. You and I shall then ride to Whorlton and see your father. I would have you as lord of the manor. If you still feel the same way, then that will be the time you can ask him for permission to wed."

He spoke in a small voice, "And you, my lord, do I have your permission?"

"I will speak to Margaret. Go about your duties. Tomorrow, we return to hard work at Egglesclif. Ask Margaret to join me."

I composed myself. It was easier talking to a squire rather than a young woman. I was not comfortable with such matters. The small knock on the door told me it was her. "Enter."

"Roger said you wished to speak to me."

I nodded, "Since your father died, I am head of the family, Roger has told me of his desire for you to be his bride. What are your views?"

"I thought I would die a spinster until you returned from Evesham, my lord. When you were all away we feared for you and for ourselves. Roger returned and, well, he was different somehow. He seemed confident and he noticed me. We began to talk and I felt my heart soar. When my father died it was Roger and not my mother who gave me comfort. We grew close. When we feasted to celebrate Samuel and Alfred's knighthood it drove us even closer together and we began to speak of marriage but he is a squire."

"And I have promised him his spurs by summer's end." She leapt to her feet and threw her arms around me. I smiled and hugged her back. "We still have to convince Lady Matilda and Roger's father that this is the right thing but…."

"Your mother knows of my feelings, my lord, and she approves. She likes Roger."

The Ripples of Rebellion

I was stunned. Eirwen had known and now I discovered that my mother was part of the conspiracy too. When I descended the news had spread and I was greeted by a sea of smiling faces. Eirwen said, "And now Robert and Myfanwy?"

I shook my head, "One crisis at a time, please. He is a squire and a young one at that. There is no urgency." She cocked an eyebrow. "If you wish to tell Myfanwy that I do not object then you may. We still have a manor to build and there are still rumblings from the rebels."

She kissed me, "You are a good father and a fine man. I will do as you ask."

The Ripples of Rebellion

Chapter 17

Henry Samuel

The Summer Storm

Although I was not approached by either my daughter or Robert there was a tacit understanding that they could court. In any event, they had little opportunity to do anything about their feelings as Robert was too busy at Egglesclif. We all were as we toiled to finish the hall, the walls and the houses. The two new brides had added urgency to the matter. Annie had a sensible head on her shoulders but sharing a home with four men was not the best of starts to a marriage. By the end of July, the hall was finished and furnished and we had a small warrior hall. At the most, it would accommodate just ten men but as Matthew only had three there was plenty of room. With Will and Leif's houses finished all that we had to do was to build a wall and a quay. We had decided that the river was a good way to travel. A quay would facilitate the journey.

William and I did not spend as long there as we had in the early days and my knights also returned to their manors. In the case of Alfred and Samuel, it was to continue to train their squires and, in my case, it was to find a replacement for Roger. Two young girls from the town offered their services as house servants to Matthew. They were friends of Annie and they saw the opportunity for a new life. The three unmarried men who were part of Matthew's retinue were also an inducement. Our world was comfortable. The king had not deteriorated any further but so long as The Lord Edward and his brother were in the Holy Land there was a threat from rebels who still lurked in every corner of the kingdom.

Roger's training was almost complete. Summer's end, for us, would be on the 1st of September. By then most of the harvest would be in and the onset of autumn seemed a good time to give him his spurs. The equinox was chosen as the day. It was the time of year when the days and nights were the same length and with crops gathered in there would be harmony in the land.

That harmony was shattered in the middle of August when a three-day storm of Biblical proportions threatened to undo our hard work. The storm had thunder and lightning as well as torrential rain. Houses were damaged, rooves were blown off and we just thanked God that no one died in the storms. Crops were flattened but, if we had better weather for the rest of the month, then the damage would be limited and we might still be able to save some of the harvest. The problem was that the river rose. The rain at the headwaters of the Tees flooded down the river. The water completely submerged the new quay at Egglesclif but the hill on which Matthew now lived was safe and dry. The farmers who used the bottom lands close to Preston lost all as the waters washed away their hard work. I would have to help them out from our reserves.

For two weeks after the storm, we did not have a moment to ourselves. The whole valley was forced to pitch in and help. Neighbour helped neighbour and the ladies of my knights spent as long out of doors as any labourer. The result was that by the end of August, we had order and we could return to the matter of a knighthood for Roger. The equinox could still be the day he won his spurs. The rider from Whorlton shattered that peace.

It was a priest who rode in on the sorriest sumpter I had ever seen. Roger recognised him immediately, "Father Abelard! What brings you all the way from Whorlton?"

The distance was just fourteen miles but the castle lay on a hill and was close to the moors. It was not a journey to be undertaken lightly, especially not on roads that had been damaged by the storm.

He dismounted in my bailey. Father Albert, recognising a fellow priest, raced over. The Whorlton priest almost fell from his saddle and he dropped to his knees, "Earl Henry, disaster, treachery and murder!"

Father Albert had a flask attached to his belt. It contained aquae vitae, "Here, brother, drink this and compose yourself. Your words make no sense."

The priest drank a little from the flask and coughed. I helped him to his feet. He did not relinquish his hold on it but said to Roger, "Your family is slaughtered. Your father, all, lie dead."

"My four brothers are killed?"

He nodded. "This is not the place for such words. Come within." I turned to Alfred, "Ask Joseph and Robert the Fletcher and my brother to join me in the Great Hall."

We swept into the hall, Roger supporting the clearly shaken priest. The women of the house all looked at us askance but Edgar was always calm under crisis and he could see that this was a crisis. "I will fetch refreshments, lord, and have a chamber prepared."

"Thank you, Edgar. Now sit and tell us calmly everything." William had heard the noise and he had a wax tablet in his hand.

The priest took a deep breath, "Your father, as you know, was a farmer. We had neither men at arms nor archers for we needed none.

The Ripples of Rebellion

The manor was prosperous. He and your brothers made the manor a rich and fertile one."

I nodded, "The income is amongst the best that we take."

"Sir Giles de Meynell of Upleatham is a soldier and not a farmer. He fought for the rebels in the civil war and lost his other manor which is in Warwickshire. There was a rumour that a cousin died in Italy and the manor was left to him. He came to Upleatham and was less than happy with the land. Your father thought that the man expected more from the manor. It had been neglected for many years. His other manor was richer. In the spring his farm suffered from a disease to his pigs and cows. They all died. He came to Sir Geoffrey to ask for help. That was when we heard his story. Sir Geoffrey was a kind man but he knew that Sir Giles was not a good farmer. He gave him two sheep and two pigs to breed. He saw it as a gesture that would grow if the animals were husbanded. That did not suit Sir Nicholas who demanded more. Sir Geoffrey said that the animals would be a new start." He shook his head. "The knight left but it was with mutterings. It is now clear that he wanted more. Sir Geoffrey thought no more about it until two days ago when a column of riders came at dawn and…" I could see him struggling to speak the unspeakable but I had already guessed the end of the tale.

Edgar had brought ale and food. The food was not needed. "Take your time, Father Abelard. You have told us already that Sir Geoffrey and his four other sons are dead. Speak on."

"Every man on the farm and many in the village were slain. Some boys escaped as did some women. The animals were all collected and driven off. The granaries were emptied and every grain of food was taken. That they left the castle whole was a miracle."

William asked, "The castle was not defended?"

"Sir Geoffrey had no warriors and the gates were always open. The castle was a place to sleep."

"And how did you escape?"

I fled to the church in the village and hid. I feared for my life. I had been a witness. They searched the church but did not find me. I waited until they had gone. By then it was almost dark and I found the bodies." He turned to Roger, "I did not, nay, I could not bury them for I had to get here. I headed north. The farmer at Crathorne, who was a friend of Sir Geoffrey, loaned me this horse and here I am."

I patted the priest's back and he drank more ale. I turned to William, "De Meynell?"

"His family fought for de Montfort. He is distantly related to de Vescy but they are not a rich family. Upleatham has no castle and is a small and mean manor. It lies to the far side of Guisborough and the Priory."

"Yet he has enough men to sack a castle." I turned back to the priest, "How many men did he have?"

"A lot."

I sighed; a soldier would have known the make up of the raiders. "Mailed, horsed, archers?"

"There were some mailed men and they had many horses. They have more now for they took every animal that Sir Geoffrey owned. They had archers and crossbowmen."

I would get no better information. Alfred and my two captains had joined us while the priest was speaking. Alfred said, "We must ride to Upleatham and impose the king's justice upon these monsters."

I shook my head, "It is not as easy as that. The land is under the rule of the Sheriff of Yorkshire. William, take a man at arms as an escort and ride to York. Tell the Sheriff, Roger Lestrange, what has happened and tell him that I will take men to recover the property of Sir Geoffrey. Seek his advice."

"Father, you cannot allow them to get away with this. You must punish them."

"And I do not have that authority, Alfred, this is a dangerous time. It would not take much to reignite the embers of rebellion. This man is a Montfortian. What he has done is beyond the pale but we must do it all legally. It is clear that he brought men from Warwickshire. It sounds like a warband. If we make the wrong move then it could begin the rebellion once more. I am the king's man and I must act accordingly. This is not about vengeance but upholding the law." I turned to Joseph and Robert, "I want half of the men ready to leave by dawn. The rest will guard here. If the rebels have planned this raid it could be to lure us from Stockton."

"Aye, my lord."

"Alfred, ride to your brother, I need him and his men. Bring them back before dark."

"Aye, Father, and I am sorry, I should learn to trust you."

"Roger, ride to Elton and Hartburn. I need my brother and Sir Richard."

Eirwen and the rest of the ladies had gathered in a cluster. All thoughts of the marriage of Margaret and Roger were pushed to the backs of our minds. The ladies always deferred to me in matters of war and this was a war. Roger was silent and I saw his hands clench and unclench. I put my arms around his shoulders, "I am sorry, Roger.

Those words are inadequate at the best of times but now they seem almost insulting."

"I could have been there, my lord. Instead, I chose the warrior's way."

"And if you had stayed then you, too, would have died. They might have left more bodies but you would be dead. In a perfect world, farmers would not need warriors to guard their lands. In a well-governed country then there would be law and such things would not happen. The rebellion, led by de Montfort, has upset the balance and with a king who is ill, a regent who is grieving and an heir who is absent, it has all the makings of a perfect storm. I will need your help, Roger, for this will require delicate handling. Now do as I ask and ride to my brother and my cousin."

"Aye, my lord."

I walked to the waiting ladies. They had not heard all but knew from the voices and actions that something serious was amiss. I told them all that I knew. Eirwen put her arm around Margaret who began to sob. All thoughts of a ceremony of knighthood and wedding were forgotten. Moreover, she had never met Roger's family and now she never would. Both had lost their parents.

My mother, as matriarch said, "And, my son, what are your plans?"

"William is riding, even as we speak for York. Durham is close but it is the Sheriff who has jurisdiction south of our river. I will recover the animals and then deliver those who committed the crime to the Sheriff."

"They will fight."

I knew that they would, too, but I wanted as little worry as possible. "They may. My problem is a delicate one. There are still rebels out there and I fought at Evesham. I can think of no other mesne from this part of England who did so. Those from the Tyne fought for de Montfort. Their leader is on the crusade but there are still dispossessed lords who will seek any chance they can to hurt those they see as the victors."

My sister, Eleanor, said, "And who will you take? Which knights?"

I knew why she asked and I took her hands in mine, "I will take bachelor knights once more and that means your sons will go to war with mine. My brother and three cousins will guard my land but I will take half of the men at arms and archers from their manors." I knew that Thomas, Matthew and Dick would want to come but I needed a strong valley and, led by my brother, we would have that.

She nodded, "Look after my boys, brother. They are all that I have left."

The Ripples of Rebellion

My wife put her arm around her shoulder, "No, for you will always have family."

My two messengers had ridden with urgency and I waited until all four knights had arrived. I gathered them in my solar. I said to Roger, "I will let you tell the squires of this tragedy. Edgar has food ready and I want you all to eat." I was giving them something to do and to keep Roger's mind occupied.

"Yes, my lord."

Once alone I told them all the details. Alfred and Roger had not had time to tell them all. My plans were firmer now. "Brother, I leave you, Richard, Matthew and Thomas to watch my land but I want your best men at arms and archers. I will use just my sons for this task. You will need to watch Redmarshal for my son, brother. From what William has told me there are rumblings from rebels to the west of us. Elton, Hartburn and Redmarshal would be the places they would attack if this is part of some cunning plan to reignite the rebellion."

Dick said, "Surely not."

I held my fingers up to illustrate my points, "The king is ill, the Regent grieves and the king's sons are in the Holy Land. We know that the rebels are still active. Henry of Almain's death shows that it is not over. I intend to tread carefully. We will ride, first to Whorlton. The dead need to be buried. Then I will ride to Upleatham." While I had waited, I had studied William's maps and now had a better idea of the geography of that part of Yorkshire. "I will move as though we are in enemy territory and look for ambushes. The dead are dead and haste will not bring them back."

Dick said, "Henry Samuel, I do not know the lands well but surely it will be a shorter journey to Upleatham than Whorlton."

"You are right but I have thought this through. Firstly, the dead need to be buried but, more importantly, Sir Giles will know that the manor is mine. Which way will he expect us to come? For he will know that we will come."

My brother said, "Along the track by the Tees towards the Red Scar."

"And there he could wait in ambush in a land which he knows and we do not. There are marshes and bogs that way. Let us go to Whorlton, bury the dead and then approach Upleatham from a direction he is not expecting. If he is waiting in ambush we may be able to take his home and then give the ambushers a surprise."

My plans were both logical and realistic. They nodded their agreement and we then spent some time identifying the men I would take.

The Ripples of Rebellion

Alfred said, "I will visit with Thomas and tell him. I will return here with his men before dark. Dick, can you ride to your brother? We will not take his men but Matthew must know that work on his manor now takes second place."

"I will." Dick nodded.

Samuel said, "I will ride back to my manor. I fear that I will only be bringing a handful of men."

"That matters not. We have plenty from Stockton, Elton and Hartburn. Are Henry and Geoffrey ready?"

Alfred nodded, "Aye, Barnard was like a rebirth for Henry."

Samuel said, "And Geoffrey has changed. I am confident that his blood will out and he will show his true nature."

"Just so long as they do not shed their own blood. I do not want to lose men on this quest. It is not a vengeance raid but the protection of the weak. Roger's father was a good farmer but I should have knighted Roger before now. If Sir Giles had seen a strong hand and defended walls he would not have risked an attack. My procrastination has caused this." I shook my head. "The priest said that Sir Geoffrey left his gates open and unguarded! What is the point of a castle if it is not defended? Our gates are open but they are guarded."

My brother smiled, "Aye, Henry Samuel, but we were trained by Sir Thomas of Arsuf. Roger will make it a stronger burgh when he is knighted."

There was much to do and after the three knights had left I went with Alfred to the warrior hall. With my two captains, we chose the men we would take. "I want only mounted men. The men who will be joining us from the other manors will all be mounted. We need speed. Do we have any men who know the land?"

Robert the Fletcher nodded, "Will of Stokesley grew up near there. He lived at Newton which is close to Roseberry."

"Then he will lead our scouts. We leave at dawn and I would be at Whorlton before Terce. Once there he and his scouts can head for Upleatham. I want to know what we are getting into before we commit men to battle."

Joseph knew Roger well and having a son who was a squire was sympathetic to such men, "How is Master Roger taking this?"

"How does any man take the loss of his father? I know that when Sir Thomas lost his father, Sir Samuel, at the Battle of Arsuf, along with the other knights of the valley, it was the making of him. It could go either way. We will need to watch him for I do not want any reckless act of revenge to end his life."

Alfred nodded, "Aye, Father, or defeat our quest."

The Ripples of Rebellion

Despite all that needed to be done I managed to get some sleep that night but, of course, I rose early. Others were of the same mind and the Great Hall was where I gathered with my sons and squires to eat. The breakfast might need to keep us going all day. We would not have the luxury of beds and servants to cook food for us. We would have to tighten our belts. We ate in silence. I knew that each of those who ate with me had different thoughts racing through their heads. Roger's would be the easiest to understand. He would be burying his family and seeking retribution. Alfred and Samuel would feel the weight of responsibility on their shoulders. They had been chosen over much more experienced knights. Their squires would also see the opportunity to test their mettle. This would be nothing like the bandit campaign at Barnard Castle. This was righting a wrong that had hurt us.

The priest, Father Abelard, was with us but I had him safely protected at the rear. We clattered through the gates as the sun broke in the east. There was no storm but the day was filled with angry clouds as the bad weather threatened from the west. It seemed ominous. The skies matched our mood. We crossed the river and passed the burnt-out manor of Thornaby and then we headed for Stainton. Will of Stokesley had chosen two camp brothers and they were far ahead of us. We rode in silence towards the high ground that was the hills. The road was a quiet one and the only sound we heard was that of our hooves and horses. We did not gallop but we made good time.

Ned Long Nose was the scout who rode back and his face was sombre, "We have found the castle." He glanced at Roger before he continued, "The dead lie where they fell. We chased away the carrion and Will is covering the bodies."

Roger's face was like white ice but anger burned in his eyes. He said nothing.

"Were there any people?"

He shrugged, "There were people in the village and hiding in the church but they did not approach, my lord."

That was understandable. The last time armed men had entered the village, their men had died.

As we neared the castle my heart sank. In the short time since Roger had come to live with us, the castle had deteriorated even further and was now dilapidated. The mortar had corroded over the years and some stones had fallen from the walls. The ditches were filled with rubbish. One of the gates hung at an angle. That could have been the result of the attack, but I suspected that Sir Geoffrey had not deemed it important enough. I dismounted in the bailey. There were more farm implements and tools than anything. I saw no weapons. Roger and I approached the

The Ripples of Rebellion

bodies. Will pulled back the cloak to reveal the butchered body of Sir Geoffrey.

Roger dropped to his knees, "There was no need, my lord, for such savagery. My father and brothers were gentle souls."

Will said, "We found the bodies of the ladies, too, my lord. They were within the hall." He shook his head as he spoke. He was hiding something and I guessed what it was. Roger was no fool and he ran into the hall before I could stop him. He found his brothers' wives. He pulled the blankets from them and saw that they had been abused.

I turned, "Father Abelard."

The priest entered the hall and when he saw the bodies he dropped to his knees and made the sign of the cross, "Dear God."

I knew the answer but asked the question anyway, "You did not know?"

He shook his head, "I saw the men were dead and I assumed the women had fled, along with the children."

Roger turned to me, "My brothers had families. Are there more bodies upstairs?" he raised his hands and screamed. "Will this horror never end?"

Will ran up the stairs and when he emerged again, he shook his head, "The rooms have been ransacked but there are none there, living or dead."

I turned to the priest, "The villagers know you and they are hiding in the church. Discover what happened to them and the children."

"Yes, my lord." He shook his head, "I am sorry, Master Roger."

I saw that Roger was fighting to hold back the tears. He merely nodded.

"Joseph, take our men to the cemetery and have graves dug. We will ride to Upleatham on the morrow when we have discovered the fate of these bairns."

"Aye, my lord."

"How many were there, Roger?"

"At the last count, I had four nephews and two nieces. The eldest would be twelve and the youngest, three."

I did not say it but the eldest was lucky not to have been slain with his father and grandfather.

The dead were carried reverently to the cemetery. It was lined with yew trees and my men had dug the graves neatly so that they would be shaded by them.

Father Abelard returned from the church with news gathered from the survivors, "The villagers saw the children taken but with their men dead they could do nothing about it. One of them, a Gammer, thinks she heard the word hostages."

I looked at my sons, "That makes sense. They know that I would not risk children's lives. These men are truly animals."

It took hours to inter the bodies and pile the soil on the graves. Each of them was given the respect that the dead deserved. Poor Roger could contain his grief no longer and he openly wept. I saw hardened warriors barely holding back their feelings. When all was done we retired to the castle. My men tidied it up as best they could and all traces of blood were removed. We cooked the food we had in our saddlebags, but no one was in the mood to eat.

"What is your plan, Father? Still the same or have the hostages made you change it?"

"I think, Samuel, that we send in our archers to the manor to scout out the building. If there are hostages there and they have not left a large number of guards, we may risk a rescue, but I will not take a chance on losing the last of Roger's family."

There was silence. My men and archers had camped outside to give the hall to us. Henry and Geoffrey had been shocked into silence and my sons were working out what we might do the next day.

I said to Roger, "Do you still wish to be a knight?"

He gave me a determined flash of his eyes, "More than ever. I will have my nieces and nephews in my care..." his eyes softened a little. I could see that something had occurred in his head, "Margaret...I cannot bring her here now."

Samuel said, "You misjudge her. She is of the Warlord's blood. She wishes to be wed to you with all that brings. It will be hard..." he shook his head, "I cannot imagine what I would do if Alfred, Myfanwy and Eleanor had all been murdered but I think I would find a way. You will be a knight and the lord of this manor. You will have a hard task ahead of you but when you do it will be a memorial to the dead."

I nodded approvingly. My son was come of age.

Before we retired for the night my sons and I met with Will and Robert the Fletcher. I explained what I wanted and asked for their opinion. Will nodded, "We can get close to the hall, my lord. It is many years since I was there but there is no high wall and it is not a castle."

Robert said, "And if we do find that the hostages are lightly held, what do we do?"

"Make sure that their guards cannot escape. We will surround the hall and you will use your bows to eliminate the guards."

My Captain of Archers shook his head and drew his dagger, "It is better that we have half of the archers watching and the other half close in and use these." He gestured his knife towards the bailey, "I know that we are the law, my lord, but these men have gone beyond the law into the darkness of anarchy. The murders were bad enough but the rape…"

"Very well, then, we have a plan. I wish to be there by dawn. Are the roads ones we can travel at night?"

Will said, "They twist and they turn but they are flat. The manor and priory at Guisborough are the only large places that we pass."

Alfred asked, "Why did the lord of the manor allow the raiders to pass?"

"It is de Brus land and he is an absent lord. He spends more time in Scotland than in his English lands."

Will said, "Aye, and the road to Upleatham does not pass close to the priory."

"And the horses?"

Joseph said, "Most have enjoyed the rest they were given in the afternoon, but Dick and Ned have animals that need a rest."

"Then they can stay when we leave. Along with Father Abelard, they will be the ones who protect what remains of the villagers," I looked at Roger, "until the new lord of the manor comes."

He nodded and I saw his shoulders and back become straighter, "I thought I would have the luxury of time. When I won my spurs, I thought that I would be able to enjoy time with my bride and learn from Matthew."

Samuel shook his head, "Each manor has different problems, Roger. Matthew's were different from mine and yours…" He waved an arm at the castle, "You have a castle to repair and a village to heal."

"And you shall have all the help that you need but first we have hostages to recover and rebels to hunt."

The plight of the youngsters was all the inducement my men needed to rise early and eat breakfast on the road. Although our archers were still ahead of us, we rode in the night with the tails of their horses just paces before us. We passed around Guisborough. There was no lord in residence but who knew its sympathies? The de Brus family was an important one in Scotland and while King Alexander appeared as a friend to us, who knew what politicking was going on? Caution was our watchword.

Upleatham was a tiny hamlet. I could understand Sir Giles' frustration, having lost the prize that was a southern manor and replaced with the kernel that was Upleatham. It made me even more suspicious about his motives. If there were few men at the manor then it would confirm my suspicions. He was seeking more than a few animals. Could this be the spark of rebellion? Had the murder of Henry of Almain given the remaining rebels hope?

We reached the village before the sun had risen. The smell and sound of the sea towards the Red Scar told us how close we were to the ocean and the mouth of the river that passed my home. I let my scouts do what they did best and we tethered the horses in the trees. We armed ourselves. None of us would wear helmets. This would not be a battle. If the low walls around the hall were well defended, then I would need to use words to win the day. If there were a few men within then they would not be mailed, and clear vision and speed would be needed. As I stood with my men at arms, knights and squires, no words were spoken, and we watched the darkness turn to light as the new day began.

The sun had risen and the day was alive when Robert the Fletcher and Will came to me and waved me further into the trees so that we could speak. "My lord, they have two men on the gate. Alan climbed a tree to spy within. They have few guards. I think that there are no more than eight men. There may be a few more we have not seen in the house but my guess is ten or twelve men is the most that we can expect."

"Thank you, Will, so we can take out the men at the gates and then assault?"

Robert shook his head, "They will slam the gates shut, my lord. Even a handful could make us bleed. The walls are just the height of a man but..."

I knew what he meant. "You have an idea?"

"There is a road that leads to the village. If we had someone walking down the road, they could distract the guards at the gate and four of my archers could creep along the ditch and take them."

"They would bar the gates and kill any man who looks like a warrior."

"Aye, my lord, but a youth, a squire who has no beard and no weapons, might appear to be a curiosity rather than a threat."

I looked at Robert. He knew the history of my nephews, "Master Henry or Master Geoffrey?"

He nodded, "Master Geoffrey would be my choice for he has a slighter build and looks like a youth."

"You know what you ask?"

"I do, my lord, but I have spoken to both boys. They are not the same ones Joseph dragged kicking and screaming into Stockton. They are ready and we will have bows on the men at the gates. If a blade is drawn, then the sentries will die." He paused, "You asked me for my opinion, my lord."

The Ripples of Rebellion

"I did. Send your men to the ditches while it is still dark and have my sons and their squires come to me." Left alone I wondered what my friend Richard would have said. I was risking the life of one of his sons. It was as though his words appeared inside my head. Of course, he would want them to take the chance for the lives of innocents depended upon them.

The four appeared and I saw questions on their faces. I saw what Robert meant. Despite the fact that he was the older, Geoffrey did not have the confident gait of his brother. Henry had become bigger. We had little time to waste on empty words and so I explained what I wanted, "So, Geoffrey, Robert the Fletcher thinks that this task should be appointed to you, but I will not order any man to risk his life. Will you do it? You will have to lose all your weapons save for a knife you can conceal in your boot and you will need to concoct a story should they question you."

"I will do it, Uncle. I owe it to you, my dead father and those children. Henry has shown that he has the blood of the Warlord in his veins and this is my chance too." He took off his coif and baldric, handing them to his brother. "I will say that I am a runaway," he smiled, "I know what that is like. I will ask for shelter and food."

I smiled; he would do, "All you need is to make them draw close to you. There will be archers with blades ready to end their lives."

Samuel said, "And your only task is to distract them and draw their eyes to you. There will be no need for recklessness. We will be waiting with blades ready to charge."

"I am ready."

"Then let us get into position. You must go down the road so that they do not see you slip from the woods."

"I will not let the family nor the children down."

He disappeared into the woods and we made our way to the edge of the trees. My sons went to whisper words in the ears of the men at arms who nodded. They would do all in their power to ensure that Geoffrey did not lose his life.

Now that the sun had risen I was able to study the gates. There were double gates but they only had one side open. Two men armed with swords and wearing helmets stood there. I saw what Robert had meant. One sentry was outside the open gate while the other stood ready to close it. I got the impression that they had it open for they were waiting for someone. I waved over Will of Stokesley. I put my mouth to his ear, "I think that they wait for someone. Go down the road and ambush any who comes on a horse."

He nodded and slipped off down the road.

The Ripples of Rebellion

We waited. It seemed an age but eventually we saw Geoffrey approaching. I smiled for he was acting a part. He staggered a little as though weary and about to collapse. I saw the two sentries as they stiffened. I was close enough to be able to hear them. One said, "Should I get Thomas?"

"Nah, he is a stripling and he is unarmed. Let us see what he wants."

"We could just kill him. One more death will not add much to our burden."

I knew that Robert and the archers would be drawing their bows a little. They could be at full draw and release before the men had the chance to draw their swords.

The other shook his head and shouted, clearly to someone within the walls that we could not see, "Harold, someone approaches. Be ready to help us close the gate if we need to."

A disembodied voice grumbled, "Aye, but I was about to go for breakfast. They have ham frying,"

The man who had spoken laughed, "Your stomach is too big in any case. When we are relieved, we can all enjoy the fine fare."

Geoffrey played his part well. He had adopted a slightly higher pitched voice to make him appear even younger, "Sir, I thank God that I have found sanctuary. I have run away from an evil master and not eaten these last days. Food I beg of you."

The one who wished him dead let go of the gate and walked threateningly towards Geoffrey, "Begone, beggar, try the village."

The attention of both sentries was on Geoffrey. I caught the sight of grasses and weeds in the ditch around the walls as they began to move. Geoffrey had played his part and the archers were edging along the ditch. He said, "Is it far?"

The other said, "Just half a mile. Now go."

Geoffrey gave an elaborate bow, "I thank you for your kindness."

The four archers rose like wraiths and with daggers drawn were on the two sentries who were still distracted by my nephew. They were fast but, even so, one shouted, "Harold!" His alarm was ended by a blade.

Before any could stop him, Geoffrey had put his shoulder to the gate and pushed it open. Samuel shouted, "Charge!" He ran, along with the four archers to complete the opening of the gates.

The man called Harold had been alerted and he raised his sword to hack at Geoffrey. Robert the Fletcher's arrow slammed into the side of his head. For once I was not the first to go to the aid of a kinsman. My sons and Henry surrounded Geoffrey in a heartbeat. Roger leapt after them. The gates now opened, my archers and men at arms raced for the door. The sentry's words told us that they were at breakfast. No one guarded the door to the hall and my four archers were the first within. Joseph, Roger and three men at arms followed and, before I had even reached the yard, my sons and their squires had entered.

As I stepped through the door, I heard the clash of arms and then heard Joseph's voice, "Hold Master Roger, they are all dead."

The dining hall was a mean one. It was small and crowded. I saw, in the corner, the frightened faces of Roger's kin. Roger was breathing heavily and his sword dripped blood. Inside the hall was like a slaughterhouse. I might have hoped for a prisoner but that was now a vain one.

Joseph put his arm around Roger, "Sheathe your sword and go to your family." He looked at me, "Edward and Egbert went to the kitchen." He shook his head, "I am sorry, my lord, I could not stop him. He was like a Viking berserker."

I nodded and looked over to the frightened youngsters. There were just five and I had expected six. I said, "Roger, who is missing?"

It was as though he suddenly saw them and he said, "Peter, where is Peter?"

The eldest boy, who looked to be no more than ten, said, "He is dead, Uncle. They killed him last night."

We had failed. I had hoped to save all the hostages but my delay had cost one his life.

Chapter 18

Henry Samuel

The Ambush

We discovered that Peter, who was the eldest, had tried to escape. He had not been killed out of hand but one of the sentries, armed with a crossbow, had slain him as he fled. Nicholas, the ten year old, told Roger that Peter had been going for help. "He said he would run all the way to Stockton to fetch you, Uncle. He said that the last warrior in the family would save us and he was right."

Roger went to his family and held his arms open. They all hugged him.

My voice gave the command that was needed, "Clear the bodies and let us leave this family to grieve. Pile the dead in the yard and cover them. We will not burn them yet for I do not want any to be alerted. Joseph, set sentries and then fetch the horses." I turned to Geoffrey, "That was bravely done. Your father would have been proud." I swear he grew six inches when I said those words. Samuel and his brother both patted his back.

We helped to clear the hall of the dead. One of the archers fetched a pail of water and swilled the blood from the furniture and the floor. Such had been our surprise that none of our men had been wounded. But for Roger's anger, we would have had a prisoner and an insight into the enemies' plans. The nine guards were not men at arms. They looked more like the bandits we had slain in the forest. Sir Giles was not amongst them.

We heard hooves coming down the road and the men who were piling bodies grabbed weapons or nocked arrows. It was Will who led the horse through the gates. The man who was seated atop the animal had an arrow in his upper arm and he was bleeding. "For the love of God, help me!"

Will snorted, "Had I wished you dead then you would be. I struck the muscle and not the bone. You whine like a baby."

"Well done, Will." Robert and Will took the wounded man from the back of his horse. They were none too gentle about it.

Will twisted the arrow and, as he pulled out the shaft, the man screamed. He looked at the arrow and nodded, "A fine arrow and I can use it again." I knew that the arrowhead would still be inside the arm.

The Ripples of Rebellion

Robert fashioned a piece of leather around the upper arm to stop the bleeding. He said, "Now if you answer the Earl's questions, we will be gentle when we take out the arrowhead. If not, then you will lose your arm. It is your choice." He meant his words. Digging out the arrow would render it less efficient.

"My arm!"

Roger snapped, "And what of my dead father and brothers? What of their wives?" He lurched towards the man.

Joseph stepped between them and said, over his shoulder, "Or I could let Master Roger loose on you. Perhaps he might inflict the fate of Simon de Montfort."

The man cowered, "I know little."

"Then telling us will not hurt anyone, will it? Where is Sir Giles?"

I watched his face as he debated the answer he would give me. "He is not here."

I shook my head, "This man is no good to us. Besides, we have the information that Harold gave us before he died. It will be enough."

I was lying, of course, but the man did not know that. I had used the name of one of the guards and the wounded man seemed to believe that I knew their plans already. "No, my lord, if you know already where the ambush lies then why do you need me to tell you?"

I smiled, "If you tell me then I will know if Harold was lying… and if you are foolish enough to lie as well."

His head drooped, "Lazenby. Just before the road enters the village there is a wood and he lies in wait there for he expects you from the west."

"Good, that confirms what Harold said. One more thing, is he not worried that I have not arrived yet?"

"Aye, my lord. He fears you are bringing a larger army. He is thinking about moving back here." The wound caused pain and he winced. "My lord!"

"Robert, see to his arm."

I turned, "Joseph, I need two men to guard the children." I nodded to my squire, "Roger, you should be one of them."

He shook his head, "No, my lord, I will be there…at the death."

"There may not yet be a death."

"My lord, I will be there. I care not if it costs me my spurs."

I nodded, "Then when the arrow is removed have the prisoner bound and the men can keep the door to the hall barred. For the rest, mount."

By the time the arrow had been removed from the man's arm, we were ready to leave. Robert had been gentle but without the usual aquae vitae, the pain had caused the man to pass out. As we headed towards the small bridge over the beck I tried to picture the maps William had shown me. There was a manor house at Wilton, but William de Bulmer had been a Montfortian and had lost the land. So far as I knew King Henry had yet to give the land to someone else. I wondered if the de Bulmer family had made an appeal. Many appeals had been successful; especially if the noble was English as opposed to French. Beyond Wilton lay small villages: Tollesby, Ormesby and Lazenby. There was also a Benedictine Priory. If the man had spoken truly then the ambush would be after the village and our approach, from the east, would come as a shock to them.

"Robert, I want Will at the fore. When he sees the ambush, he is to return and tell us. Your archers can dismount. I want them to flank the ambush. I will give Sir Giles the opportunity to surrender."

"My lord!"

"Roger, I must remain within the law. Sir Giles is a knight and entitled to a trial. That may be trial by combat or he may make a plea to the Sheriff but I must offer him a trial. It is the law."

"Then I will fight him."

"You cannot. You are not yet a knight." His shoulders sagged.

It was a bare six miles to the village and we stopped half a mile shy of the village. The trees through which we were passing were not thick but they did afford some cover. Will rode back and dismounted. "They have ten crossbowmen and fifteen archers," he snorted, "piss poor ones, my lord. Their bows are already strung!" There was pride in my archers. "I counted four knights and twenty men at arms. They are dismounted and have their coifs about their shoulders."

"Captain Robert."

"Dismount and tether your horses."

It was only when their horses were tethered that they strung their bows, each with a fresh string and then followed my Captain of Archers through the trees. I gave them time to get into position and then waved my men forward. I wore no helmet and my coif was about my shoulders. I would talk first.

The clattering of our hooves alerted Sir Giles and his men to our presence. He saw just knights and our squires along with Joseph approaching along the road. As we appeared their archers were already nocking arrows and their crossbowmen raised their cumbersome weapons. The warriors were raising their coifs to cover their heads. I reined in forty paces from them. There were just four of us abreast on the road with our three squires behind but I knew that the men at arms would be spread out in the woods. The attention was on those of us on the road. It was Joseph, me and my sons who were in danger but, with the best mail that was an acceptable risk.

Behind me were our three squires. They had coifs and helmets.

"Sir Giles de Meynell, I am Earl Henry of Stockton, and I am here to arrest you for the murder of Sir Geoffrey of Whorlton, his sons and their wives."

He laughed, "You are outnumbered, Earl, and my men have weapons aimed at you."

"So, you would add the murder of an earl to your crimes. I have no weapon in my hand but you have a sword ready to strike." I saw the doubt on his face. "We have the hostages. You have nothing to bargain with and we have witnesses. I have sent word to the Sheriff of Yorkshire."

The two crossbowmen who raised their crossbows were not given an order by Sir Giles. It could have been in preparation for an order or, perhaps, they thought to take matters into their own hands. Whatever the reason, when one pulled the release mechanism, half a dozen arrows flew from the woods and slammed into the two men. The bolt flew just over my shoulder and Joseph shouted, "Cowardly cur."

I held up my hand for silence, "As you can see, Sir Giles, your ambush has been ambushed and my archers are itching to end the lives of murderers and rapists. Surrender or you and your men will die here and now."

The two crossbowmen's bodies lay oozing blood. One of the knights said, "Brother, perhaps a trial might be the answer. We are surrounded."

"He is bluffing, Gurth. We would all lie dead if there were archers all around." It was clear that his own archers and crossbowmen did not share the knight's opinion. They stared around them in fear. He jabbed a finger at me, "Your family owes me blood. My cousin was slain in Italy by one of your family. I would have blood for that loss of my cousin. Earl Henry, I will have trial but trial by combat. What say you? We will let God decide the right of this. I promise that I will give you a better end than was given to my friend, the Earl of Leicester."

Samuel said, "You do not need to do this, Father."

I dismounted, "Yes I do." I took my sword out. "What weapons, Sir Giles?"

"I choose axe and dagger."

"Then I will have sword and dagger. Roger, helm me."

Roger had dismounted and he placed my open sallet on my head. It gave protection to my neck but not my face. The simple nasal was the only metal to cover my nose. He had a visored bascinet. While I had been speaking, I had studied him. He was stocky and broad. Younger by

The Ripples of Rebellion

a year or two than I was he was clearly confident. The difference was that I had fought and won at Evesham. He had fought and lost.

His men and knights formed a half circle behind him. Joseph, my sons and squires stood behind me. My men at arms remained mounted. We both knelt and I kissed the crosspiece of my sword. He did the same with his dagger.

"God give me the right. Amen."

We both said the same words but I knew that I had a clear conscience. I had never murdered.

We stood and he showed his intentions from the first blow. Even as I was rising, he was swinging his axe at my head. He intended to end this quickly. I stepped back and the axe head missed me by barely a handspan. He lunged at my face with his dagger. My open helmet was a tempting target. I flicked it away with my sword. I kept my left arm by my side. I wanted him to forget it. He swung his axe again but this time it was in a sweeping arc. I was unable to step back so I did the unexpected, I stepped forward and partly blocked the blow with my dagger. The axe head, instead of striking at my side just tore some links on the back of my hauberk. The weaponsmith would have work to do. I was so close to him that he took his chance and butted his head at me. With a visor, it would not hurt him. I jerked my head back but he still connected. I saw stars and blood spurted from my nose.

He thought he had me, "First blood and here is revenge for the Earl of Leicester and my cousin."

My eyes were streaming but I had natural reactions, honed over the years, and it was they that saved me. My dagger came up to block his dagger and sparks flew as they ground together but it bought me time. He had to step back to use his axe and as he did so I made my first offensive blow. I hacked at his leg with my sword. I did not break flesh but I did tear through links and the blow was so hard that I hurt his muscle, perhaps even a bone for he screamed. It was a muffled one from behind his visor. It stopped his blow in mid-air, and I was able to swing a second time, this time at his mittened left hand. The blow was so hard that despite the mail it broke his hand and the dagger fell to the floor.

He was losing and I said, "Yield!"

"Never! Gurth, at them!"

It was treacherous and dishonourable but it was also a mistake. As his knights and squires charged my men, my archers released arrows at his archers and crossbowmen and my men at arms spurred their horses. When the axe came at my head again, I spun. I was able to do so while his wounded leg slowed him. His axe struck air and I was able to bring

The Ripples of Rebellion

my sword across his back. The momentum of my swing and my strength smashed the weapon into his back. He sank to his knees and dropped his axe. He was without a weapon and the trial by combat was over. God had decided.

I shouted, "Enough! It is over!"

It was too late for the knights. Joseph and my sons had killed three of them and the archers slew the last knight and two of the squires. My men at arms rode down the rest. Two men at arms, three archers and the squire managed to race and mount their horses. I turned to see that my sons were unhurt and as I did Samuel shouted, "Father!"

Even as I whirled Sir Giles had taken his sword and had lunged at my unprotected back. I could not avoid the blow. The four arrows that struck him in the back were all bodkins. His sword struck my chausse as he fell dead at my feet. "So dies a snake." I sheathed my weapons and took off my helmet. I would need a new one.

Roger walked up to the body. I saw the anger on his face. He had his sword drawn and it was bloody. He raised his hand as though to mutilate his face and I put my hand on his.

"No, he is dead."

"It is not enough, not for what he did to my family."

"God will punish him and the others." The blood had stopped flowing from my nose but I knew that I looked a mess. "Fetch water, I need to be cleaned."

It was as though he saw, for the first time, my injuries, "I am sorry, my lord, of course."

Samuel said, "What do we do with the dead?"

"Take the weapons and mail from the men at arms. We will make a funeral pyre for the ones who are not knights. The knights we will bury at Upleatham."

Geoffrey said, "Why do they get special treatment, Uncle?"

"Politics, Geoffrey. If we burned them then their families might bear a grudge. If we bury them then their families can rebury them in whatever manner they choose. We did no wrong this day and I hope that by speaking first we have dampened the embers of rebellion. We will tell the Sheriff what we have done and he can let their families know." Roger returned and he washed my face. I said, "His sword is yours, Roger. Take it as payment for blood. It is a well made sword and in your hands will do good."

It took some time to do as I had asked. I sent Alfred to the Benedictine Priory where he told them what had happened. Samuel did the same in the village. I did not pursue the survivors but they were the kind of men who might cause mischief and my warning would make

The Ripples of Rebellion

everyone vigilant. It was late afternoon and the funeral pyre had burnt to embers before we left. We headed back to Upleatham. As we rode, I gave more instructions. The blow had given me a headache and I just wanted to lie down. "Samuel, ride ahead to Upleatham and tell the villagers the fate of their lord. Alfred, set a good watch this night. We have done all that we might have hoped this day. Let us not undo it with a lack of vigilance." They both nodded. "And you, Roger, have no more duties than to offer counsel and comfort to your family. I cannot conceive of the pain that they must be enduring."

Joseph said, "And you, my lord, will do nothing. Are you Atlas that carries the world upon your shoulders?"

I smiled, "My grandfather was the same. A man cannot change his nature, can he?"

Once back at the manor, I took off my mail. The spoiled links meant I would need it repaired before I went to war again. I lay down in the master bedchamber and I slept. When I woke it was dark and Geoffrey sat next to the bed with a candle.

"How are you, Uncle?"

"Better for the sleep. Why are you here?"

"Joseph said that you needed to be watched. Blows to the head can often be fatal, he said, and I was to summon help if your condition changed." He smiled, "Joseph is a good man. You are lucky to have such a loyal man serving you."

"It is not luck, Geoffrey. I was taught to treat every man as though he was a noble. I am no better than the next man." I smiled. "Anyway, I am now starving. Is there any food?"

He frowned, "There is but it has angered some of the others."

"Why?"

"They slaughtered some of the animals taken from Roger's father's manor. They were good animals. Robert said it was a sin but it would be a greater sin if we did not eat it."

"And there he is right. Let us descend."

What should have been a celebration of victory was a sombre occasion. The five survivors from Roger's family and Roger were tearful and it cast a pall on any celebration of a victory. With sentries set and the gates barred, we retired.

Roger had slept in the same room as his family. It was the hall and with a fire burning all night, it was cosy. My men tiptoed around the house preparing food for they slept on. When they woke it was after terce. While they made water the squires set the table and I was able to talk to Alfred and Samuel. Henry and Geoffrey fetched food and ale.

"Do we return to Whorlton, Father?"

The Ripples of Rebellion

I shook my head, "These children, and that is what they are, Samuel, children, will need more than the rough touch of a soldier. Your mother, grandmother and the ladies of Stockton know how to heal their hurts. However, we need to send the animals back to Whorlton and men will be needed to watch the castle until…"

Behind me, Roger said, "Until I can take over."

I nodded and gestured for him to join us, "Aye, Roger, in a world without the likes of Sir Giles there would be no need for haste but autumn will soon be here and your manor, if you still want it, needs to be ruled."

"My mind is the same, my lord, but the question is, is yours?"

I frowned, "What do you mean?"

"In the last two days I have questioned you and not behaved as I should. Do you still wish to give me my spurs?"

I sighed, "You reacted as any man would when he is hurt. When Sir Thomas returned from Arsuf such was his anger at the desecration of his grandmother's tomb that…well, we all know that tale. I will still dub you. I hope that the wedding will still go ahead."

His face fell, "Can I ask Margaret to take on this task? It is more than any lady should have to bear."

The food and ale had arrived. The children had returned from making water. I gave the slightest of nods to my nephews who took charge of the bairns and arranged them along the benches. I said to Roger, "You know that the knights of the valley have in their veins the blood and history of warriors who serve England and protect this land. That blood also runs through the women of the family. They are stronger than you think. Margaret will shoulder this burden. Indeed, she will probably relish it."

His face brightened, "Thank you, my lord, then the sooner I am knighted and married the sooner I can return to Whorlton and begin to give order to a manor whose heart has been torn from it."

"There is, Roger, a problem. You are alone. With no squire, no men at arms and no archers…"

Robert the Fletcher put food down on the table and said, "My lord, forgive my impertinence but I could not help but overhear. May I speak?"

"Of course, Robert."

"These last days have been as trying for the archers as the men at arms. We have seen sights that have made hardened men sick. Master Roger is popular. Some of the archers and men at arms would follow Master Roger when he is knighted. There are some who served Lady Margaret's father. It is not that they wish to leave you, my lord, but

The Ripples of Rebellion

there is a sense of duty which is ingrained. Will of Stokesley was an archer of the old earl. He would return to his home. There are others too. Rafe Poleaxe has a wife and a son in Stockton. He has been looking for land to farm. He thought about offering his services to Sir Matthew, but he came from Osmotherley, and this land is like the land of his home. There are three others too."

I smiled, "As much as I am loath to lose such men I am touched by their loyalty to my uncle. Tell them that I am happy for them to do so."

I had planned on leaving early but Robert the Fletcher's words meant we had to speak to the men. Roger and the five men joined me, and we worked out the best approach. It was decided that the five of them would take the animals that had been captured and not eaten and return to Whorlton. They would secure the manor and we would return to Stockton. The dubbing and the wedding would have to be hastily arranged and while that might not please the ladies I knew that it was necessary.

It was noon when we finished and we were about to leave when we heard the clatter of hooves in the yard. Hands went to weapons until Joseph shouted, "It is Master William, my lord."

We went into the yard and there was William, his escort, Bill Longsword and twelve riders I did not recognise. He dismounted and embraced me, "We left Whorlton an hour since. The Sheriff sent these men to secure the manor and help you to defeat Sir Giles. I can see that is unnecessary." He handed me a parchment, "This is his authority to do all that you did in the name of the king. He will punish the wrongdoers."

I shook my head, "There is only one who remains to be punished. He has a wounded shoulder. The rest are buried here in the manor."

William turned to the knight who was with him, "Sir Ralph, you have, it seems, a manor."

The knight dismounted, "I can see that there is a tale to tell here. Earl, if you would spare the time, I would know all. I am a young knight and this is my first manor."

"Of course. Come within."

By the time the whole story was told it was the middle of the afternoon. The manor was to have a new lord. The de Meynell family had forfeited the right to own the land. They had supported de Montfort and they had spurned the chance to redeem themselves by slaughtering Roger's family. The Sheriff was taking a stance. Sir Ralph asked three of his men to help Roger's five men take the animals to Whorlton. He had a manor to organise. We mounted our horses to return home to Stockton. Roger, Alfred, Samuel, Henry and Geoffrey were each given

The Ripples of Rebellion

a child to ride behind or, in the case of the younger children, before them. It was safer and more comforting. With a chill wind from the river, the rider's cloaks kept them warm. We had spare horses and they were led by my archers. I rode with William. Joseph and Robert followed behind. William needed more detail for his records and we paused, briefly, at the sight of the battle. The trees, leaves, rocks and the road were still blood-spattered. The blackened earth where the pyre had been still stank of death. When the autumn rains came they would wash away the evidence of the skirmish.

We passed the Benedictine Priory and headed, along the river, to take the ferry. The journey home would be shorter than the outward one.

William spoke as we rode, "The Sheriff was pleased with your prompt action. He had been less than happy when Sir Giles was given Upleatham but he was powerless to prevent it. It was done to appease the dispossessed. He confided in me that the king worsens each day and there is a rumour that the Regent has retreated into a shell of remorse. Such lack of order only encourages the rebels. He asks you to be vigilant. He has written to the Bishop of Durham to warn him too. Sir Ralph's appointment might seem hasty but Sir Giles was already seen as a threat to the stability of the county. The Sheriff is winkling out the rebels close to York but the Tees is a different matter."

"Thank you, brother." I said, over my shoulder, "And with men taken from Stockton to serve at Whorlton and Egglesclif, we are not in a position to be overly aggressive." The words were intended for Robert and Joseph.

Robert said, "My lord, there are young men who are almost ready to be archers. We can replace our losses and more."

"But will they be good enough, Robert? The men we are losing have been tempered in battle."

"We still have more than enough quality left. Trust your senior archers, my lord. The gift of land from Master Roger can only encourage others to be loyal. You have rewarded them and that makes others wish to join such an august body of archers."

"Joseph?"

"Robert sees the archers at the mark on Sunday morning, my lord. We see the ones who wield a spear. There are not as many prospective men at arms but enough. I cannot replace our losses as quickly as Robert but if I have the autumn to work with them then by spring I might be able to replace our losses and have more men. The weapons and mail we took will help."

William said, "If the rebels give us time."

The Ripples of Rebellion

"Aye, brother, there's the rub. We do not know whence will the danger come. Waiting is always hard. We will do what we must do and trust to God."

Chapter 19

Henry Samuel

The bountiful autumn

I did not spring the arrival of refugees on those in the castle. I sent a rider ahead so that when we arrived the ladies of the house were ready to welcome the orphaned children. Edgar had rooms arranged and there was food ready. My mother and my wife had thought of things that did not occur to me. There were clean clothes waiting for the children and Lady Rebekah had arranged for musicians to play as they entered. It was as though there was a feast day and the children were greeted by smiles. The smiles were reciprocated. The full news would have to wait but I needed to speak to Margaret. Roger would, perforce, need to be there, too. Roger ensured that his family was happy before he joined me. Myfanwy and Eleanor were entertaining them. "I cannot thank your family enough, Earl."

"Roger, this is your family. You are not of our blood but you are of our heart. Besides you will be part of the family when you wed." Almost as though she had been waiting Margaret appeared. I waved her over and Roger took her hands and kissed them.

Margaret said, "I cannot imagine what you must be going through. When I saw those children…"

I knew that I was almost in the way but I was needed there and I remained.

Roger said, "I must ask you, Margaret, if you wish to take on this burden? A marriage to me is one thing but to take on five children…"

Margaret's face changed. I hid my smile for she had become Lady Mary, her mother. She had the same steely glint in her eye and her voice was just as authoritative, "Roger of Whorlton, if you think I am so shallow that I would change my mind because of this then perhaps we should not wed. I do not shirk from responsibility. Just because we women do not go to war does not make us weak. If anything, it makes us stronger for we do not know if our men will come back. Aunt Rebekah lost her whole family, yet she is still a rock."

Roger said, "I am sorry, my love, I meant no disrespect. Of course, I know that you are strong, but I am asking much of you."

Her face softened, "You are asking me to be part of your life for now and forever. I am happy to do so and if I be as a mother to your

The Ripples of Rebellion

nieces and nephews then so much the better." She smiled, "Great Aunt Rebekah had no children of her own, but she was a mother to many. I hope to be a mother to our own and to your family too."

I was no longer needed and I was able to go to my chamber and change from the clothes of war. When I descended the hall was filled as food was prepared and bed chambers allocated. Such was the activity in the hall that my mother and I, along with Eirwen and William, had to wait until quite late to speak of the events of the last week. When we were finally alone, I shook my head, "None could see this coming and it has caused such upheaval that I do not know how it will change our lives."

My mother smiled and sipped some of the fortified wine from Portugal that she liked. She reserved it for special occasions and this one was such. "Change, my son, comes into every life, and it is how you deal with it that matters. When I lost your father to a murderer in York I thought my life was over. It was not. It was never the same but different is not always a bad thing. The haste for the knighting and the marriage is not unseemly, it is necessary. Margaret will not have the day that Thomasina and Matthew enjoyed but a year ago she could only dream of such a marriage."

I could see that my mother was right. "I am happy for them both and I know that they will make it work. Roger is not a farmer, but his dead family left the manor in good order and Roger is sensible enough to appoint those who can farm it. What surprised me were the men who chose to go with Roger."

Eirwen put her hand on mine, "Do not take it as a rejection of you, husband."

I shook my head, "I do not. I am just honoured that our men value our family as much as we do."

"It is the way of this family and what makes us strong."

"And we shall need that strength will we not, Henry Samuel?" William had been silent. He was a master of many things, but marriages and family relationships were not two of them. He nodded, "A storm is coming. It will not be like the civil war, but it will hurt the lives of many. My big brother will have his work cut out to keep order, even here, in the north."

"You must ride to Durham on the morrow, William. Speak to the Bishop and ask what his plans are. He is not a military man but he has a good mind. I am happy to fall in with them."

My mother stood, "And now, my sons, it is time for bed. You have both worked hard and I see no rest in the future. You, Henry Samuel, cannot be allowed to weaken. You are the rock on which this family stands." She came over to kiss me on the forehead. "So, no more trial by combats, eh? You are getting no younger and one day will come someone with faster hands or more cunning."

I sighed, "Yes, Mother." I might be the Earl of Cleveland, but I could still be chastised by my mother.

I slept the sleep of a man who is getting old and takes longer to recover. While others organised the wedding I rode, alone, to speak to my lords. They needed to know what I knew and what had happened at Whorlton and Upleatham. Egglesclif had changed since I had been away and there was a happy buzz such as one gets from a healthy hive.

When I spoke to Matthew he and Robert exchanged a look, "This is my fault, uncle. The knight who was killed in Italy was killed by me. He had land at Upleatham."

"You were protecting your lord and no fault can be attached to you. Even had we known of the knight's death we could not have foreseen what his cousin would do. You have done no wrong."

He nodded and they showed me around the manor and I saw what a change there was. The plough fields had a haze of green. Seeds had been sown and there would be a winter crop. The storm had not damaged the crop. The houses were now finished and there was an air of hope. Walter of Egglesclif was still lazy and objectionable but his son, Ralph, had thrown himself into being as much help to Matthew as he could. He and his sons now practised on the green each Sunday. It was too late for him to be an archer but Jack was happy to make him a spearman.

Norton, Elton and Hartburn had all managed to recover from the effects of the storm. My brother and my two cousins heeded my warning and promised to try to acquire more men or train young men to be warriors. William was right. If we had time, the time to train men, then all would be well, but if the pot boiled over then we could be hurt.

The spectre of death still hung over the valley but the summer storms were forgotten as we enjoyed long days of sun. We harvested well and stored great bounty for the winter. All the time our farmers worked the women did their best to ensure that the hasty marriage of Roger and Margaret would be a good one. I knighted Roger on the day before his marriage. I gave him spurs and my mother gave him Margaret's father's sword. He had the one taken from Sir Giles but the sentimental value of William of Stockton's blade was a rich gift.

He still had no squire but, as we walked from the chapel on the morning after the vigil he said, "I know that he is young, too young for war, but Nicholas, my nephew, can be trained. I would rather have family, Earl. Is that a bad thing?"

The Ripples of Rebellion

I shook my head, "You are the first squire I have had who was not related to me. It cannot hurt," I stopped in the middle of the bailey, "If there is war then I want you and your men to hunker down in your castle. Your men are mortaring the walls and repairing the gates in preparation for your return but you must maintain the walls and the building."

"Will you not need me?"

I shook my head, "If danger comes then the knights and men of the valley will have to suffice. We have the promise of help from York and the Bishop told my brother that he will give us aid if he can."

The wedding, for all that it was a hurried affair, was a joyous day. Margaret looked radiant and the orphans all bore smiles. The hurt was still within them but my family had made them more than welcome and lavished love and care on them. The test would come when they returned to Whorlton with all the attendant memories. Margaret told me that she knew it would be her appointed duty to deal with the tears and the nightmares but she was prepared for that. "When I think of what poor cousin Isabelle endured with the monster that was Sir Robert, I know that I have the easier task. I am there to heal. It will be good preparation for my own family. I am marrying a good man, Henry Samuel, and I thank you for all that you did to make him so." She smiled and said, "And if you had not visited Abel the Horse then Roger would never have come into our lives so I am grateful that you did. If not for the horses I would be a spinster yet."

The day after the wedding I had an escort of my men for the wagons that took the family to Whorlton. It was not that I expected trouble but I planned on using my men to improve the defences of the castle. It was my most isolated manor and the one that could not be reached quickly. I would not abandon my knight or my cousin.

My men had come to know the children and we all ensured that there was laughter, jokes and banter as we rode to the hilltop castle. However, once we neared it, I could feel the tension and the fear in the children. Roger said, "I know that there are bad memories of what happened in our home but we will make happy ones, I promise. If any of you wish to ride back to Stockton with the earl then they may do so." He had not asked my permission, but he knew I would not refuse. It was a way out for the children. Margaret's smiling face helped and I doubted that there would be any takers.

When we reached the castle, it was much improved. The gates worked and I saw that most of the stones which had fallen had been replaced and mortared. It could be defended. All traces of the massacre were gone. The five men I had sent were good men and they had

The Ripples of Rebellion

whitewashed the stains of slaughter where they needed to. Roger set the children to work as soon as they entered the castle and they were too busy to dwell on the past. The men who were to stay in the castle, and their families, were accommodated and we cooked food. We would stay the night and so, while it was crowded, it was cosy too. Roger kept the children up late and that was wise as they were so exhausted that they fell asleep quickly. Margaret retired at the same time. I sat with him and Alfred after the rest had gone to bed.

Roger smiled, "It is hard work being a lord, my lord."

"Harder for you than for me. I had a steward and servants, you have none."

"There are widows and young people in the village. I can use them."

Alfred said, "This will be a hard winter."

"I know but I owe it to my father and my brothers to rebuild the manor. It may never be as productive as it once was, but it will be safe. I curse Sir Giles and all like him."

I nodded, "And there are others, like Sir Giles, who crawl and slither about this land looking to cause mischief and benefit from the misfortune of others. The rebels thought, after Lewes, that they had won and then came Evesham. I believed that they would have given up their dream of removing the king but, it seems, I was wrong. Perhaps the murder of Henry of Almain gave them some kind of hope. At least the Sheriff is aware of the danger. Sir Ralph will be vigilant and the Bishop of Durham promised to send word to de Brus to remind him of his duties in Guisborough."

We left the next day. Margaret gave me a hug and whispered in my ear, "Thank you, Henry Samuel, you have been as a father to me and I shall not forget it. This place of sadness shall be filled with joy. I have a task and I will not shirk from the work."

I nodded, "And I am happy that you have found happiness too."

Roger had grown and the knight who put his arm around his wife and waved us off was more than ready to take on any who would threaten the peace.

Alfred was pensive as we rode home, "Roger and Matthew both found brides, Father, yet I see none for Samuel and me."

"I found your mother in Wales. Thomas found his just up the road in Herterpol. Be patient, Alfred. You are still learning to be a knight. Roger has been thrust into the position as has your brother and Matthew has had to build from nothing. You are lucky. You do not need to worry about tenants or land. The seasons, to you, merely means having to change the clothes that you wear. Your brother knights have to wonder how it will affect their people. I was in your position when I served with my grandfather. I used my time well. Do the same."

I meant the advice well but it was harder for Alfred than it had been for me. I could do little to help him as I was too busy running Stockton and ensuring that Matthew, at his new manor, and Samuel, at Redmarshal, were supported. I could offer little to Whorlton and its new lord and lady. In the end, it was Alfred who came up with a solution to both problems. He volunteered to ride, once a week, to Whorlton. He stayed overnight and was able to show my former squire and my cousin that they were not forgotten. It also helped him as he saw, at first hand, the problems of being the lord of the manor.

The ship that put into Stockton, the last one before the winter, brought some interesting news. It was of such import that I delivered it myself to Matthew, for it touched him the most. He was surprised when I rode in. Now that I had no squire my knights were used to my arrival alone but visits to Egglesclif normally meant my wife and daughters would be with me.

"My lord, what brings you here this chill morning?"

We stood before the roaring fire and Thomasina poured us ale. I said, "Thank you, Thomasina. A ship brought news. Simon de Montfort's son, one of the murderers of Henry of Almain, died in Siena."

Thomasina made the sign of the cross.

"Died, my lord? He was not killed?"

"The captain of the ship said that he died a horrible death from some disease which struck him and yet killed no others. It is said he was killed by God."

"But his cousin remains alive?" I nodded. "Then I am pleased that one murderer has been punished but until the other dies then Henry of Almain is unavenged."

The bountiful harvest was followed by an early cold snap. The trees we had copsed at all my manors gave us the fuel to warm homes and halls. Preparations were made for Christmas and the Winter Solstice. For Thomasina, this was a real change from what she had known. Italy might have been cold in winter but the white frosts that came in November were a shock to her. It was at about that time that we learned she was pregnant. Eirwen and my mother began to make a weekly visit to Egglesclif and, of course, my daughters went with them. In Myfanwy's case, it was also an opportunity to see Robert. Since the wedding, she had mooned around the hall. When Matthew, along with his squire, had visited Stockton, she changed and became radiant sunshine. The pregnancy was a joy to my daughter but for a different reason to the rest of my family.

My preparations for Christmas were spoiled by one piece of especially bad news. Richard of Cornwall was paralysed and lost the ability to speak. Matthew had told me that the death of Henry of Almain had affected the King of the Romans badly. Whatever the reason the kingdom had lost its regent. That left just Eleanor, the queen, to take the reins of power for the king was still too ill to do so. I knew that she was hated by the people of London and that hatred was reciprocated. When sailing her barge along the Thames she had been pelted by the populace. As London was filled with those who had Montfortian sympathies then I knew England was, once more, poised on the brink of civil war. The one man who could do something about it was halfway around the world, fighting in the crusades.

I summoned, as usual, the knights of the valley to our Christmas feast. I told no one, except William, the news until after we had feasted. St Stephen's Day was soon enough to give them the dire news. I took them hawking in the woods of Hartburn. They were all in high spirits. I waited until we stopped for food, at noon, before I told them what I had learned. I had told Rafe the Codger that I would need privacy while we ate and so he took his men and the cadge to gut the birds the hawks had caught in the morning. Those like my brother, Alfred and my cousin Dick, knew that something was amiss but when I told them their faces told me that they all understood the ramifications.

"Do the Bishop and the Sheriff know?"

I nodded, "They do, brother, for the messenger came from the Sheriff and was headed to Durham."

"Then they will be prepared for any unrest."

I pointed to the rock-hard ground, "This cold weather is our ally. However, once spring comes and our enemies have had the time to plot and plan then we will need to be vigilant. I wanted to tell you here that we do not need the ladies to be worried. When you return to your manors, we prepare our warriors. We have many new ones who will not have the luxury of time to become veterans. You will need to temper them as quickly as you can. Alfred, when you make your weekly visits to Whorlton, use that ride to watch the land. Look for strangers. Matthew, you will need to keep a good watch on the river. It can be crossed and you must be vigilant. Samuel, Redmarshal is our westernmost outpost. The Montfortians who lost their manors to the west of us to the Neville family may well try to take them back."

Dick said, "It has been many years since Evesham, Henry Samuel, surely the embers of rebellion are doused."

The Ripples of Rebellion

Matthew said, "Aye, Simon de Montfort the Younger, is dead."

"But his cousin, Guy, lives. There may not be a rising but the Sheriff warned me of the dangers and only a fool ignores such warnings."

Chapter 20

Henry Samuel

The Last Spark of Rebellion

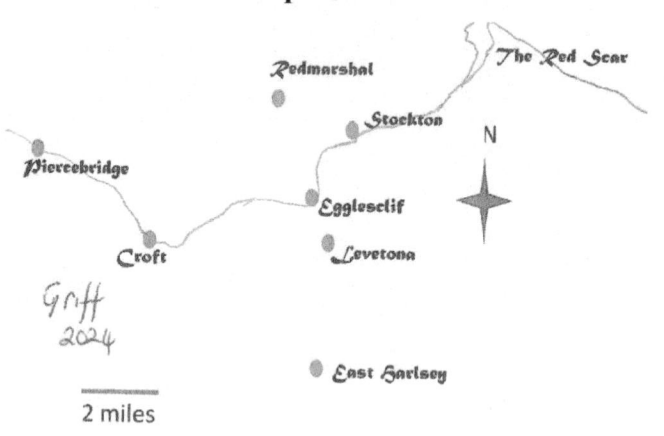

The news that Richard of Cornwall had died reached us at the end of the first week of April. He had lingered on the edge of life since December, but God had finally granted him peace. That peace, however, was not to be enjoyed by the rest of us. With the news came other warnings and threats. Londoners had refused to pay their taxes and there were rebels on the Welsh border. Baron Mortimer was under attack. There were rumours of knights who had supported Simon de Montfort rebelling. They saw a land without a strong hand on the reins. Our land was quiet but I put my knights on a war footing.

I rode out with new men as well as seasoned veterans. I had decided to be as visible as I could and use that as a deterrent. It also helped me to get to know my new men. Alfred came with me and he did as I had done with my grandfather, he learned by watching. One of the things we had done was to build, at Egglesclif, a ferry. It was actually a detachable part of the quay but we used it to cross the river closer to York than Stockton. It allowed us to reach the road south more quickly.

I organised patrols. They were a weekly event although we changed the days on which we rode. Samuel, Dick and my brother Alfred led patrols west to Sadberge while Thomas had the easier task of watching the road to Durham. I led the patrol to Whorlton and the south. By crossing the river Matthew was able to come with us. There had been much debate about my decision. I persuaded my knights that our patrols would deter enemies. I wanted us to be seen as vigilant.

It was May and the days were growing longer. The trees were laden with leaves and the hedges blossomed. It was a good time to be abroad and yet we rode under the threat of war. Joseph had found us some good men. One of the men at arms was Baldwin, the son of Joseph's shield brother, Edward. Edward had died, not in battle, as all such warriors should, but from a wasting disease within. He had been a loss to the castle and Baldwin had been a boy when he was left without a father. Joseph became his foster father and it was he who had suggested he would make a good replacement. Many thought him young for he was barely seventeen and his frame was not yet filled out. I did not agree for he had a keen energy about him. Robert the Fletcher had also brought a youth with us, his son, Stephen. Like Baldwin, he was not yet fully grown but he had his father's eye and skill. Baldwin and Stephen rode behind my two captains.

As we headed past the tiny hamlet of Levetona I looked west and pointed, "There used to be a prosperous manor there, Low Worsall. It had a lord and sent men to fight at the Battle of the Standards."

"But there is nothing there now, Henry Samuel. I have ridden there and it is just humps and bumps."

"Those humps and bumps are the remains of the houses. It is a lesson to be heeded. A lord must keep his land and his people alive. Levetona has no lord and the people here could be wiped out in a heartbeat."

Matthew nodded, "You are saying that as I am the lord who is closest to them I should offer aid."

I shook my head, "You have barely enough people to keep your own land safe, Matthew, but the gift from Richard of Cornwall is one which will become heavier with time."

Henry asked, "Earl, where do we ride this day?"

"Why, is it so tiresome to be out with your cousins and uncles?"

"No, but we have not ridden this road yet. We normally head east to Whorlton."

"Roger and his men have made that land secure." I waved a hand around us, "Do you see a castle?" He shook his head. "That is because there is none until Richmond to the southwest and Helmsley to the southeast. Whorlton guards the northern part of those hills but this vale is without defences. To answer you, young Henry, we ride to East Harlsey. In the time of the Warlord, it had a lord who served Stockton. He died along with Sir Samuel at Arsuf. King John appointed another. His son, Sir Mawdsley, is the lord of that manor. The last messenger we had from the Sheriff asked if we would look in on him. We have not yet done so."

The road was not a straight one. We passed through the hamlet of Picton first, then Appleton and Rounton. Each of them had just a couple of farmers eking out a living in land hacked from the forests but the farmers seemed happy enough and were reassured by the blue banner of the earl of Stockton. Since the time of the Warlord, it had been a sign of protection.

East Harlsey was bigger than the hamlets we had passed. The manor house was walled and while there were no sentries I counted enough men in the village to offer a defence to an attacker. Sir Mawdsley was working in his fields with his men. They were using his oxen to plough what looked to be a new field. As we dismounted to walk over to them Matthew smiled, "I now know how hard that can be."

"Earl, this is an honour, what brings you here?"

I went closer to him, "Did you hear of the death of Richard of Cornwall?"

"I did, my lord. I had business in York and that was the sole topic of conversation."

"The Sheriff and the Bishop of Durham both fear the rise of rebels. I am riding the land with my men as well as Sir Matthew and Sir Alfred to ensure that we snuff out any potential threat."

He suddenly stopped, "Sir Matthew?"

My cousin said, "Do you know me, Sir Mawdsley?"

"No, but I heard your name. Come within my hall out of the sun." he turned, "Ned, have ale brought out for the earl's men."

His wife had seen our approach and by the time we entered the cool hall, there was wine. Goblets, bread, ham and cheese were on the table. She was clearly flustered at the arrival of an earl and she apologised, "My lord, had I known I would have…"

I smiled, "My lady, we came unannounced and this fare is more than generous."

Just then there was a wail and a shout, "I must go my lord. Our sons…"

Sir Mawdsley smiled, "They are a pair of imps, my lord. Too young to be trained and they are wild."

I glanced at Henry who looked shamefaced, "I know of such boys but I know that they can be redeemed. Now, Sir Mawdsley, how did you come to hear of Sir Matthew?"

"It was not me but my brother. He farms at Osmotherley and he met with me in York. We dined at the inn called the Saddle and enjoyed a meal. While we talked, he asked me if I had heard of a knight called Sir

Matthew of Redmarshal. I said I had not but I knew the manor. He said that he would not like to be in Sir Matthew's manor as there was a knight he had heard had sworn to have vengeance on him for some slight he had suffered."

"Who was this knight, Sir Mawdsley?" My cousin's question suggested that he had an idea of the answer.

"It was Sir Marmaduke Fitzwilliam."

Matthew nodded, "Henry of Almain's household knight. He blamed me for being dismissed before we even got to France. I had forgotten him."

Robert said, "Surely, he cannot hurt us, my lord. He was on his own."

Sir Mawdsley shook his head, "No, he was not. My brother came across him at Leicester where he was hiring swords."

"When was this, Sir Mawdsley?"

"My brother was in Leicester buying sheep and that would have been, oh, the middle of April."

"Round about the time that the Regent died."

"I suppose."

Alfred asked, "But why call him Matthew of Redmarshal? He is Matthew of Egglesclif."

Matthew shook his head, "I was called Matthew of Redmarshal when I went on the crusades. He would not have known of my new manor."

Sir Mawdsley said, "But Leicester is far from here. Surely you are safe, Sir Matthew."

I shook my head, "Leicester is the heartland of support for Simon de Montfort. If this knight is recruiting there then it is rebels he will bring. As the death of Henry of Almain shows us, if rebels cannot touch their real enemies, the king and his sons, then they will strike at any who they think are vulnerable. It is Samuel who might suffer for he is now lord of Redmarshal. We must return home as soon as we can." I thought quickly, "Matthew and Alfred, ride back to Egglesclif and send word to Stockton. Matthew, protect your manor. Alfred, mount men and meet me at Redmarshal. Take my banner with you. It will act as a rally for the men of Stockton. I will take my men and ride to Croft. That is the closest place that they can cross the Tees. I would discover if they have crossed already."

"Father, that is a long ride."

"And I am happy to undertake it. Thank you, Sir Mawdsley, for the information and your hospitality. We are in your debt."

The Ripples of Rebellion

We had a difficult ride to make. As we headed north and east, I explained to Joseph and Robert the Fletcher what I had learned. Joseph was sceptical, "It seems a long way to come for vengeance, my lord. What has he to gain?"

"He expects to find Sir Matthew alone in his manor with few men around him. Redmarshal is small and could be taken easily. Using those with rebel sympathies he strikes a blow for rebels. The north is seen as loyal and safe to the king. A blow here serves both Sir Marmaduke and the rebels. It may be that there are others, spread around the country, who will rise at the same time. Remember that the three manors to the west of Redmarshal were given to the Neville family. The supporters of de Montfort lost them. In any case, I care not about the reasons. There is a threat to Redmarshal and we have to quash it before any of our people are hurt."

We followed the road to the river and headed along it. There was a pack horse bridge at Croft. It was not one used by armies but locals travelled across it. The land was owned by the king and it was the Constable of Richmond who was responsible for its maintenance. He was in the Holy Land. The wounded men we found in the village told us that Sir Marmaduke had, indeed, crossed the bridge. The wounds had been caused when the villagers objected to the column of men who had crossed and had taken ale and food.

"How many men were there?"

The headman, Edmund, who had a nasty cut to his face, said, "Forty or so, my lord. It was last night they arrived and they left this morning. They were mercenaries. I only saw one set of spurs but most of them were mailed."

"I am sorry that you suffered. We will catch them and they will be punished."

We headed north and east. We had eight miles to go but while the horses of our enemies were fresh, ours were weary. I had taken the defenders of Redmarshal away. My son and his men were with Dick and Alfred to the west. They would be doing as I had done and travel until noon and then return to the manor.

The smoke rising ahead of us told us the story before we reached Redmarshal. We left the road at Whinny Hill and headed across the fields. The road twisted around the well-worked fields and we needed speed. Crops could be resown. We saw villagers fleeing across the fields away from the burning manor house. We would be outnumbered but that did not stop us. We drew our swords. We did have two advantages. One was that we were mounted and some of the mercenaries would be on foot. The other was that we had archers and from what Edmund had told me they did not.

"Robert, when we close with them then dismount. Use our archers to thin their ranks."

Our thundering hooves acted like a warning for Sir Marmaduke and his men. They heard us coming across the fields and left off from their destruction of the manor to grab shields and spears. My shield and helmet hung from my cantle. It meant I had clear vision but no protection for my head.

"Shield wall!" The cry came from the mercenaries.

Sir Marmaduke knew his business. A shield wall would make our horses stop and my ten men would then be at a disadvantage. There was only one thing to do and I led by example. My courser was well trained and I wheeled him and rode along the line of shields. A spear jabbed at my leg and drew blood but my sword, held horizontally, smacked into one head and I saw the man fall. When I reached the end of their line, I whirled my horse and shouted, "Reform!" If I still had Roger as my squire then he would have used the horn. I saw that one of the new men, Henry, had been speared and was writhing on the ground. I steadied my horse, as my men at arms obeyed me and reformed. The mercenary who raced from the line to finish off Henry paid with his life as a bodkin-tipped arrow slammed into him. The rest of my handful of archers sent their missiles towards the shield wall.

It was time for me to lead my men and I shouted, "Dismount. Shields. We will make a wedge!" My right leg was bleeding but the spear had not penetrated too far. However, I knew that the longer the fight went on the weaker I would become.

A wedge was a way to use my skills and those of Joseph to our advantage. With me at the fore and Joseph and Baldwin behind, the ten of us marched at their line. It seemed a foolish thing to do as there were too many for us to defeat but the alternative was to wait for them to attack us. Robert and the archers used their arrows wisely. They wasted not a one. Whenever they saw a target, an arrow flew and struck flesh. It ensured that the enemy kept up the shields and that restricted their vision. I went for Sir Marmaduke. He was the one wearing livery and had spurs.

He confirmed his identity when he shouted, "Vengeance for the Earl of Leicester!" The men with him cheered.

I shouted, "For King Henry and England. Death to all traitors."

Protected from our archers by my men at arms, Sir Marmaduke and those around him surged forward. I kept my shield up and thrust with my sword. Spears were jabbed at me but my shield took most of the blows while Baldwin showed that he had his father's eye as he slashed down and severed the head of one spear. My sword slid off Sir Marmaduke's shield and sliced into the cheek of the man next to him. The mercenary line lapped around our wedge. In doing so some of the enemy were exposed to my archers' arrows. Even so, it was hard fought. We were so close that full swings were impossible and the enemy warriors who had chosen spears now discarded them for swords. I had learned many tricks over the years and I used one on the knight. I brought my shield up sharply to ram under his visored helmet. As his head jerked back, I punched his head with the hilt of my sword. The combination knocked the helmet from his head. I smacked him in the chest with my shield as a sword from behind Sir Marmaduke came at my head. It scored a line across my cheek and blood flowed. It looked worse than it was and the mercenary who cheered had his life ended when Baldwin's sword was rammed into his laughing mouth. It was then that his foster father was wounded. I heard the grunt and felt a lessening of the pressure behind me. If he fell, then our wedge would disintegrate and we would lose.

 I stepped forward and, lowering my sword as I did so, I punched again with my shield. When Sir Marmaduke stepped back it allowed me to bring up my sword, unseen. It tore through some links and into his gambeson. It was a blind strike and not fatal but it went into his side and when I pulled it out I saw that it was bloody.

 I heard Baldwin cry, "Joseph!"

 Our wedge was not beyond redemption and I shouted, "Watch your foster father and I will end this." It was neither rash nor reckless. I calculated that if I could take the head from the snake then the rest would crumble. As I moved closer to the wounded knight more arrows flew from behind me. The mercenary with the poleaxe poised to end my life never saw the arrow that killed him. It was then that I heard the horn of Stockton. It came from behind the enemy and they did what any warrior does when he fears an attack from behind, they halted and their whole line hesitated. Some even glanced behind. I did not falter but brought my sword from above. Sir Marmaduke blocked the blow with his shield but the force of it made him reel and step back. I moved forward punching with my shield as I did so. I caught his hand with a blow and he could not use his sword. I slashed diagonally across his body and my blade tore through his surcoat and cut some links in his hauberk. More importantly I hurt his shoulder. My son, Alfred, Sir Matthew and Sir Thomas were leading the men of Stockton and Norton into the rear of the enemy line and they were broken. They started to flee. Sir Marmaduke could have yielded and asked for mercy. I would have given it to him but instead he lunged at me with his sword. I blocked with mine and as I pushed forward the edge of my blade found an unprotected throat. The blood that spurted told me he was dead even as he fell at my feet.

I looked up and saw Matthew. He had disobeyed me and followed my brother. He looked harrowed and shook his head, "I am sorry that I brought this upon my home."

"You did not. This is just the last act of a rebellion that should have ended at Evesham. Now it is done."

"Sir Henry!"

I turned and saw Baldwin cradling his foster father. Robert jumped from his horse to help him. My Captain of Sergeants was wounded. I saw that his left hand was cut to the bone and hanging by tendons. The blood was pooling on the ground. Robert tore the surcoat from Sir Marmaduke and fashioned a tourniquet. I said, "Get him to the doctor."

"I fear, Sir Henry, that my days as Captain of Sergeants are over."

Robert lifted his father to his feet and placed one foot in the stirrup. I said to Matthew, "Go with Joseph and help your squire. Warn the castle that there are more injured."

The three left us and Alfred and Thomas dismounted. Alfred said, "You should have waited, Father."

I shook my head, "It was too late for they heard our hooves and, besides," I pointed to the people who had hidden during the attack and now emerged, "warriors accept death as part of their lives. Sir Samuel's people should not have to."

Just then we heard hooves and our hands went to our weapons. It was my brother, son and cousin with their men. My brother said, "We came when we saw the smoke. How did you get here first, brother?"

"We heard of this threat from Sir Mawdsley of East Harlsey. Joseph was badly wounded."

He nodded at the three other men at arms who had fallen. "And we have paid a price. Is this all of those who came to attack us?"

"No, others fled. They need to be either apprehended and hanged or chased from our lands. I will not have a nest of rebels festering in the valley."

My brother mounted his horse, "Leave that to us. You have done enough this day."

Samuel leapt from his horse, "Paul!" His reeve was wounded. My son ran to help him.

Robert the Fletcher and his archers had fetched their horses and were now stripping the dead of weapons and mail. Samuel was speaking to his people and organising the dousing of the fires. Alfred and Henry were, along with Geoffrey, tending to our wounded. Baldwin was standing close to me. His surcoat was spattered with blood and I saw that his sword was notched.

"You did well, Baldwin, in your first fight and for one so young. You have hidden skills. I shall replace that sword when we return to the castle."

"Will my foster father live? It was a terrible wound, Earl."

"Doctor Erasmus is a good healer and he knows how to tend wounds. He may not be able to save Joseph's left hand but he will try."

"What will he do if he cannot fight?"

"He needs to do nothing for he has earned a place of comfort at the castle but I know Joseph. He still has a right hand and he can still train men. He might not be Captain of Sergeants any longer but he will have a position."

"And me, my lord?"

"You?"

"I am not yet fully grown and Joseph was using me as a sort of squire. A new captain might not see a place for one so young."

I looked at the young man with new eyes. This had been the first time he had come on patrol. I saw now, a little more clearly, that he was more slightly built than the other men at arms. A thought drifted into my head. It may have been the battle or the serious wound that had almost ended Joseph's life but I heard, in my head, the word '*squire*'. I voiced it, "Baldwin, I have no squire. Would you consider taking on the responsibility?"

"But I am not noble born, my lord."

"Neither is Robert yet he is a squire. You showed great courage today. You guarded my back and Joseph's side. If I were to choose another squire, he would need more training just to get to where you are now."

"Then I accept, my lord."

When the fires were doused, Samuel came over.

"How is your reeve?"

"He is wounded but it will heal. He is no warrior."

"Your manor will need work."

"I know, we will take the enemy dead and make a pyre on that field yonder. It has yet to be ploughed. When the dead are burned we will plough their ash into the ground and that field will be a reminder of how close we came to losing the manor."

"Your hall will need to be rebuilt."

He nodded. "We will pull it down and begin again. Perhaps this is a good thing. Thomas and Isabelle were unhappy in that hall. Geoffrey and I can use Uncle William's active mind and design something better. He did a good job at Egglesclif." I nodded. "And we can make this one stronger and better able to resist such attacks. I will make sure that Paul and my other men know how to fight. If nothing else this has been a lesson. The fires of rebellion are not yet doused."

"I can see now that I made a mistake by looking further afield. I should have kept my eye on my valley. It is a lesson learned." I pointed to the cloak covered bodies, "And before we do anything else, let us give these dead warriors a decent burial in your church yard."

I saw that Henry and Geoffrey were the first to gently lift the dead. My nephews had completed the journey begun at Hartburn. Perhaps the raid was necessary. It had tempered them and been as a warning to us. The rebellion was almost over but it had rippled on for too long. When we had a new king he would need a firmer hand. Despite the fact that he did not like me, we would have to work together, for England and for the valley.

Epilogue

The Valley 1272

By the time it was September, the new hall had been built at Redmarshal. The scars of war were repaired. It helped that Thomasina had given birth to a son, William. It seemed symbolic and when we heard that Margaret was also with child then the future of the family was assured. My sons still had to find brides but they were actively seeking them. They hoped for love but knew their duties. There were the daughters of nobles who lived within riding distance and marriages would be arranged. That discussion caused the first argument I can remember between my mother and my wife. My wife wanted her sons to marry for love but my mother felt that they had a duty to marry well. They could not rely on the vagaries of chance.

I rode with my new squire and a new Captain of Sergeants, Richard of Thorpe. We travelled to Whorlton, Egglesclif and Redmarshal to look at the new manors. William came with us for he had a hand in the design of all of them. At Whorlton I was glad to see that the orphans now seemed happier and more content. As William said, after we had visited, one never knew what lay in their heads but both of us were pleased that Roger and Margaret had the necessary skills to cope with any future problems.

Joseph, as I had predicted, was not willing to simply retire. The doctor had been forced to amputate the hand but the blade that had caused the damage had cut cleanly. Sealed by fire, Joseph's stump healed and he took over the duties of sword master. While Captain Richard could tend to other duties it was Joseph who worked with the sergeants each day to make them as skilled as he had been. On Sunday he and Robert the Fletcher worked with the men of Stockton. The land was at peace but when they were needed then the men of the valley would show that the legacy of the Warlord lived on. What he had begun when he came from the east was built on rock and made of stone. When Sir Thomas had returned from the east, he had made the phoenix rise again. I hoped that when, eventually, The Lord Edward returned from the Holy Land, he would emulate the last great king who had ruled England, King Henry 2nd. If he was as strong then there would be peace in England and prosperity would be there for all.

The End

Glossary

Archae - legal documents relating to usury
Carter's Bread - dark brown or black bread eaten by the poorest people
Caparison or trapper - a cloth covering for a horse
Chevauchée - a mounted raid
Egglesclif - Egglescliffe
Folcanstan - Folkestone
Levetona - Kirklevington
Manchet - the best bread made with wheat flour and a little added bran
Raveled or yeoman's bread - coarse bread made with wholemeal flour with bran
Raygate - Reigate, Surrey
Sergeant - man at arms
Shaffron - protection for a horse's head, leather cuir-bouilli with a metal strip
Socce - socks
Wallintun - Warrington

Canonical Hours
- Matins (nighttime)
- Lauds (early morning)
- Prime (first hour of daylight)
- Terce (third hour)
- Sext (noon)
- Nones (ninth hour)
- Vespers (sunset evening)
- Compline (end of the day)

Classes of hawk
This is the list of the hunting birds and the class of people who could fly them. It is taken from the 15th-century Book of St Albans.
Emperor: eagle, vulture, merlin
King: gyrfalcon
Prince: gentle falcon: a female peregrine falcon
Duke: falcon of the loch
Earl: peregrine falcon
Baron: buzzard
Knight: Saker Falcon
Squire: Lanner Falcon
Lady: merlin

The Ripples of Rebellion

Young man: hobby
Yeoman: goshawk
Knave: kestrel
Poor man: male falcon
Priest: sparrowhawk
Holy water clerk: sparrowhawk

The Ripples of Rebellion

Historical Note

Jews were savagely persecuted by the de Montfort faction. Two high-ranking Jews were murdered by the bare hands of one Montfortian supporter. Northampton did fall because of a weakened priory wall but there was talk of collusion with the prior who was a Poitevin.

The royalists should have won at Lewes but The Lord Edward's pursuit of the Londoners cost them dearly. There were few knights killed at Lewes which, in comparison to Evesham, seems almost a civilised affair. When The Lord Edward was kept prisoner, it was Lady Maude Braose, Sir Roger's wife, who arranged his escape. He was sent a good horse and when he was out riding, he switched to the better horse and outran his guards. King Henry was kept close by Simon de Montfort after Lewes as was The Lord Edward's wife, Eleanor.

There were two spies who passed on valuable information. One was Margoth who was a cross-dressing woman. I made up the relationship with the other spy for convenience. It made for a tighter story. King Henry was mistaken for a rebel and was almost slain. Again, in the interest of storytelling, I have Henry Samuel rescue him.

The butchering of de Montfort and his leaders took place as I described it and Sir Roger Mortimer did all that I ascribe to him. It is not sure if the future King Edward condoned the act for all the men who went with Sir Roger were his men. The sons of de Montfort who escaped both went to France where they spent the rest of their lives trying to undermine King Henry and his son.

The scouring of the forests of Chesterfield did take place and it is from this time that the legend of Robin Hood began. The Dictum of Kenilworth did end the war but Sir John de Vescy objected and the last battle of the civil war took place at Alnwick Castle. Sir John not only changed sides after that battle, but he also joined The Lord Edward on the crusade.

This book references the crusade undertaken by The Lord Edward. I will not be writing about that for I have already done so in the book, 'The Archer's Crusade' (Lord Edward's Archer series). The story of Lord Edward's Crusade is a fascinating one. When I wrote that series, I thought that the title, The Lord Edward, was optional and omitted the The. I have read original thirteenth-century documents since then and realised that the future king of England was always referred to with the definite article before his name.

The Ripples of Rebellion

The murder of Henry of Almain sounds shocking even today. It was committed in a church and in front of nobles and princes. He had no opportunity to defend himself. As an act of revenge for the way Simon de Montfort was killed, it fails as Henry of Almain was not even at the battle. He was a prisoner of the rebels! Two of the characters mentioned in this book, Simon de Montfort the Younger and Ugolino della Gherardesca both became immortalised in Dante's Divine Comedy written many years after these events.

Roland's song

Under a pine tree, by a rosebush,
there is a throne made entirely of gold.
There sits the king who rules sweet France;
his beard is white, with a full head of hair.
He is noble in carriage, and proud of bearing.
If anyone is looking for the King, he doesn't need to be pointed out.

This is only part of the song. Readers of my other books will know who Taillefer was. He was a troubadour and knight who famously asked Duke William of Normandy if he could begin the Battle of Hastings. The book is the first in the series, Conquest, and is called, **Hastings**.

All the maps used were made by me. Apologies, as usual, for any mistakes. They are honest ones!

A typical ship as used by Genoa and Pisa in the 12th Century. Notice the steering board which had not changed much since the Viking drekar. They were not much bigger than a Viking ship but they were much wider in the beam and, of course, higher. The two castles at the bow and stern are augmented on this one with a small nest on the foremast.

Books used in the research:

- A Great and Terrible King-Edward 1 - Marc Morris
- The Crusades - David Nicholle
- Norman Stone Castles - Gravett
- English Castles 1200-1300 - Gravett
- The Normans - David Nicolle
- Norman Knight AD 950-1204 - Christopher Gravett
- The Norman Conquest of the North - William A Kappelle
- The Knight in History - Francis Gies
- The Norman Achievement - Richard F Cassady
- Knights - Constance Brittain Bouchard
- Knight Templar 1120-1312 - Helen Nicholson
- Feudal England: Historical Studies on the Eleventh and Twelfth Centuries - J. H. Round
- English Medieval Knight 1200-1300
- The Scottish and Welsh Wars 1250-1400 - Rothero
- Chronicles of the Age of Chivalry ed Hallam
- Lewes and Evesham- 1264-65 - Richard Brooks
- The Tower of London - Lapper and Parnell
- Knight Hospitaller 1100-1306 Nicolle and Hook
- Old Series Ordnance Survey Maps 93 Middlesbrough
- Pickering Castle - English Heritage
- British Kings and Queens - Mike Ashley
- Alnwick Castle
- Old Series Ordnance Survey Map 92 Barnard Castle
- Barnard Castle, Bowes Castle, and Egglestone Abbey - English Heritage

Griff Hosker February 2024

Other books by Griff Hosker

If you enjoyed reading this book, then why not read another one by the author?

Ancient History

The Sword of Cartimandua Series
(Germania and Britannia 50 A.D. – 128 A.D.)
Ulpius Felix- Roman Warrior (prequel)
The Sword of Cartimandua
The Horse Warriors
Invasion Caledonia
Roman Retreat
Revolt of the Red Witch
Druid's Gold
Trajan's Hunters
The Last Frontier
Hero of Rome
Roman Hawk
Roman Treachery
Roman Wall
Roman Courage

The Wolf Warrior series
(Britain in the late 6th Century)
Saxon Dawn
Saxon Revenge
Saxon England
Saxon Blood
Saxon Slayer
Saxon Slaughter
Saxon Bane
Saxon Fall: Rise of the Warlord
Saxon Throne
Saxon Sword

The Ripples of Rebellion

Medieval History

The Dragon Heart Series
Viking Slave *
Viking Warrior *
Viking Jarl *
Viking Kingdom *
Viking Wolf *
Viking War*
Viking Sword
Viking Wrath
Viking Raid
Viking Legend
Viking Vengeance
Viking Dragon
Viking Treasure
Viking Enemy
Viking Witch
Viking Blood
Viking Weregeld
Viking Storm
Viking Warband
Viking Shadow
Viking Legacy
Viking Clan
Viking Bravery

The Norman Genesis Series
Hrolf the Viking *
Horseman *
The Battle for a Home *
Revenge of the Franks *
The Land of the Northmen
Ragnvald Hrolfsson
Brothers in Blood
Lord of Rouen
Drekar in the Seine
Duke of Normandy
The Duke and the King

The Ripples of Rebellion

Danelaw
(England and Denmark in the 11th Century)
Dragon Sword *
Oathsword *
Bloodsword *
Danish Sword*
The Sword of Cnut

New World Series
Blood on the Blade *
Across the Seas *
The Savage Wilderness *
The Bear and the Wolf *
Erik The Navigator *
Erik's Clan *
The Last Viking*

The Vengeance Trail *

The Conquest Series
(Normandy and England 1050-1100)
Hastings
Conquest

The Aelfraed Series
(Britain and Byzantium 1050 A.D. - 1085 A.D.)
Housecarl *
Outlaw *
Varangian *

The Reconquista Chronicles
Castilian Knight *
El Campeador *
The Lord of Valencia *

The Anarchy Series England
1120-1180
English Knight *
Knight of the Empress *
Northern Knight *
Baron of the North *
Earl *

The Ripples of Rebellion

King Henry's Champion *
The King is Dead *
Warlord of the North*
Enemy at the Gate*
The Fallen Crown*
Warlord's War
Kingmaker
Henry II
Crusader
The Welsh Marches
Irish War
Poisonous Plots
The Princes' Revolt
Earl Marshal
The Perfect Knight

Border Knight
1182-1300
Sword for Hire *
Return of the Knight *
Baron's War *
Magna Carta *
Welsh Wars *
Henry III *
The Bloody Border *
Baron's Crusade*
Sentinel of the North*
War in the West*
Debt of Honour
The Blood of the Warlord
The Fettered King
de Montfort's Crown
The Ripples of Rebellion

Sir John Hawkwood Series
France and Italy 1339- 1387
Crécy: The Age of the Archer *
Man At Arms *
The White Company *
Leader of Men *
Tuscan Warlord *
Condottiere*

The Ripples of Rebellion

Lord Edward's Archer
Lord Edward's Archer *
King in Waiting *
An Archer's Crusade *
Targets of Treachery *
The Great Cause *
Wallace's War *
The Hunt*

Struggle for a Crown
1360- 1485
Blood on the Crown *
To Murder a King *
The Throne *
King Henry IV *
The Road to Agincourt *
St Crispin's Day *
The Battle for France *
The Last Knight *
Queen's Knight *
The Knight's Tale

Tales from the Sword I
(Short stories from the Medieval period)

Tudor Warrior series
England and Scotland in the late 15th and early 16th century
Tudor Warrior *
Tudor Spy *
Flodden*

Conquistador
England and America in the 16th Century
Conquistador *
The English Adventurer *

English Mercenary
The 30 Years War and the English Civil War
Horse and Pistol

The Ripples of Rebellion

Modern History

The Napoleonic Horseman Series
Chasseur à Cheval
Napoleon's Guard
British Light Dragoon
Soldier Spy
1808: The Road to Coruña
Talavera
The Lines of Torres Vedras
Bloody Badajoz
The Road to France
Waterloo

The Lucky Jack American Civil War series
Rebel Raiders
Confederate Rangers
The Road to Gettysburg

Soldier of the Queen series
Soldier of the Queen*
Redcoat's Rifle*
Omdurman*

The British Ace Series
1914
1915 Fokker Scourge
1916 Angels over the Somme
1917 Eagles Fall
1918 We will remember them
From Arctic Snow to Desert Sand
Wings over Persia

Combined Operations series
1940-1945
Commando *
Raider *
Behind Enemy Lines
Dieppe
Toehold in Europe
Sword Beach

The Ripples of Rebellion
Breakout
The Battle for Antwerp
King Tiger
Beyond the Rhine
Korea
Korean Winter

Tales from the Sword II
(Short stories from the Modern period)

Books marked thus *, are also available in the audio format. For more information on all of the books then please visit the author's website at www.griffhosker.com where there is a link to contact him or visit his Facebook page: Griff Hosker at Sword Books or follow him on Twitter: @HoskerGriff or Sword (@swordbooksltd) If you wish to be on the mailing list then contact the author through his website.: Griff Hosker at Sword Books